Disney

# FROZEN

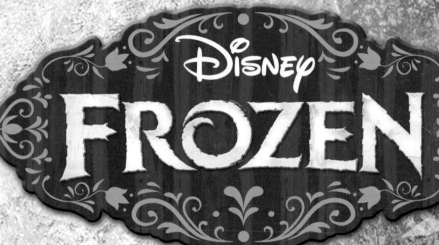

**ALSO FROM JOE BOOKS**

Disney Frozen Cinestory Comic
Disney Frozen Fun Book
Disney Cinderella Cinestory Comic
Disney The Little Mermaid Cinestory Comic
Disney Aladdin Cinestory Comic
Disney Tangled Cinestory Comic
Disney Alice in Wonderland Cinestory Comic
Disney Descendants Wicked World Cinestory Comic Volume One
Disney Descendants Wicked World Cinestory Comic Volume Two
Disney Descendants Wicked World Cinestory Comic Volume Three
Disney Princess Comics Treasury
Disney Princess Comic Strips Collection Volume One
Disney Elena of Avalor Cinestory Comic: Ready to Rule
Disney Star Darlings: Becoming Star Darlings Cinestory Comic
Disney Moana Comics Collection
Disney Beauty and the Beast Cinestory Comic

**Don't miss our monthly comics...**

Disney Frozen
Disney Princess
Disney Star vs the Forces of Evil

# Disney FROZEN

## COMICS COLLECTION

### HEARTS FULL OF SUNSHINE

JOE BOOKS LTD.

# JOE BOOKS LTD

CEO — Jay Firestone
COO — Jody Colero
President — Steve Osgoode
Associate Publisher — Deanna McFadden
Executive Editor — Amy Weingartner
Creative Manager — Jason Flores-Holz
Production Manager — Sarah Salomon
Associate Editor — Steffie Davis
Associate Designer — Nicole Dalcin
Publishing Assistant — Emma Hambly
Sales and Marketing Assistant — Samantha Carr

Book Design by AndWorld Design

Disney Frozen Comics Collection, March 2017. ISBN #978-1-77275-465-0. Published by Joe Books Ltd. 489 College Street, Suite 203, Toronto, Ontario, M6G 1A5.

# CONTENTS

# Special Break

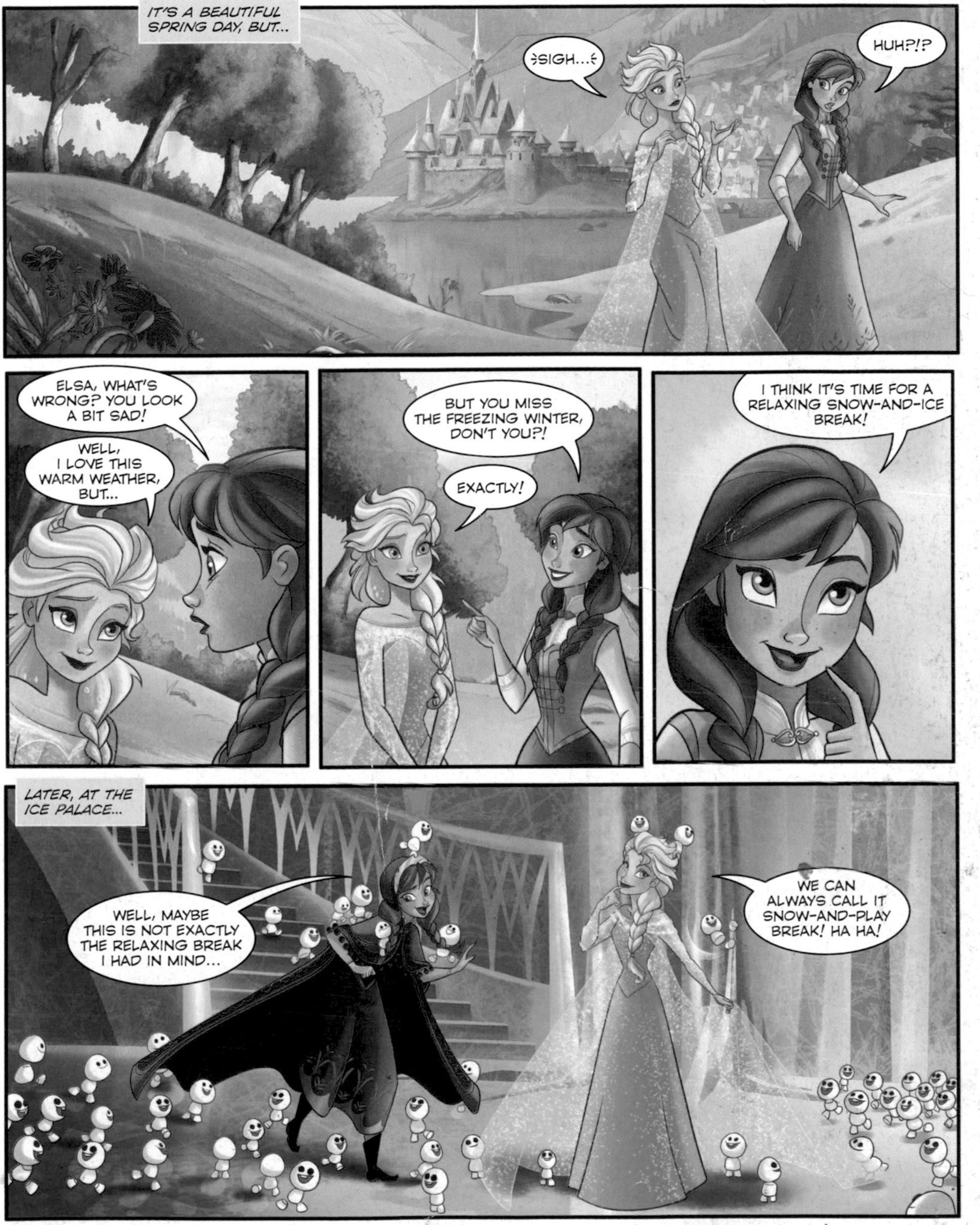

IT'S A BEAUTIFUL SPRING DAY, BUT...
SIGH...
HUH?!?
ELSA, WHAT'S WRONG? YOU LOOK A BIT SAD!
WELL, I LOVE THIS WARM WEATHER, BUT...
BUT YOU MISS THE FREEZING WINTER, DON'T YOU?!
EXACTLY!
I THINK IT'S TIME FOR A RELAXING SNOW-AND-ICE BREAK!
LATER, AT THE ICE PALACE...
WELL, MAYBE THIS IS NOT EXACTLY THE RELAXING BREAK I HAD IN MIND...
WE CAN ALWAYS CALL IT SNOW-AND-PLAY BREAK! HA HA!

# Morning Bike Ride

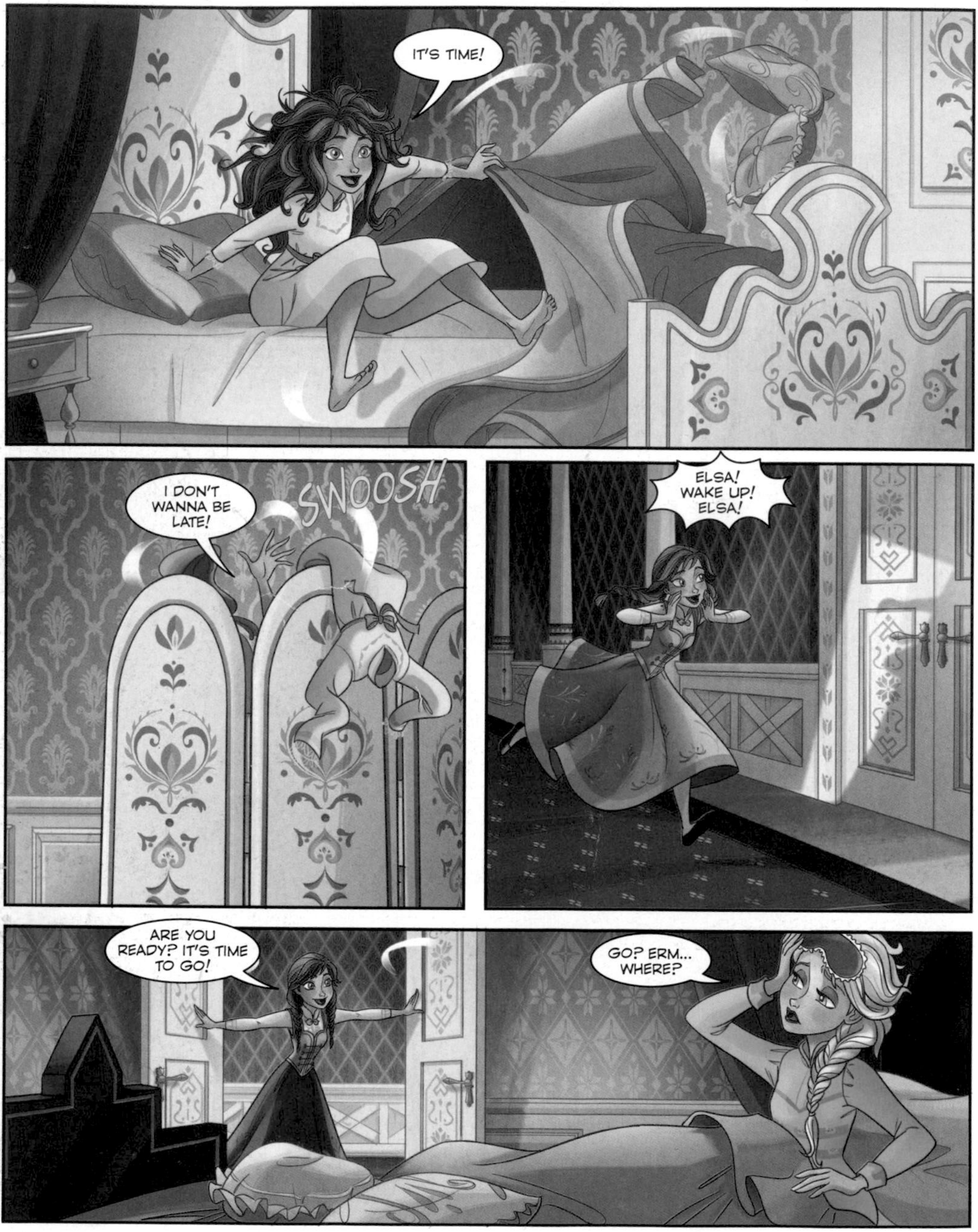
IT'S TIME!
I DON'T WANNA BE LATE!
SWOOSH
ELSA! WAKE UP! ELSA!
ARE YOU READY? IT'S TIME TO GO!
GO? ERM... WHERE?

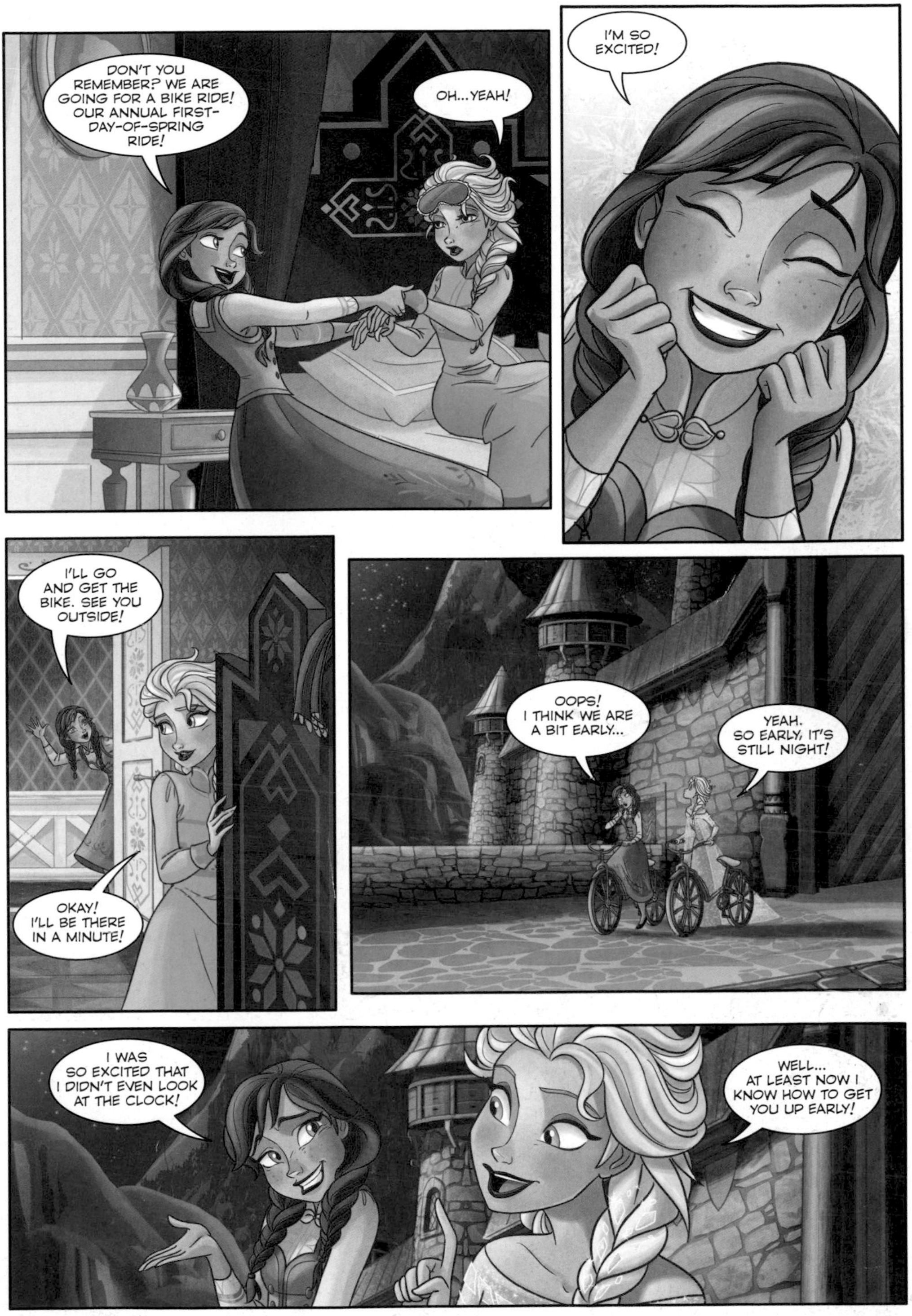
DON'T YOU REMEMBER? WE ARE GOING FOR A BIKE RIDE! OUR ANNUAL FIRST-DAY-OF-SPRING RIDE!
OH...YEAH!
I'M SO EXCITED!
I'LL GO AND GET THE BIKE. SEE YOU OUTSIDE!
OKAY! I'LL BE THERE IN A MINUTE!
OOPS! I THINK WE ARE A BIT EARLY...
YEAH. SO EARLY, IT'S STILL NIGHT!
I WAS SO EXCITED THAT I DIDN'T EVEN LOOK AT THE CLOCK!
WELL... AT LEAST NOW I KNOW HOW TO GET YOU UP EARLY!

# A Mysterious Invitation

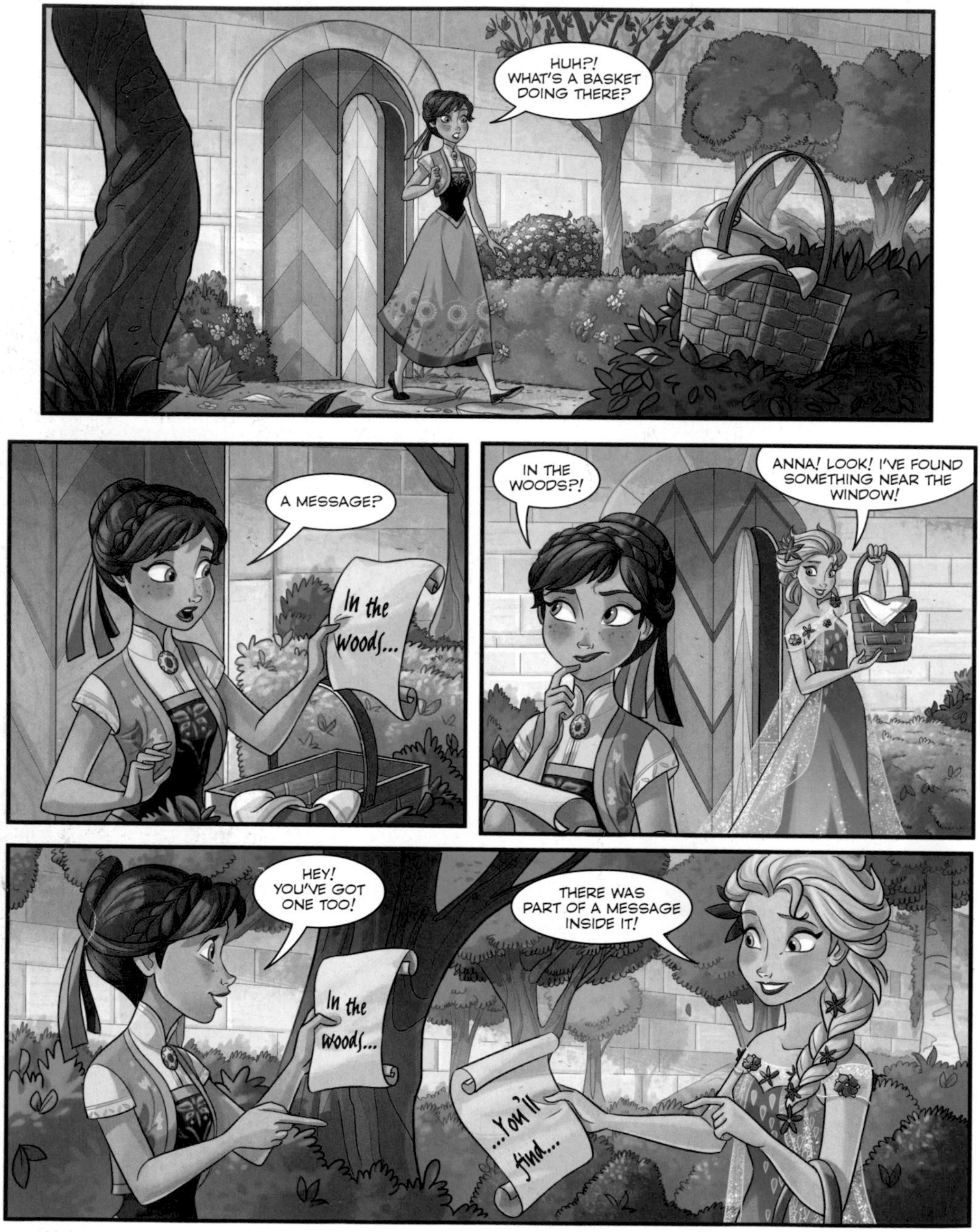
HUH?! WHAT'S A BASKET DOING THERE?
A MESSAGE?
In the woods...
IN THE WOODS?!
ANNA! LOOK! I'VE FOUND SOMETHING NEAR THE WINDOW!
HEY! YOU'VE GOT ONE TOO!
In the woods...
THERE WAS PART OF A MESSAGE INSIDE IT!
...You'll find...

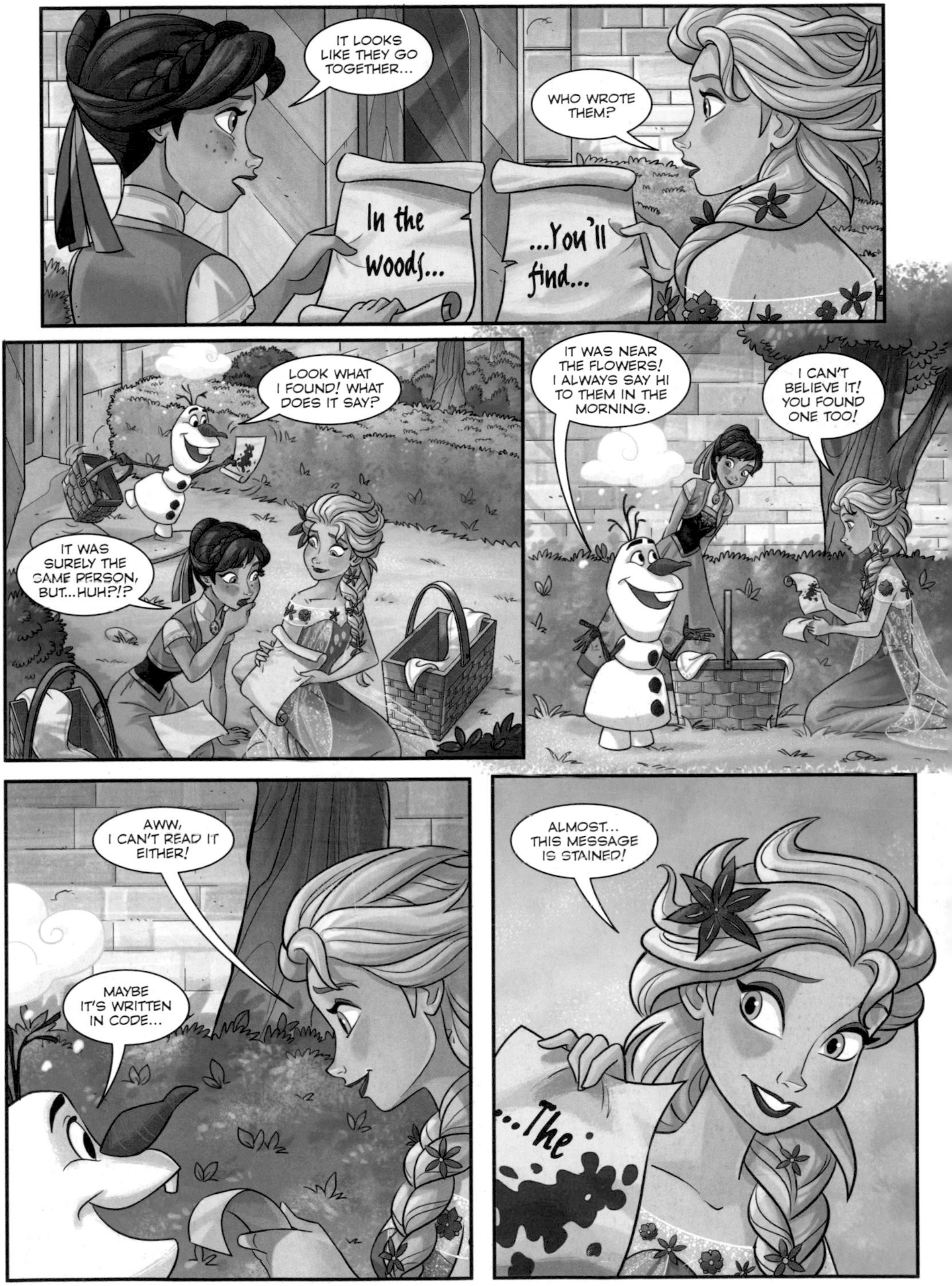
IT LOOKS LIKE THEY GO TOGETHER...
In the woods...
WHO WROTE THEM?
...You'll find...
LOOK WHAT I FOUND! WHAT DOES IT SAY?
IT WAS SURELY THE SAME PERSON, BUT...HUH?!?
IT WAS NEAR THE FLOWERS! I ALWAYS SAY HI TO THEM IN THE MORNING.
I CAN'T BELIEVE IT! YOU FOUND ONE TOO!
AWW, I CAN'T READ IT EITHER!
MAYBE IT'S WRITTEN IN CODE...
ALMOST... THIS MESSAGE IS STAINED!
...The

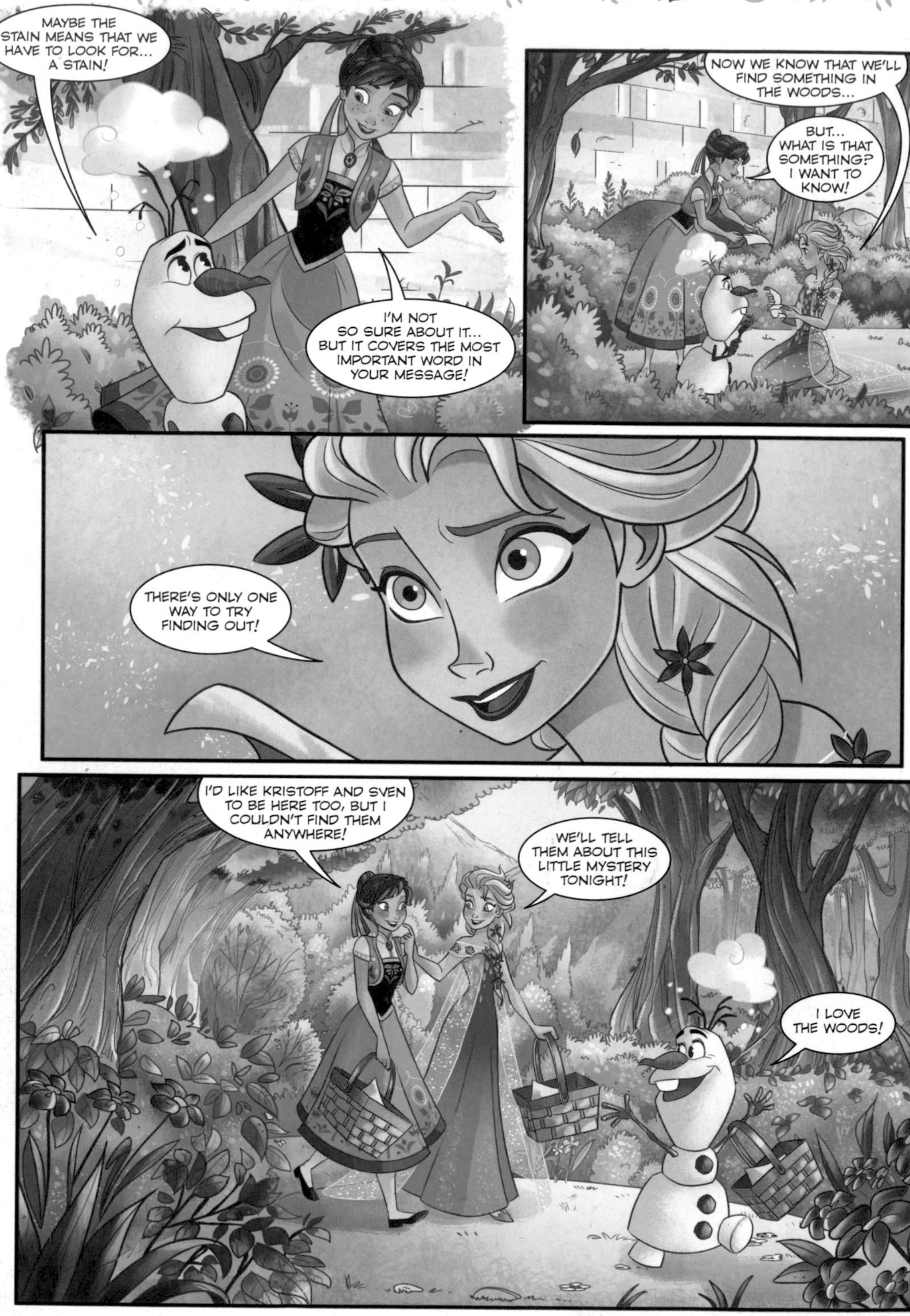
MAYBE THE STAIN MEANS THAT WE HAVE TO LOOK FOR... A STAIN!
I'M NOT SO SURE ABOUT IT... BUT IT COVERS THE MOST IMPORTANT WORD IN YOUR MESSAGE!
NOW WE KNOW THAT WE'LL FIND SOMETHING IN THE WOODS...
BUT... WHAT IS THAT SOMETHING? I WANT TO KNOW!
THERE'S ONLY ONE WAY TO TRY FINDING OUT!
I'D LIKE KRISTOFF AND SVEN TO BE HERE TOO, BUT I COULDN'T FIND THEM ANYWHERE!
WE'LL TELL THEM ABOUT THIS LITTLE MYSTERY TONIGHT!
I LOVE THE WOODS!

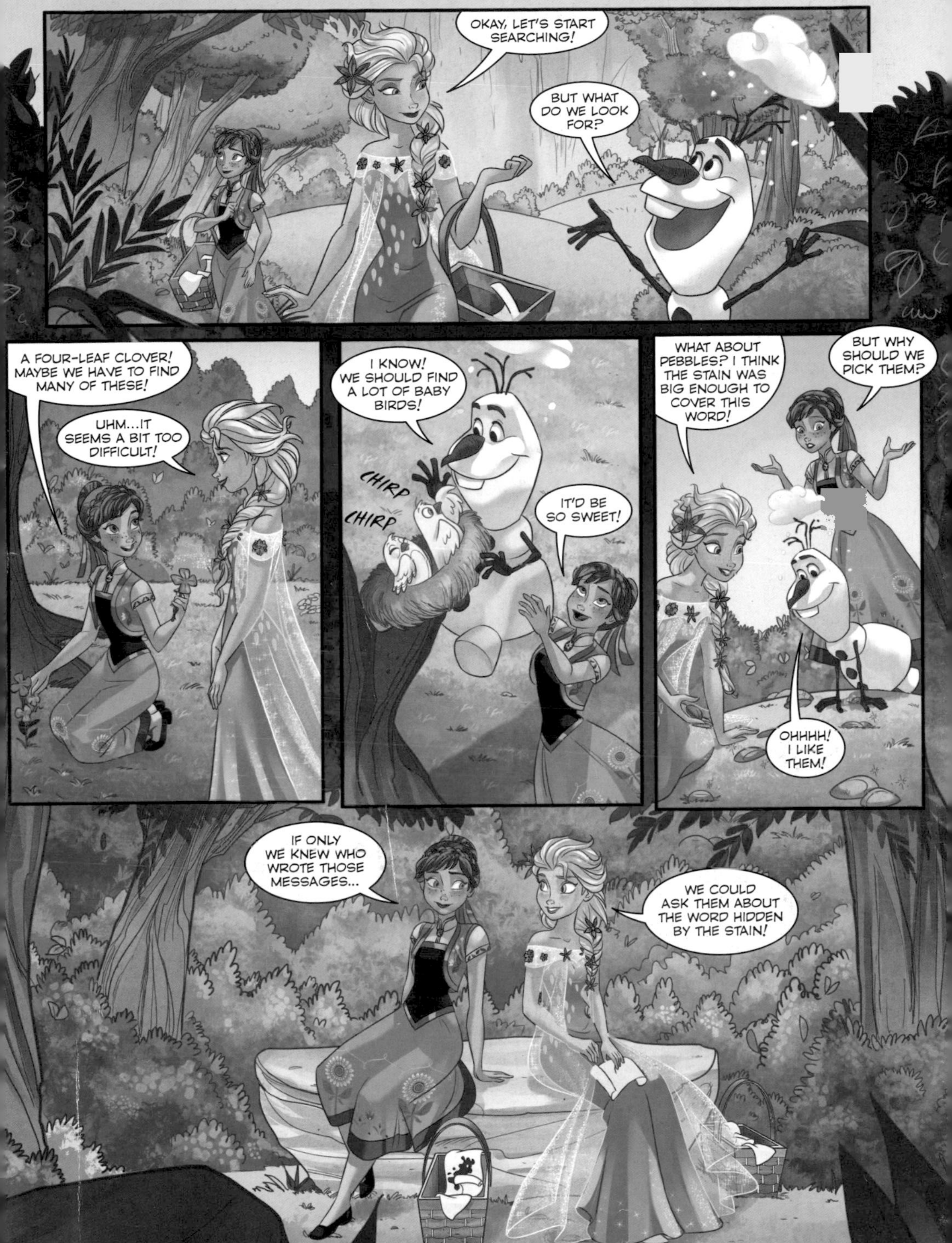

OKAY, LET'S START SEARCHING!
BUT WHAT DO WE LOOK FOR?
A FOUR-LEAF CLOVER! MAYBE WE HAVE TO FIND MANY OF THESE!
UHM...IT SEEMS A BIT TOO DIFFICULT!
I KNOW! WE SHOULD FIND A LOT OF BABY BIRDS!
CHIRP
CHIRP
IT'D BE SO SWEET!
WHAT ABOUT PEBBLES? I THINK THE STAIN WAS BIG ENOUGH TO COVER THIS WORD!
BUT WHY SHOULD WE PICK THEM?
OHHHH! I LIKE THEM!
IF ONLY WE KNEW WHO WROTE THOSE MESSAGES...
WE COULD ASK THEM ABOUT THE WORD HIDDEN BY THE STAIN!

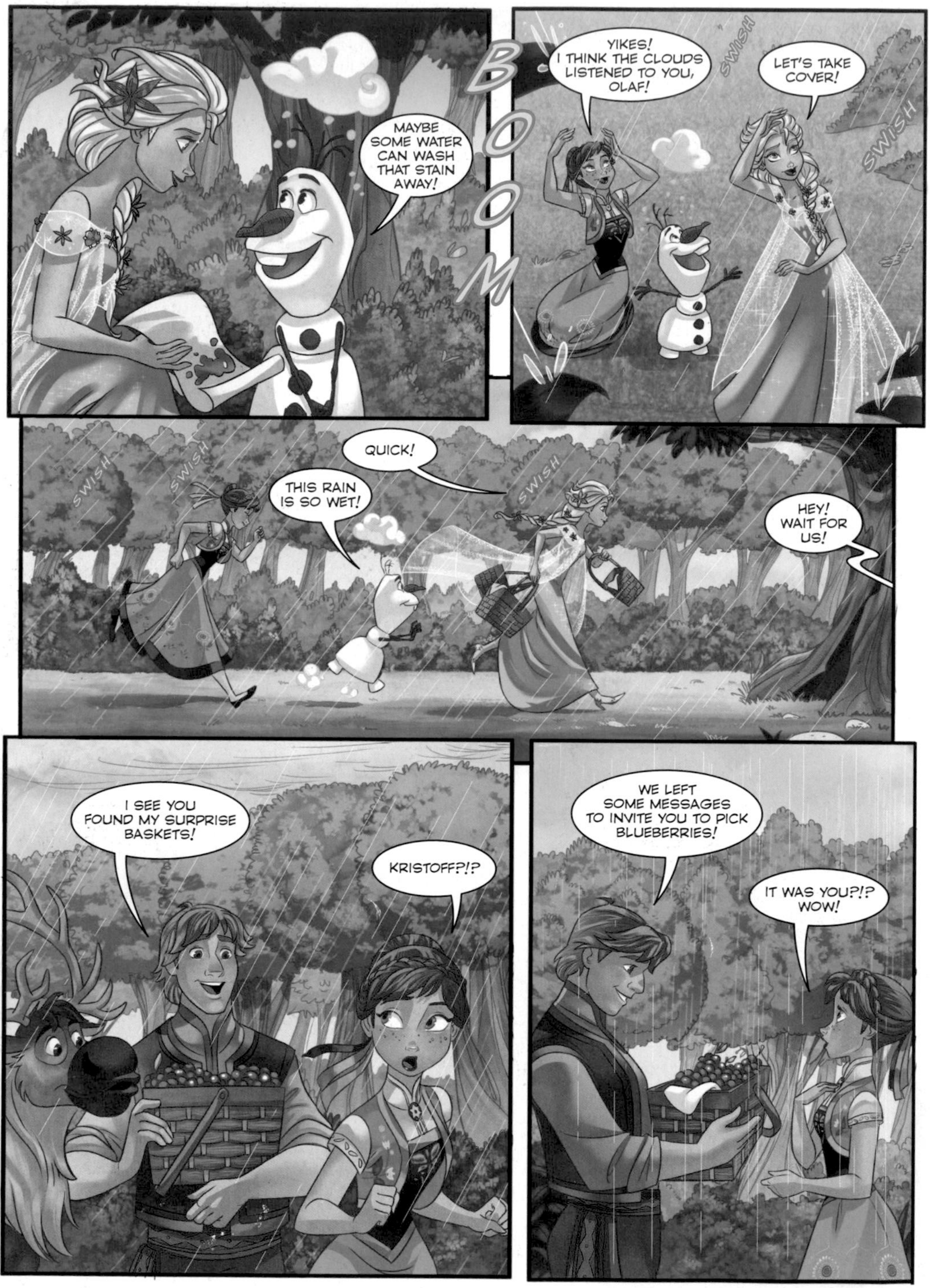
MAYBE SOME WATER CAN WASH THAT STAIN AWAY!
BOOM
YIKES! I THINK THE CLOUDS LISTENED TO YOU, OLAF!
SWISH
LET'S TAKE COVER!
SWISH
SWISH
SWISH
SWISH
QUICK!
THIS RAIN IS SO WET!
SWISH
HEY! WAIT FOR US!
I SEE YOU FOUND MY SURPRISE BASKETS!
KRISTOFF?!?
WE LEFT SOME MESSAGES TO INVITE YOU TO PICK BLUEBERRIES!
IT WAS YOU?!? WOW!

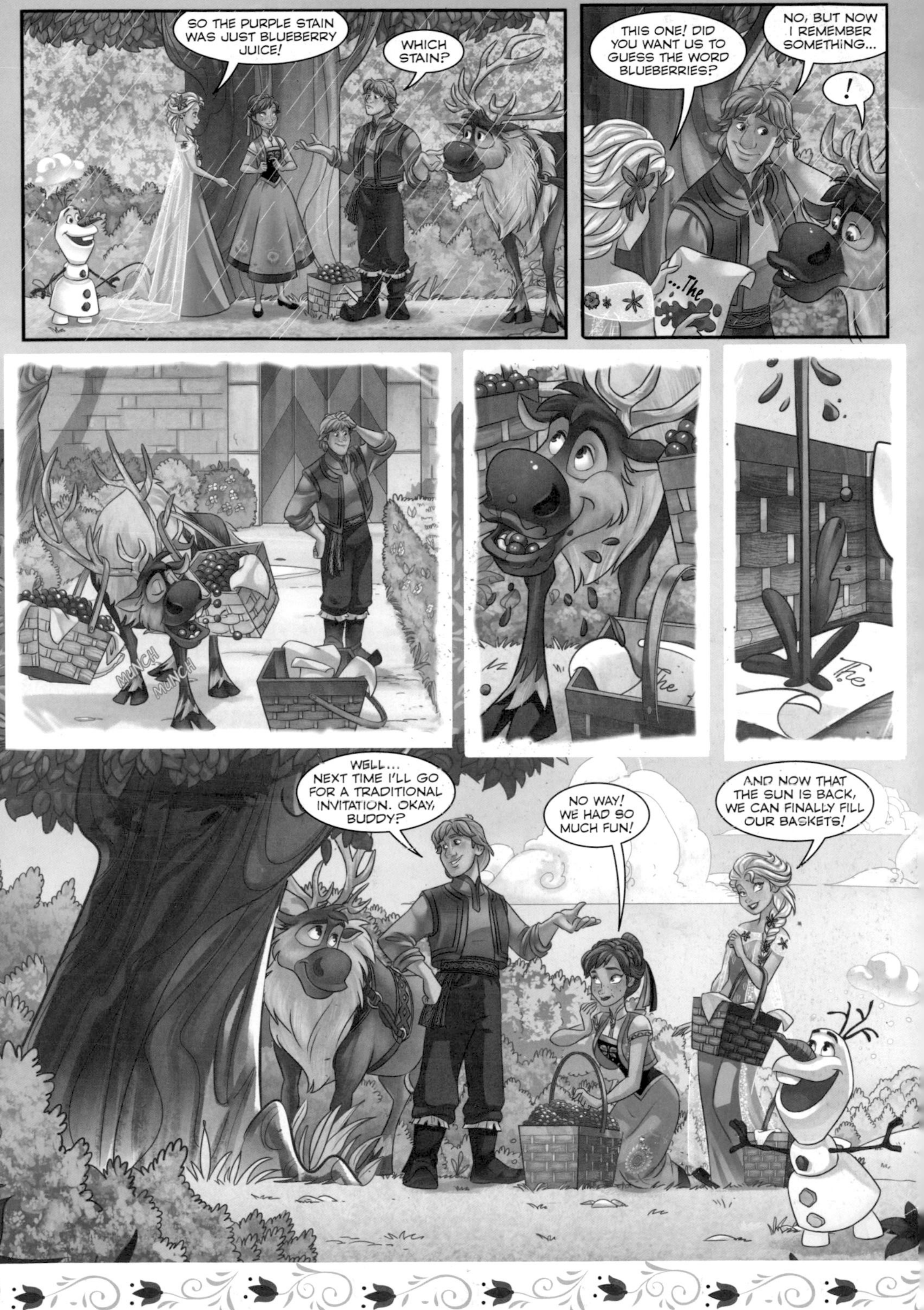
SO THE PURPLE STAIN WAS JUST BLUEBERRY JUICE!
WHICH STAIN?
THIS ONE! DID YOU WANT US TO GUESS THE WORD BLUEBERRIES?
NO, BUT NOW I REMEMBER SOMETHING...
!
...The
MUNCH
MUNCH
The
The
WELL... NEXT TIME I'LL GO FOR A TRADITIONAL INVITATION. OKAY, BUDDY?
NO WAY! WE HAD SO MUCH FUN!
AND NOW THAT THE SUN IS BACK, WE CAN FINALLY FILL OUR BASKETS!

# New Branches

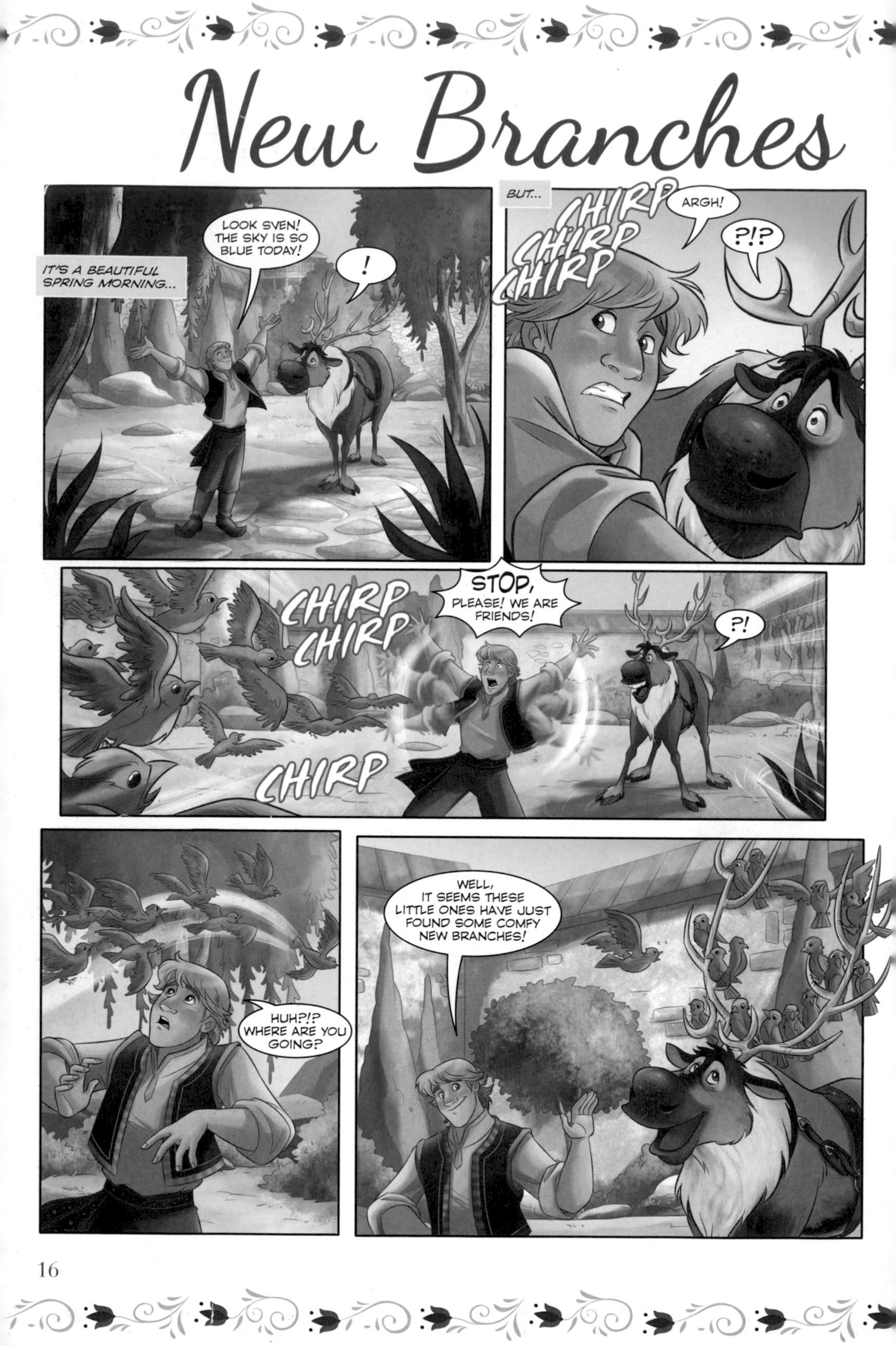
IT'S A BEAUTIFUL SPRING MORNING...
LOOK SVEN! THE SKY IS SO BLUE TODAY!
!
BUT...
CHIRP CHIRP CHIRP
ARGH!
?!?
CHIRP CHIRP
STOP, PLEASE! WE ARE FRIENDS!
?!
CHIRP
HUH?!? WHERE ARE YOU GOING?
WELL, IT SEEMS THESE LITTLE ONES HAVE JUST FOUND SOME COMFY NEW BRANCHES!

# Almost Ready

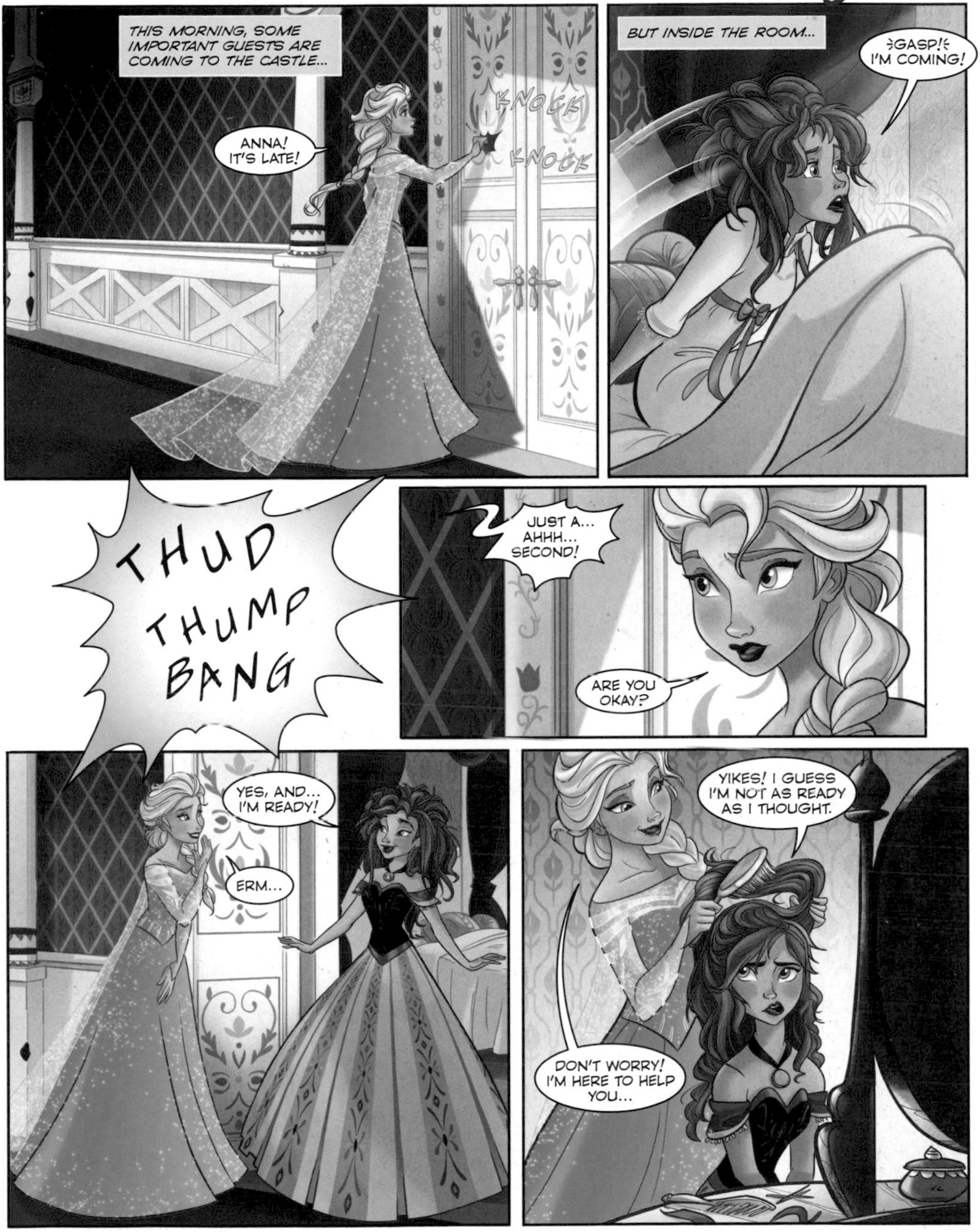

THIS MORNING, SOME IMPORTANT GUESTS ARE COMING TO THE CASTLE...
KNOCK
KNOCK
ANNA! IT'S LATE!
BUT INSIDE THE ROOM...
GASP! I'M COMING!
THUD
THUMP
BANG
JUST A... AHHH... SECOND!
ARE YOU OKAY?
YES, AND... I'M READY!
ERM...
YIKES! I GUESS I'M NOT AS READY AS I THOUGHT.
DON'T WORRY! I'M HERE TO HELP YOU...

# Question of Balance

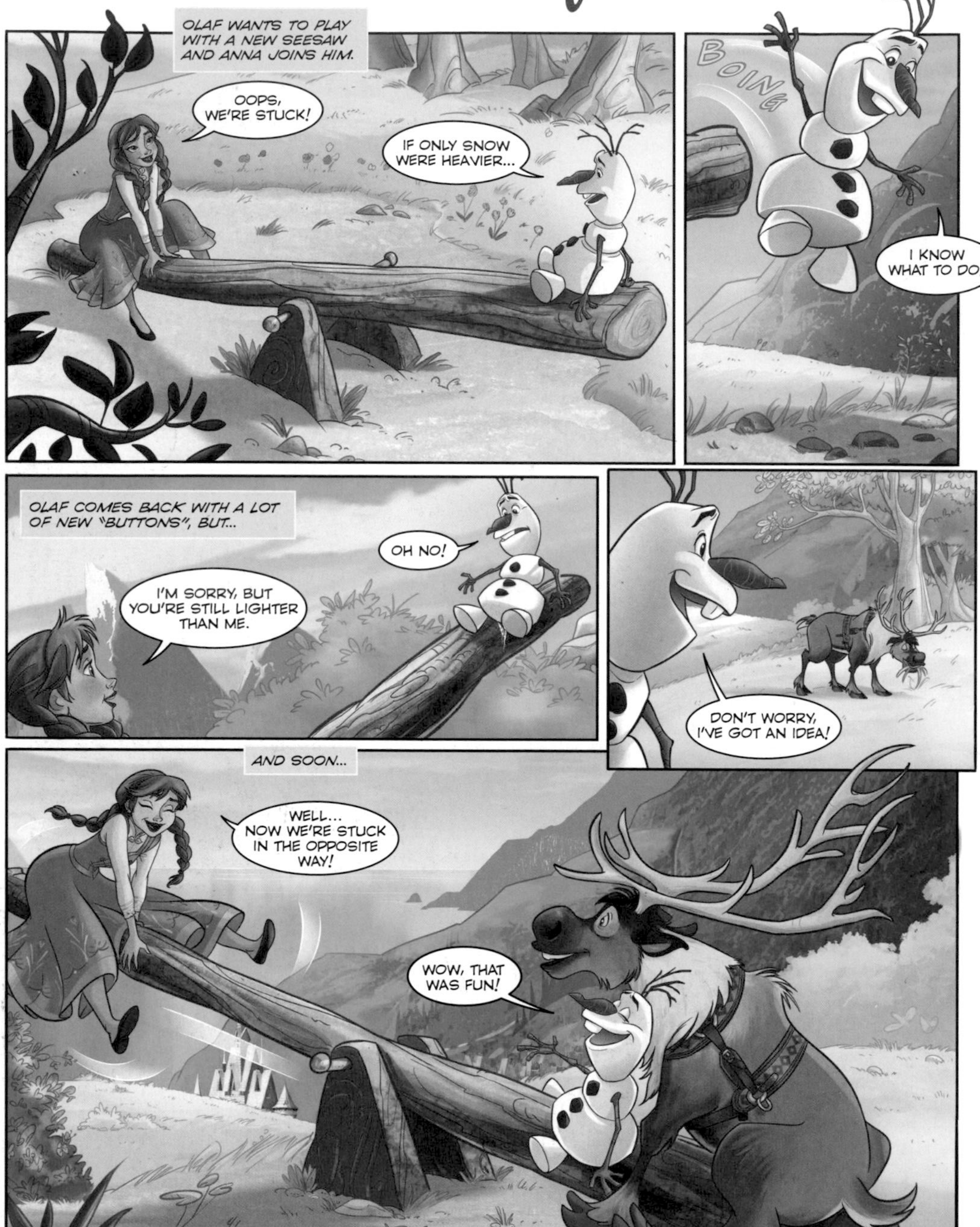

OLAF WANTS TO PLAY WITH A NEW SEESAW AND ANNA JOINS HIM.
OOPS, WE'RE STUCK!
IF ONLY SNOW WERE HEAVIER...
BOING
I KNOW WHAT TO DO!
OLAF COMES BACK WITH A LOT OF NEW "BUTTONS", BUT...
OH NO!
I'M SORRY, BUT YOU'RE STILL LIGHTER THAN ME.
DON'T WORRY, I'VE GOT AN IDEA!
AND SOON...
WELL... NOW WE'RE STUCK IN THE OPPOSITE WAY!
WOW, THAT WAS FUN!

# Spring Trolls

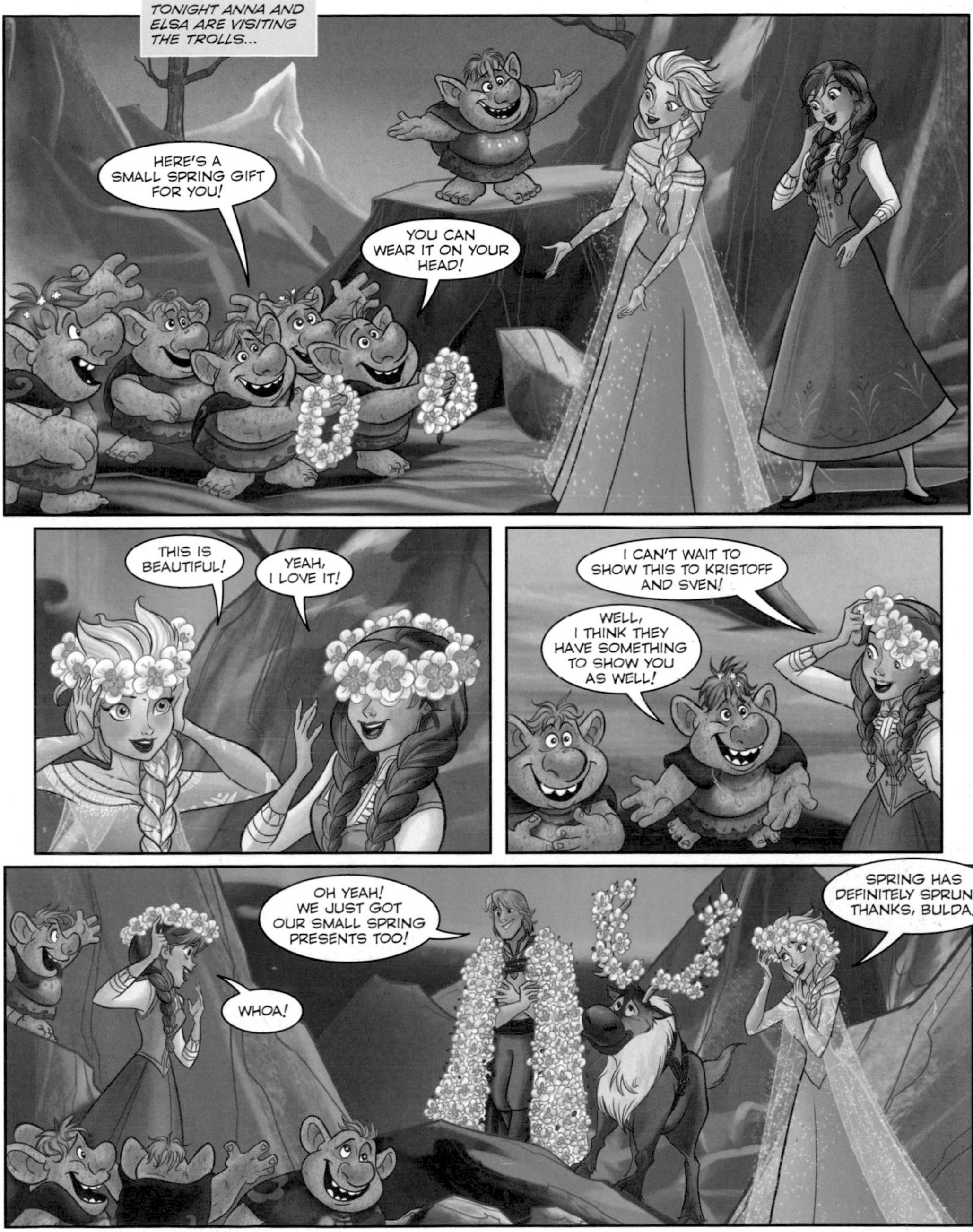

TONIGHT ANNA AND ELSA ARE VISITING THE TROLLS...
HERE'S A SMALL SPRING GIFT FOR YOU!
YOU CAN WEAR IT ON YOUR HEAD!
THIS IS BEAUTIFUL!
YEAH, I LOVE IT!
I CAN'T WAIT TO SHOW THIS TO KRISTOFF AND SVEN!
WELL, I THINK THEY HAVE SOMETHING TO SHOW YOU AS WELL!
OH YEAH! WE JUST GOT OUR SMALL SPRING PRESENTS TOO!
WHOA!
SPRING HAS DEFINITELY SPRUNG! THANKS, BULDA!

# A New Reindeer Friend

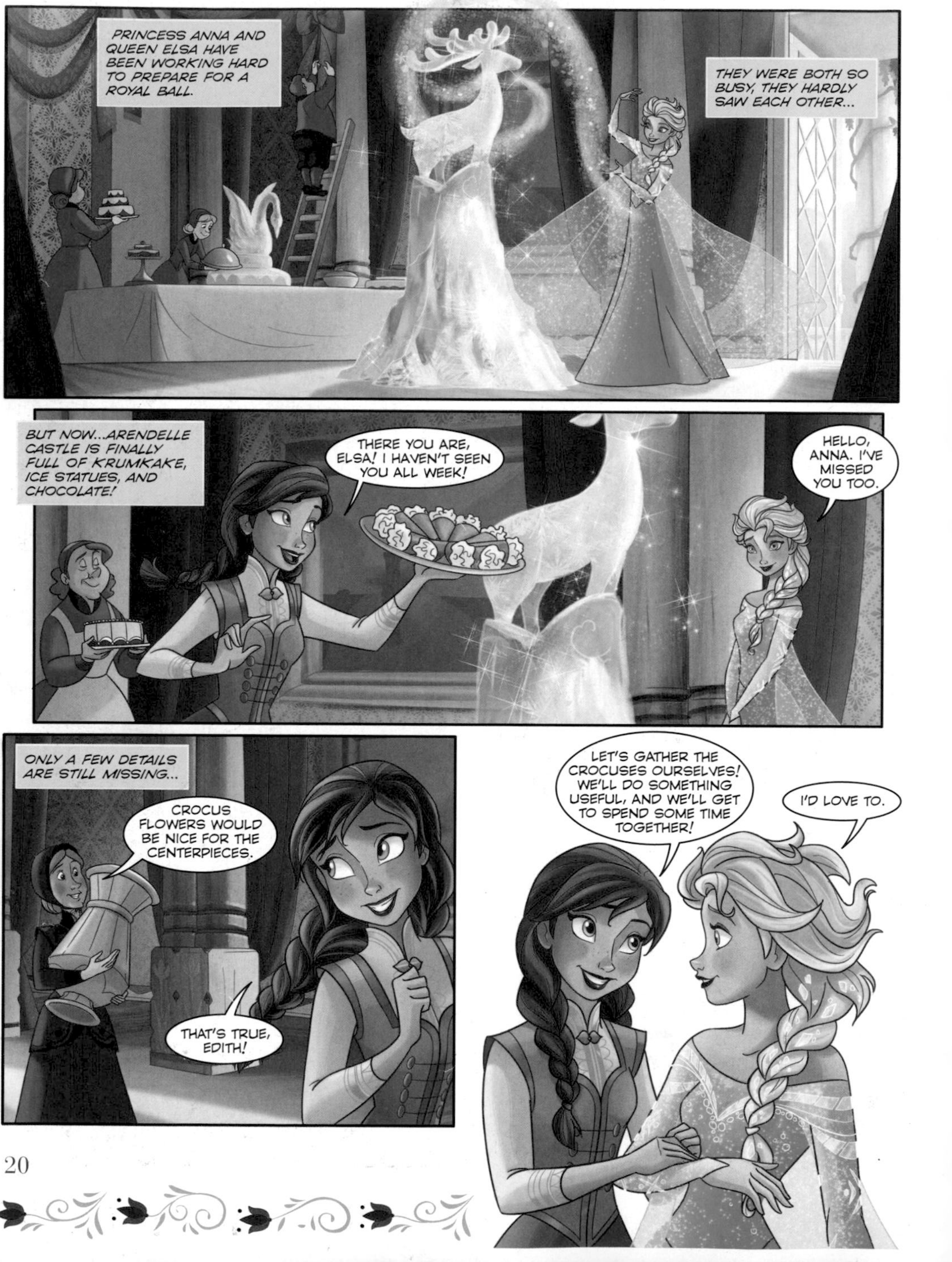
PRINCESS ANNA AND QUEEN ELSA HAVE BEEN WORKING HARD TO PREPARE FOR A ROYAL BALL.
THEY WERE BOTH SO BUSY, THEY HARDLY SAW EACH OTHER...
BUT NOW...ARENDELLE CASTLE IS FINALLY FULL OF KRUMKAKE, ICE STATUES, AND CHOCOLATE!
THERE YOU ARE, ELSA! I HAVEN'T SEEN YOU ALL WEEK!
HELLO, ANNA. I'VE MISSED YOU TOO.
ONLY A FEW DETAILS ARE STILL MISSING...
CROCUS FLOWERS WOULD BE NICE FOR THE CENTERPIECES.
THAT'S TRUE, EDITH!
LET'S GATHER THE CROCUSES OURSELVES! WE'LL DO SOMETHING USEFUL, AND WE'LL GET TO SPEND SOME TIME TOGETHER!
I'D LOVE TO.

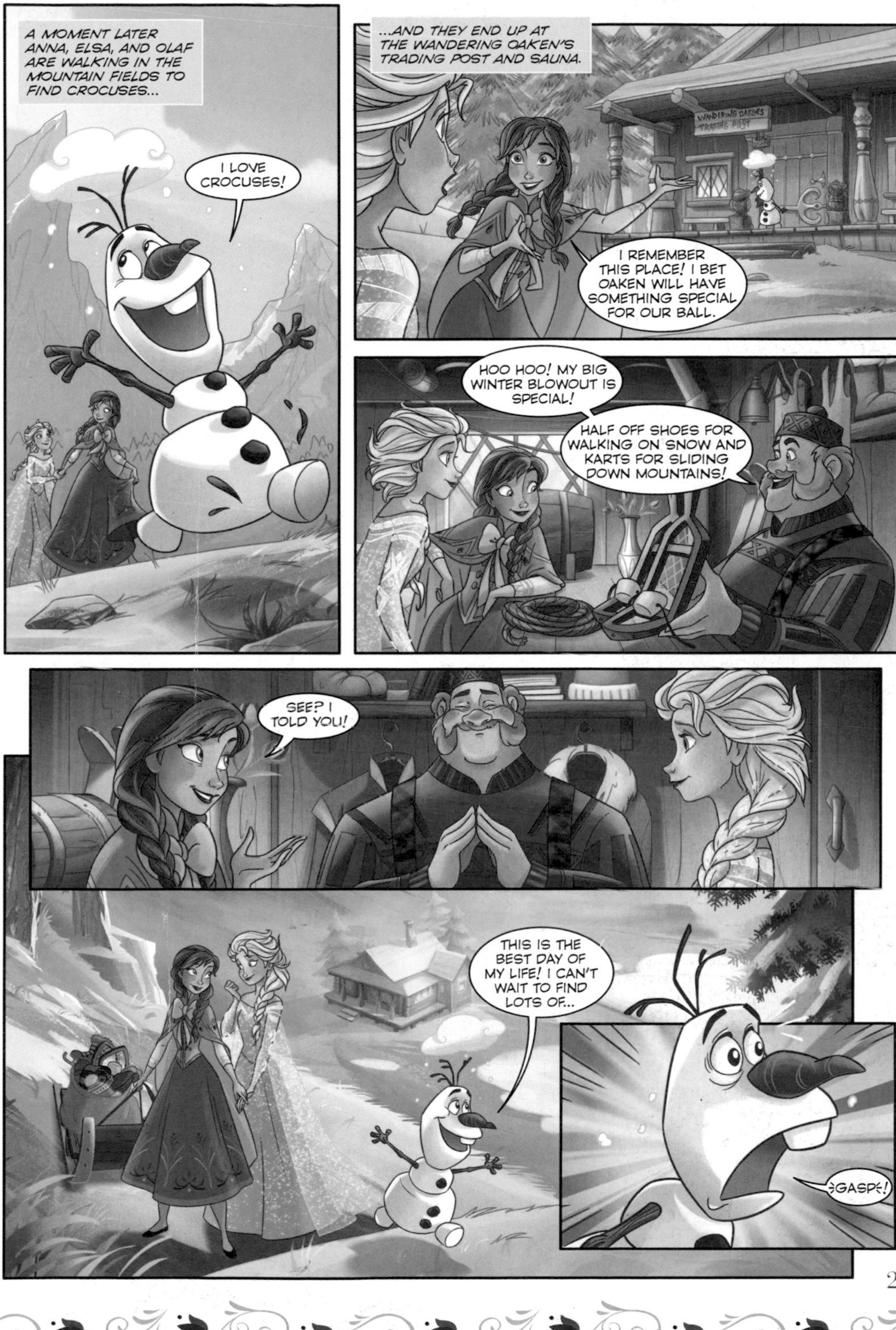
A MOMENT LATER ANNA, ELSA, AND OLAF ARE WALKING IN THE MOUNTAIN FIELDS TO FIND CROCUSES...
I LOVE CROCUSES!
...AND THEY END UP AT THE WANDERING OAKEN'S TRADING POST AND SAUNA.
I REMEMBER THIS PLACE! I BET OAKEN WILL HAVE SOMETHING SPECIAL FOR OUR BALL.
HOO HOO! MY BIG WINTER BLOWOUT IS SPECIAL!
HALF OFF SHOES FOR WALKING ON SNOW AND KARTS FOR SLIDING DOWN MOUNTAINS!
SEE? I TOLD YOU!
THIS IS THE BEST DAY OF MY LIFE! I CAN'T WAIT TO FIND LOTS OF...
GASP!

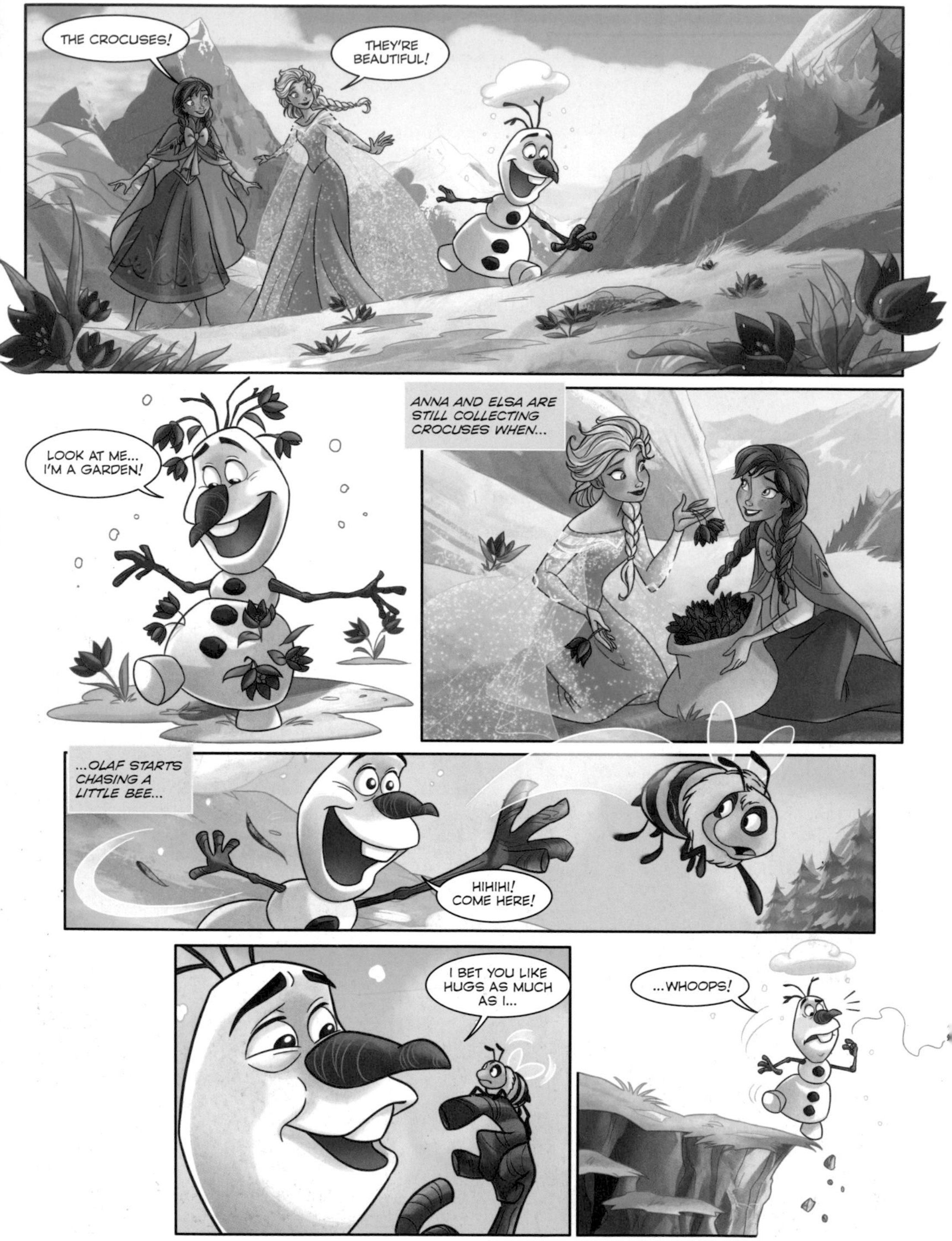
THE CROCUSES!
THEY'RE BEAUTIFUL!
LOOK AT ME... I'M A GARDEN!
ANNA AND ELSA ARE STILL COLLECTING CROCUSES WHEN...
...OLAF STARTS CHASING A LITTLE BEE...
HIHIHI! COME HERE!
I BET YOU LIKE HUGS AS MUCH AS I...
...WHOOPS!

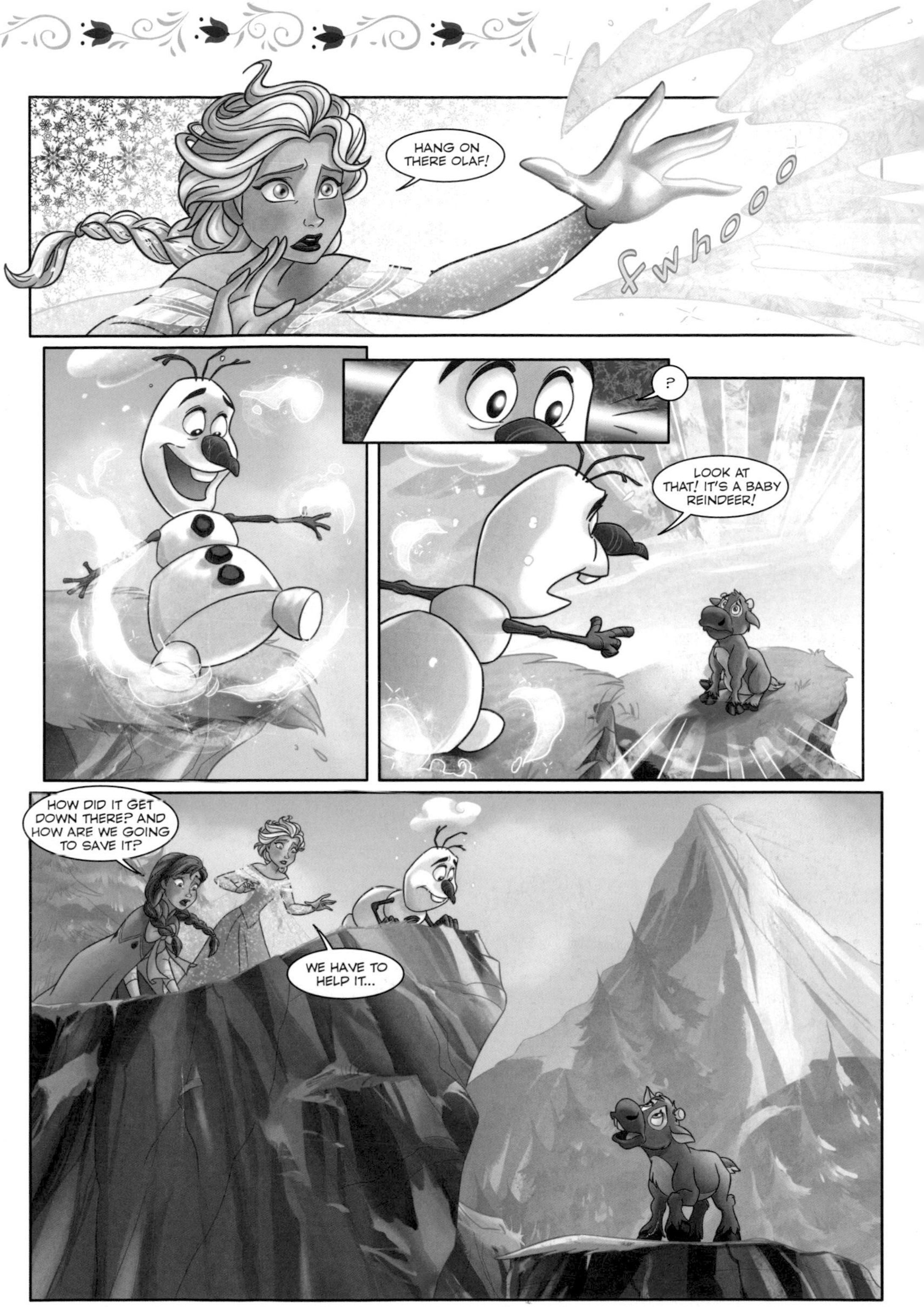
HANG ON THERE OLAF!
fwhoooo
?
LOOK AT THAT! IT'S A BABY REINDEER!
HOW DID IT GET DOWN THERE? AND HOW ARE WE GOING TO SAVE IT?
WE HAVE TO HELP IT...

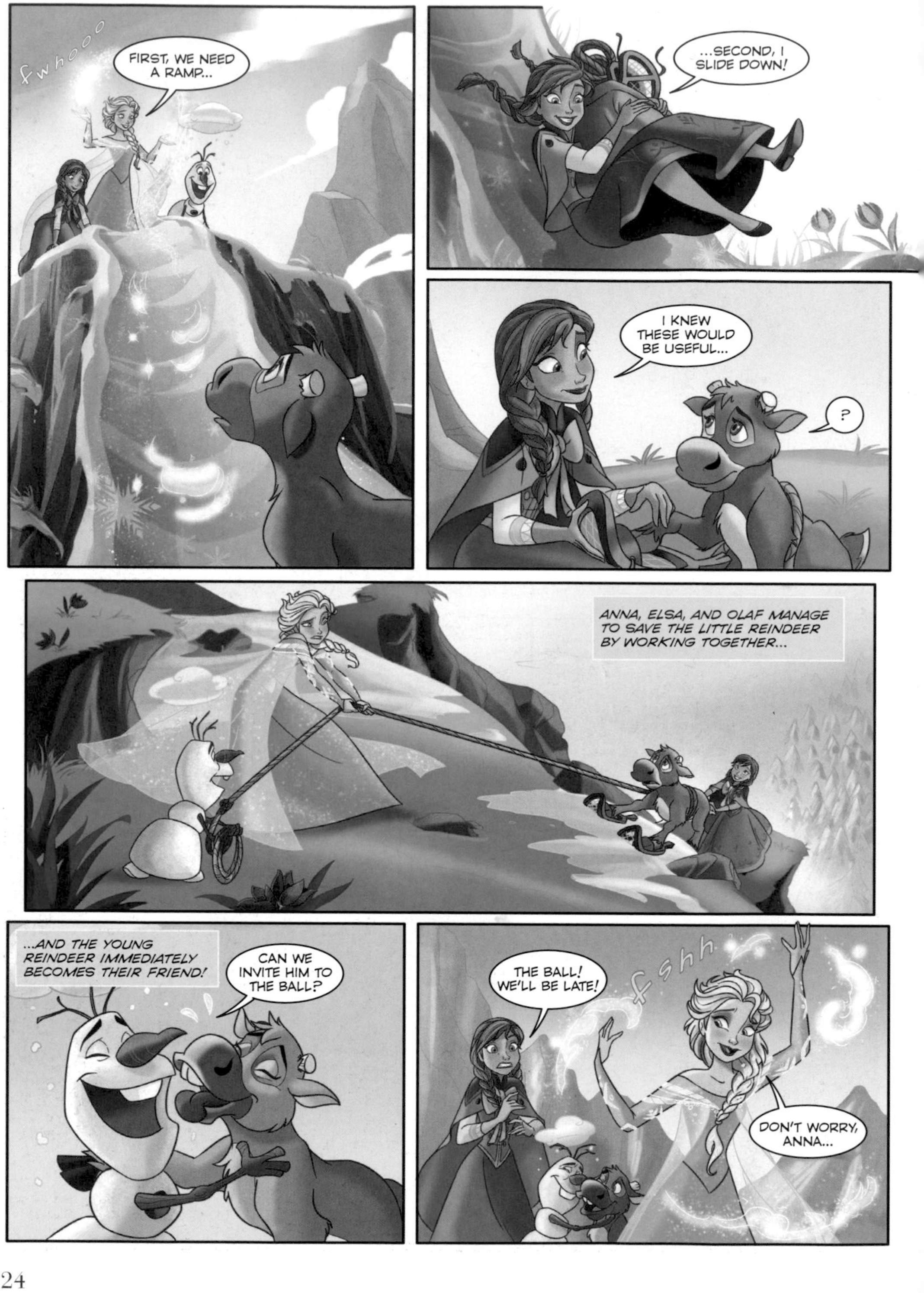

fwhooo
FIRST, WE NEED A RAMP...
...SECOND, I SLIDE DOWN!
I KNEW THESE WOULD BE USEFUL...
?
ANNA, ELSA, AND OLAF MANAGE TO SAVE THE LITTLE REINDEER BY WORKING TOGETHER...
...AND THE YOUNG REINDEER IMMEDIATELY BECOMES THEIR FRIEND!
CAN WE INVITE HIM TO THE BALL?
THE BALL! WE'LL BE LATE!
fshh
DON'T WORRY, ANNA...

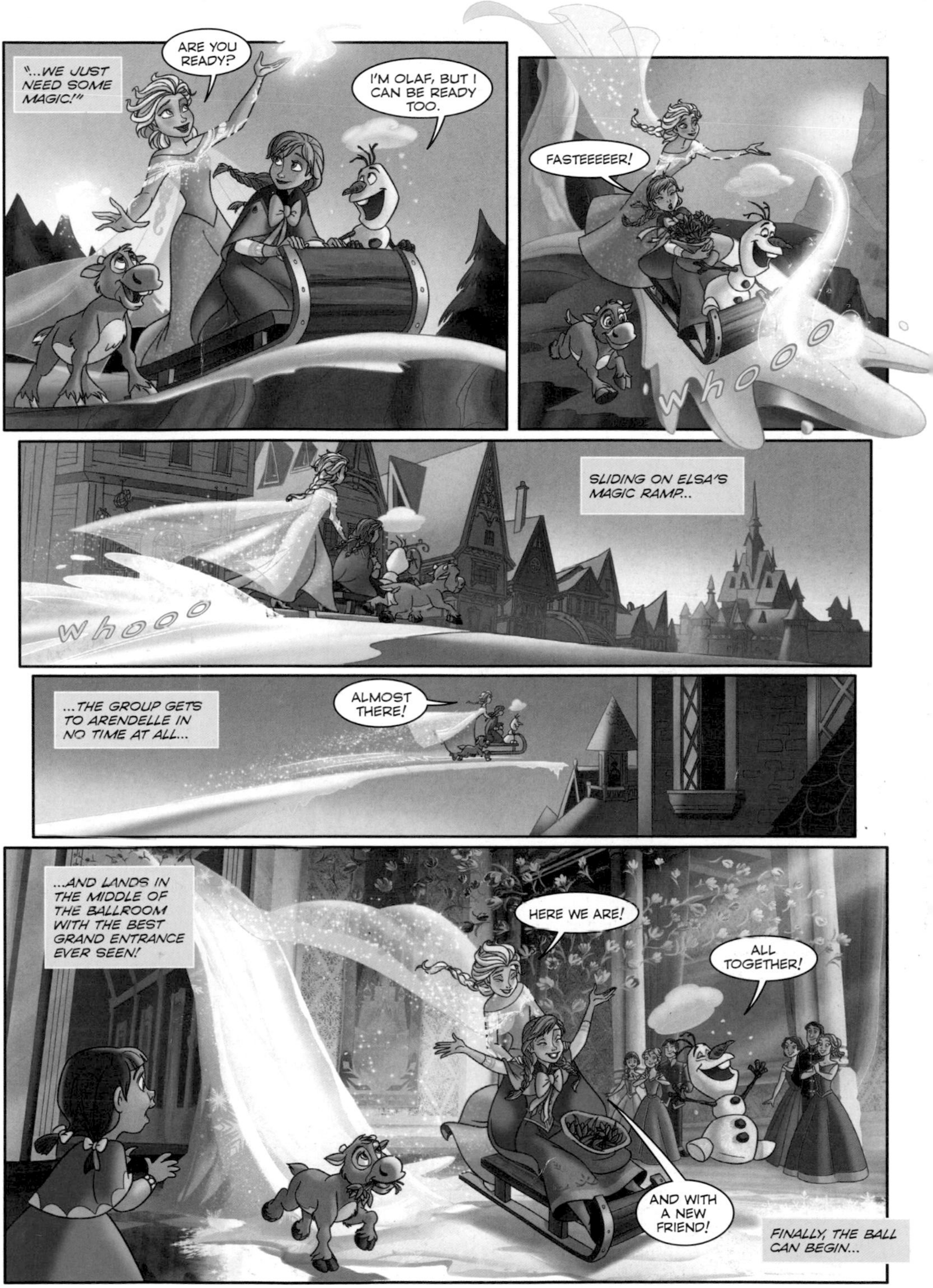
"...WE JUST NEED SOME MAGIC!"
ARE YOU READY?
I'M OLAF, BUT I CAN BE READY TOO.
FASTEEEEER!
WHOOOO
SLIDING ON ELSA'S MAGIC RAMP...
WHOOO
...THE GROUP GETS TO ARENDELLE IN NO TIME AT ALL...
ALMOST THERE!
...AND LANDS IN THE MIDDLE OF THE BALLROOM WITH THE BEST GRAND ENTRANCE EVER SEEN!
HERE WE ARE!
ALL TOGETHER!
AND WITH A NEW FRIEND!
FINALLY, THE BALL CAN BEGIN...

# The Right Season

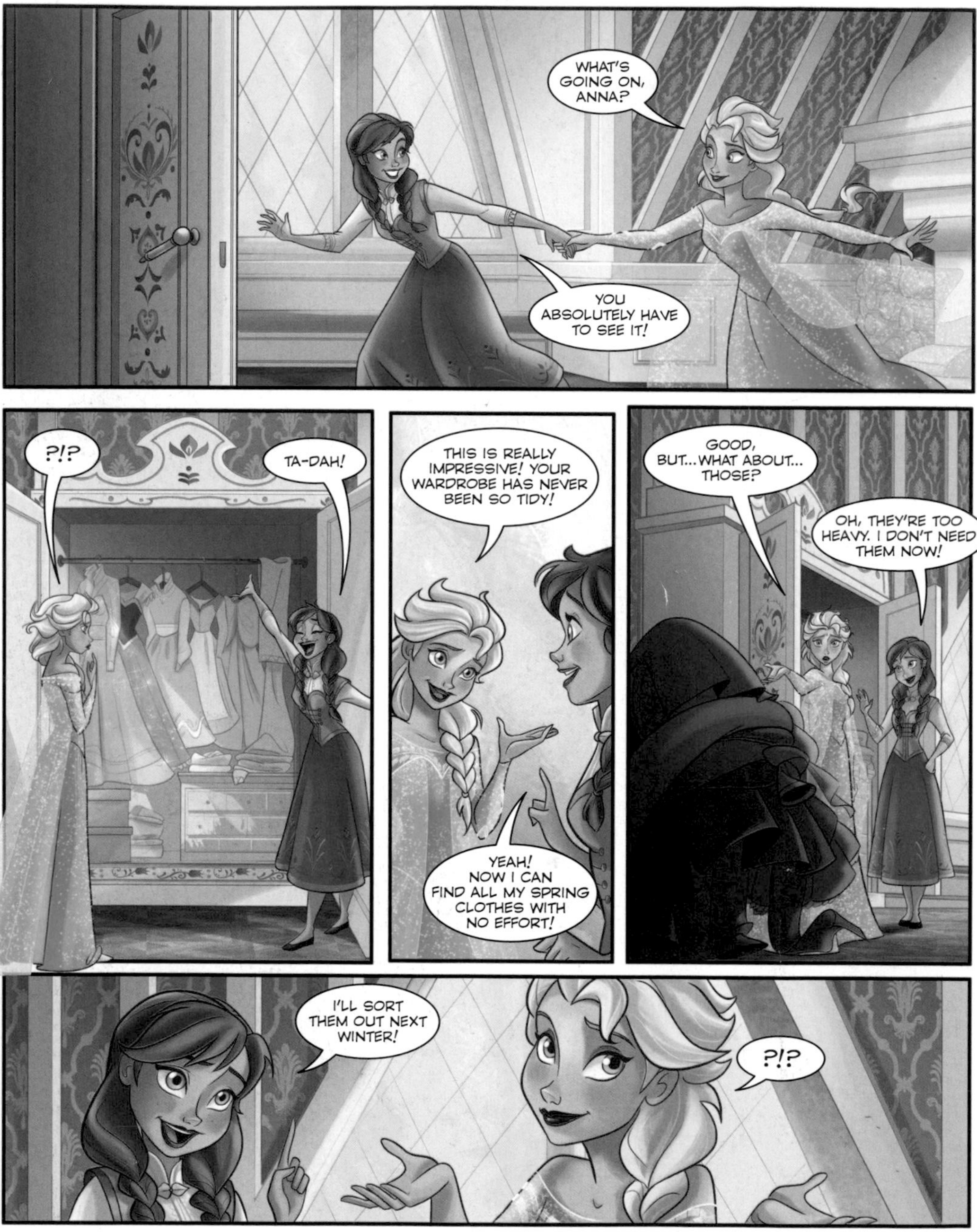
WHAT'S GOING ON, ANNA?
YOU ABSOLUTELY HAVE TO SEE IT!
?!?
TA-DAH!
THIS IS REALLY IMPRESSIVE! YOUR WARDROBE HAS NEVER BEEN SO TIDY!
YEAH! NOW I CAN FIND ALL MY SPRING CLOTHES WITH NO EFFORT!
GOOD, BUT...WHAT ABOUT... THOSE?
OH, THEY'RE TOO HEAVY. I DON'T NEED THEM NOW!
I'LL SORT THEM OUT NEXT WINTER!
?!?

# A Touch of Spring

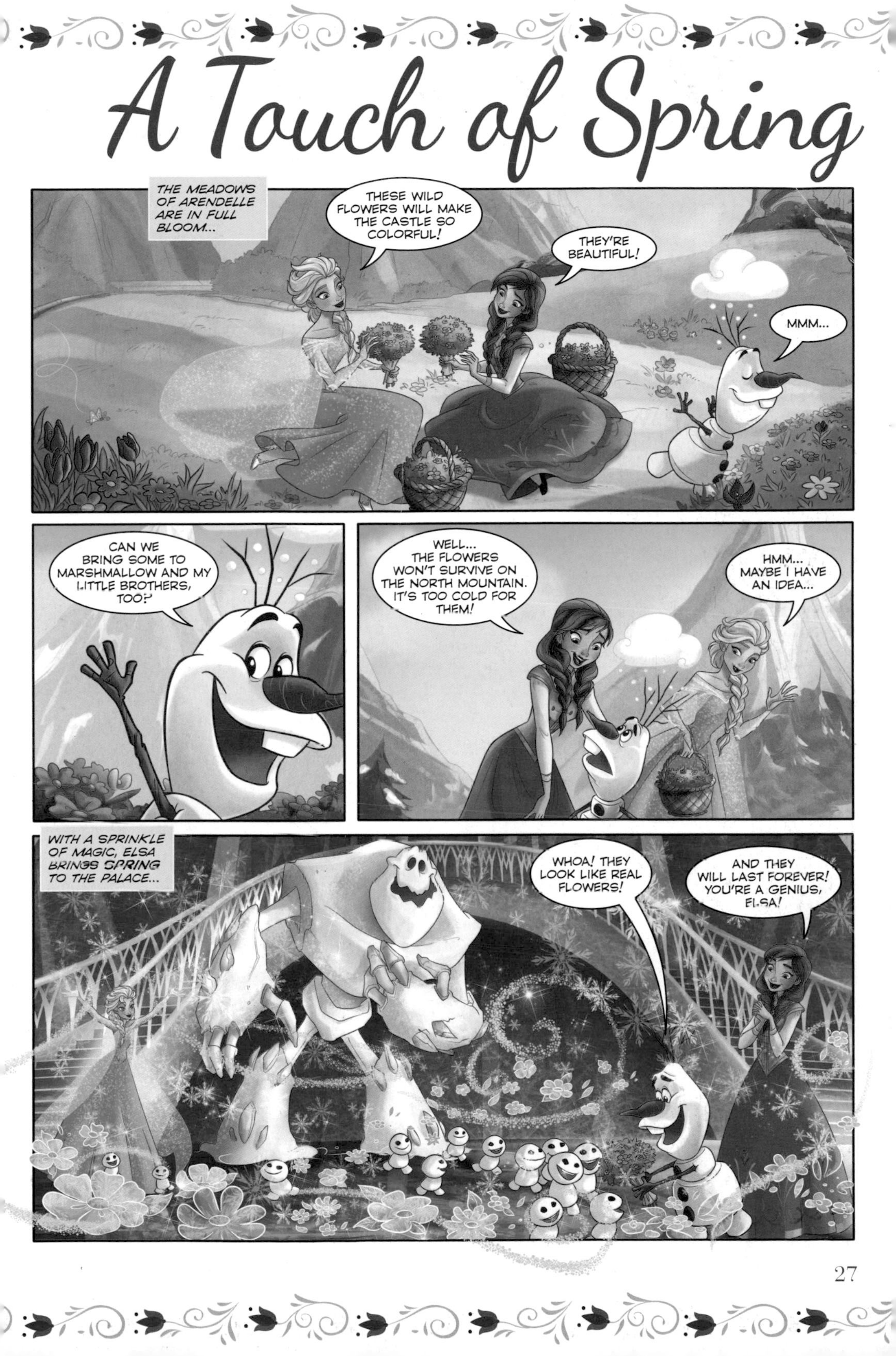
THE MEADOWS OF ARENDELLE ARE IN FULL BLOOM...
THESE WILD FLOWERS WILL MAKE THE CASTLE SO COLORFUL!
THEY'RE BEAUTIFUL!
MMM...
CAN WE BRING SOME TO MARSHMALLOW AND MY LITTLE BROTHERS, TOO?
WELL... THE FLOWERS WON'T SURVIVE ON THE NORTH MOUNTAIN. IT'S TOO COLD FOR THEM!
HMM... MAYBE I HAVE AN IDEA...
WITH A SPRINKLE OF MAGIC, ELSA BRINGS SPRING TO THE PALACE...
WHOA! THEY LOOK LIKE REAL FLOWERS!
AND THEY WILL LAST FOREVER! YOU'RE A GENIUS, ELSA!

# The Carrot Guard

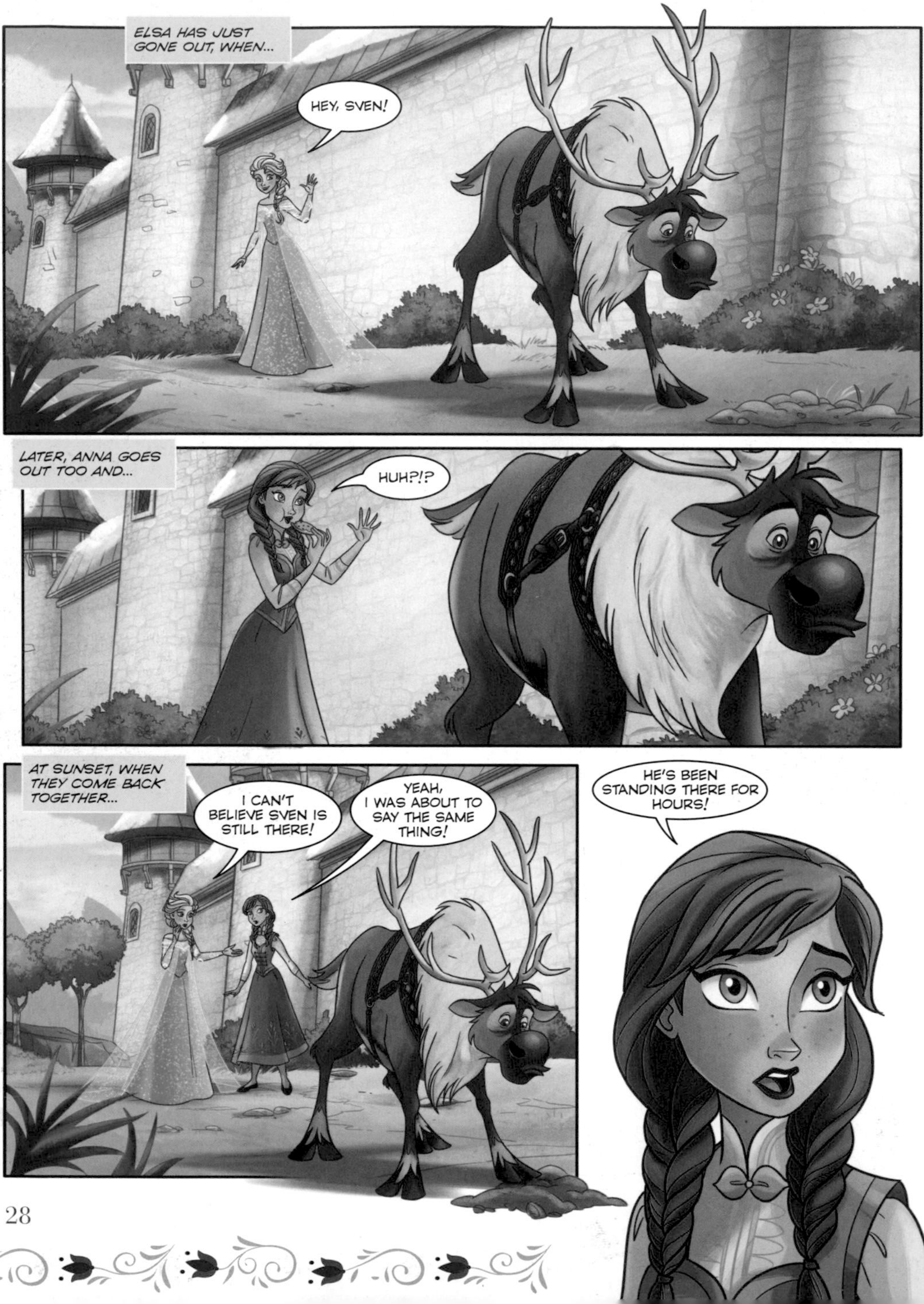
ELSA HAS JUST GONE OUT, WHEN...
HEY, SVEN!
LATER, ANNA GOES OUT TOO AND...
HUH?!?
AT SUNSET, WHEN THEY COME BACK TOGETHER...
I CAN'T BELIEVE SVEN IS STILL THERE!
YEAH, I WAS ABOUT TO SAY THE SAME THING!
HE'S BEEN STANDING THERE FOR HOURS!

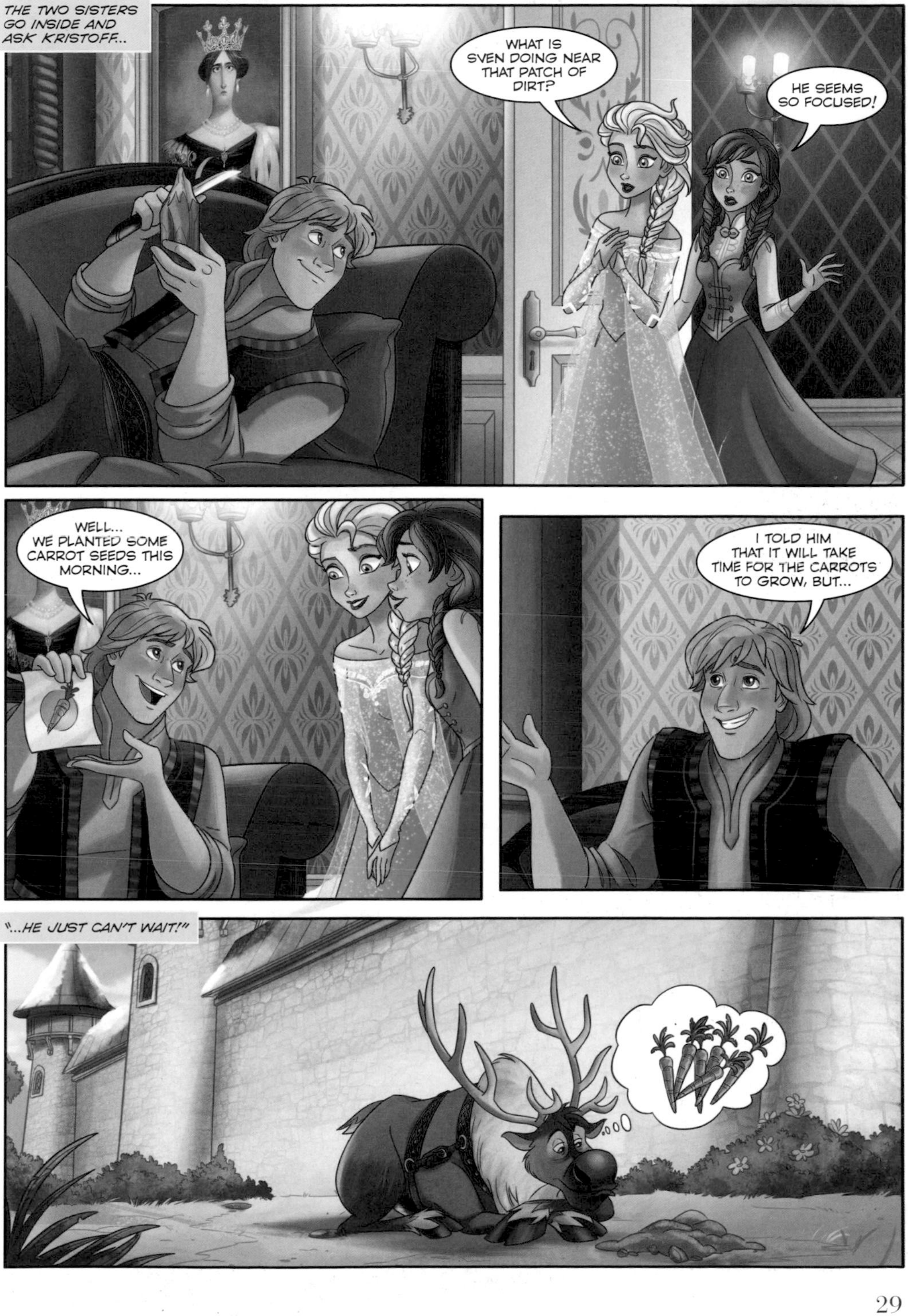
THE TWO SISTERS GO INSIDE AND ASK KRISTOFF...
WHAT IS SVEN DOING NEAR THAT PATCH OF DIRT?
HE SEEMS SO FOCUSED!
WELL... WE PLANTED SOME CARROT SEEDS THIS MORNING...
I TOLD HIM THAT IT WILL TAKE TIME FOR THE CARROTS TO GROW, BUT...
"...HE JUST CAN'T WAIT!"

# A Great Spring Game

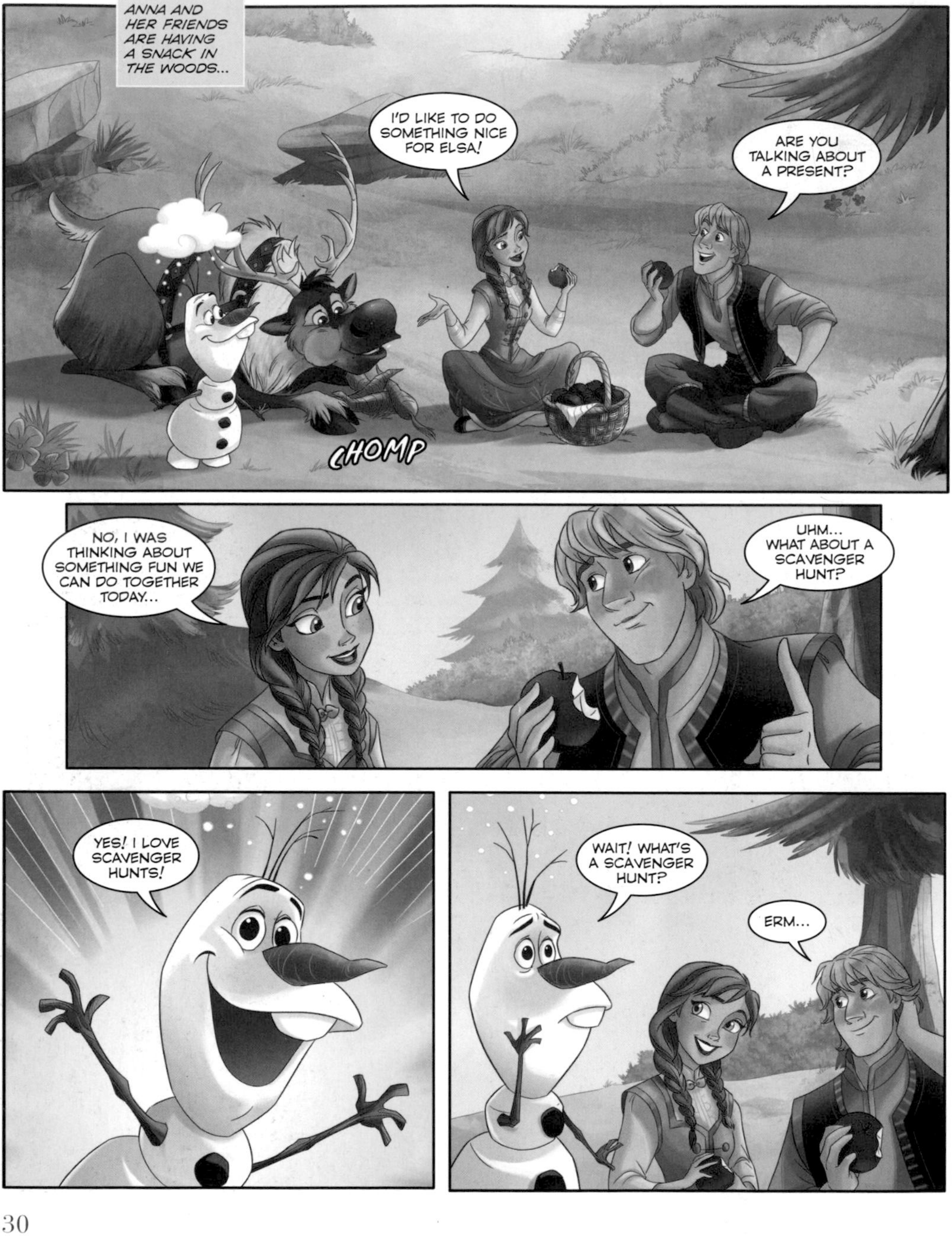
ANNA AND HER FRIENDS ARE HAVING A SNACK IN THE WOODS...
I'D LIKE TO DO SOMETHING NICE FOR ELSA!
ARE YOU TALKING ABOUT A PRESENT?
CHOMP
NO, I WAS THINKING ABOUT SOMETHING FUN WE CAN DO TOGETHER TODAY...
UHM... WHAT ABOUT A SCAVENGER HUNT?
YES! I LOVE SCAVENGER HUNTS!
WAIT! WHAT'S A SCAVENGER HUNT?
ERM...

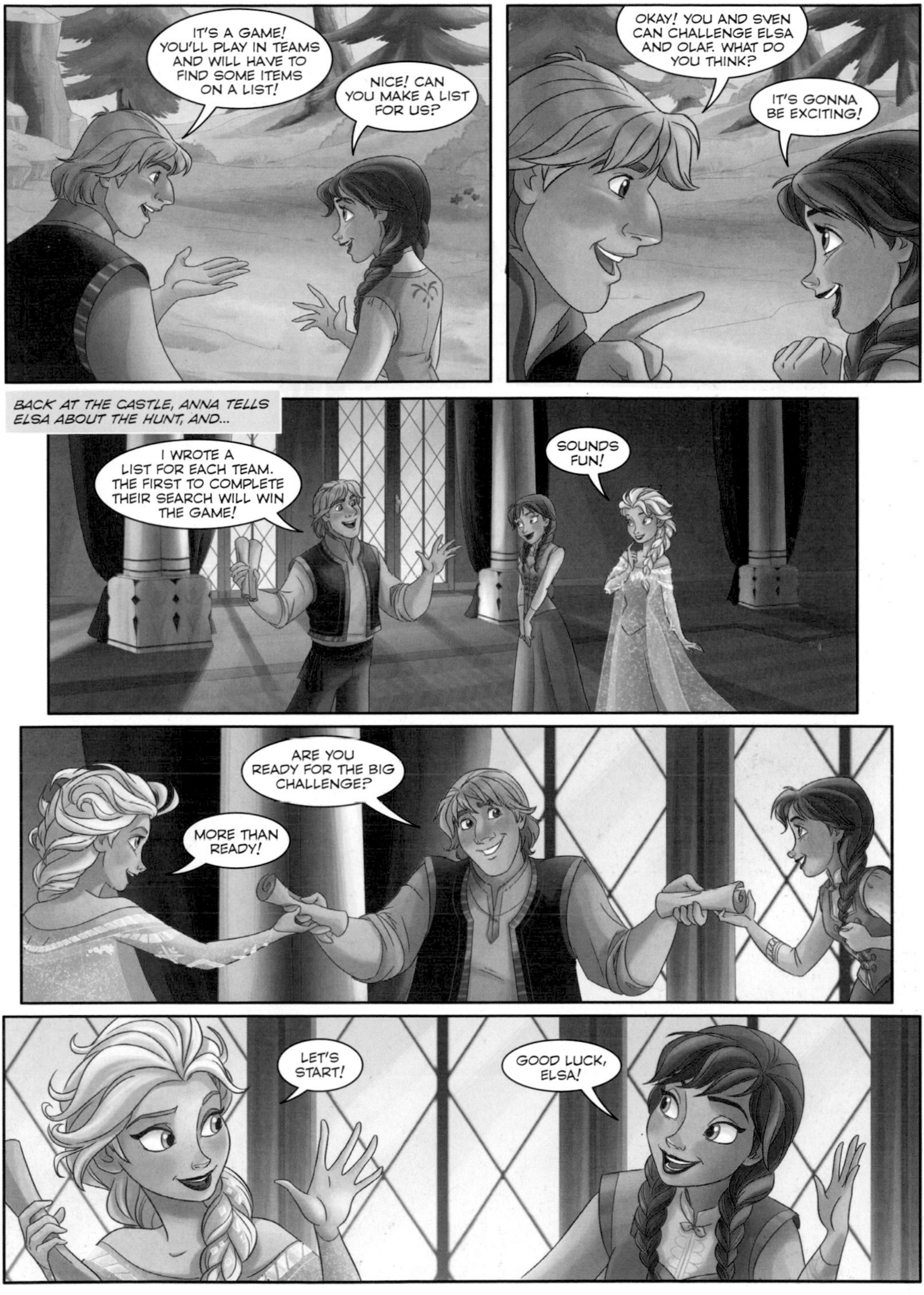
IT'S A GAME! YOU'LL PLAY IN TEAMS AND WILL HAVE TO FIND SOME ITEMS ON A LIST!
NICE! CAN YOU MAKE A LIST FOR US?
OKAY! YOU AND SVEN CAN CHALLENGE ELSA AND OLAF. WHAT DO YOU THINK?
IT'S GONNA BE EXCITING!
BACK AT THE CASTLE, ANNA TELLS ELSA ABOUT THE HUNT, AND...
I WROTE A LIST FOR EACH TEAM. THE FIRST TO COMPLETE THEIR SEARCH WILL WIN THE GAME!
SOUNDS FUN!
ARE YOU READY FOR THE BIG CHALLENGE?
MORE THAN READY!
LET'S START!
GOOD LUCK, ELSA!

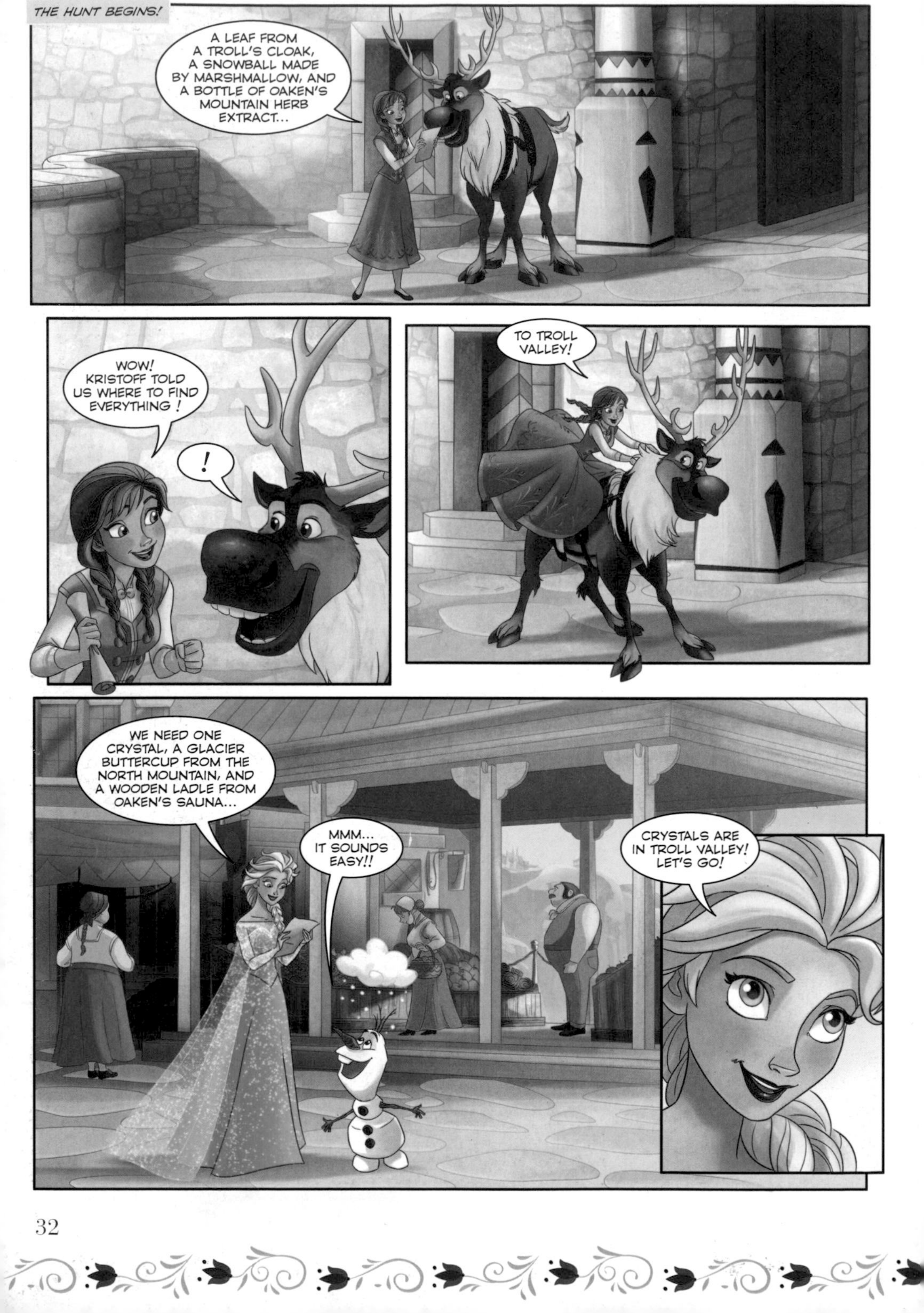
THE HUNT BEGINS!
A LEAF FROM A TROLL'S CLOAK, A SNOWBALL MADE BY MARSHMALLOW, AND A BOTTLE OF OAKEN'S MOUNTAIN HERB EXTRACT...
WOW! KRISTOFF TOLD US WHERE TO FIND EVERYTHING!
!
TO TROLL VALLEY!
WE NEED ONE CRYSTAL, A GLACIER BUTTERCUP FROM THE NORTH MOUNTAIN, AND A WOODEN LADLE FROM OAKEN'S SAUNA...
MMM... IT SOUNDS EASY!!
CRYSTALS ARE IN TROLL VALLEY! LET'S GO!

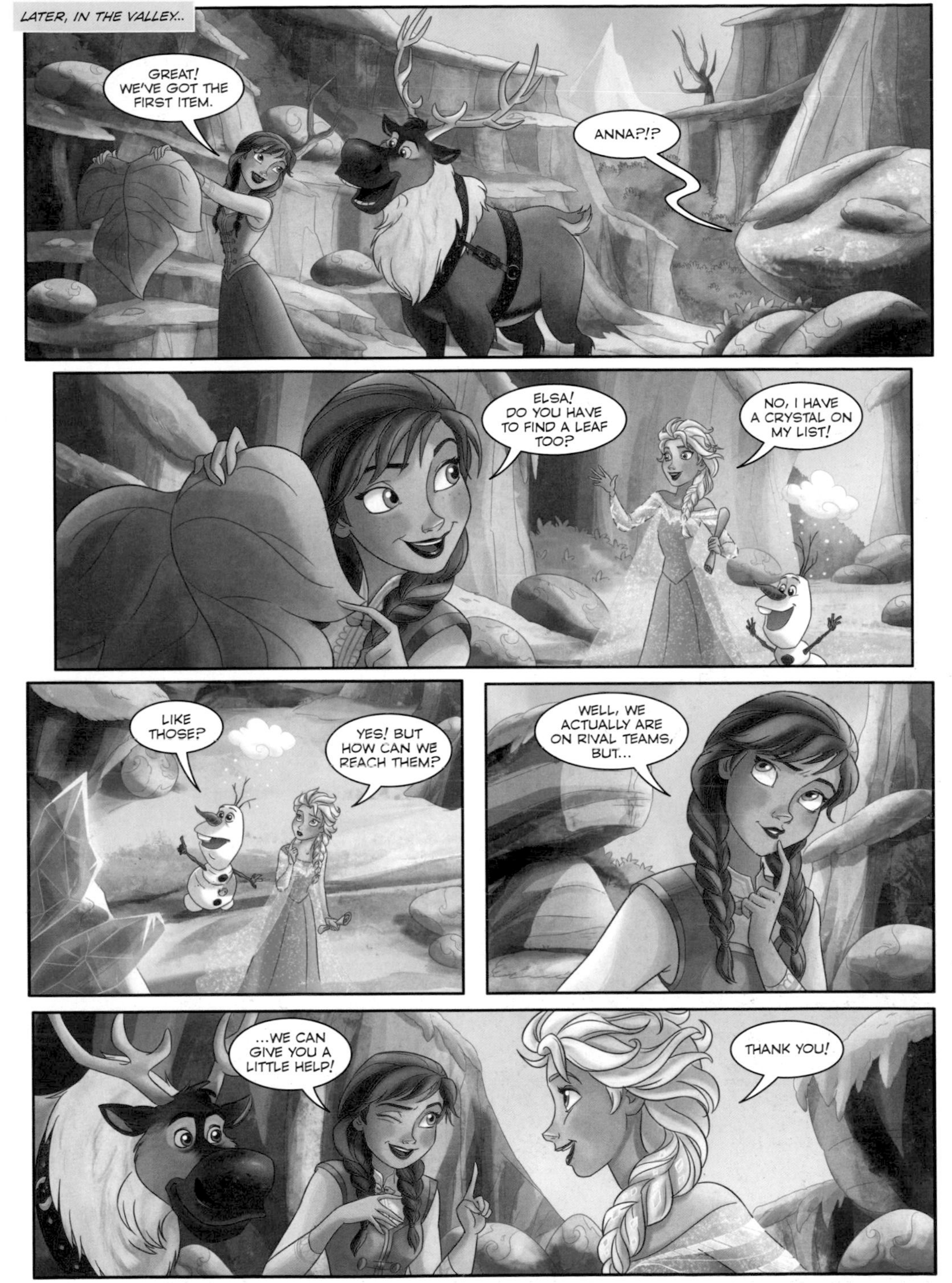
LATER, IN THE VALLEY...
GREAT! WE'VE GOT THE FIRST ITEM.
ANNA?!?
ELSA! DO YOU HAVE TO FIND A LEAF TOO?
NO, I HAVE A CRYSTAL ON MY LIST!
LIKE THOSE?
YES! BUT HOW CAN WE REACH THEM?
WELL, WE ACTUALLY ARE ON RIVAL TEAMS, BUT...
...WE CAN GIVE YOU A LITTLE HELP!
THANK YOU!

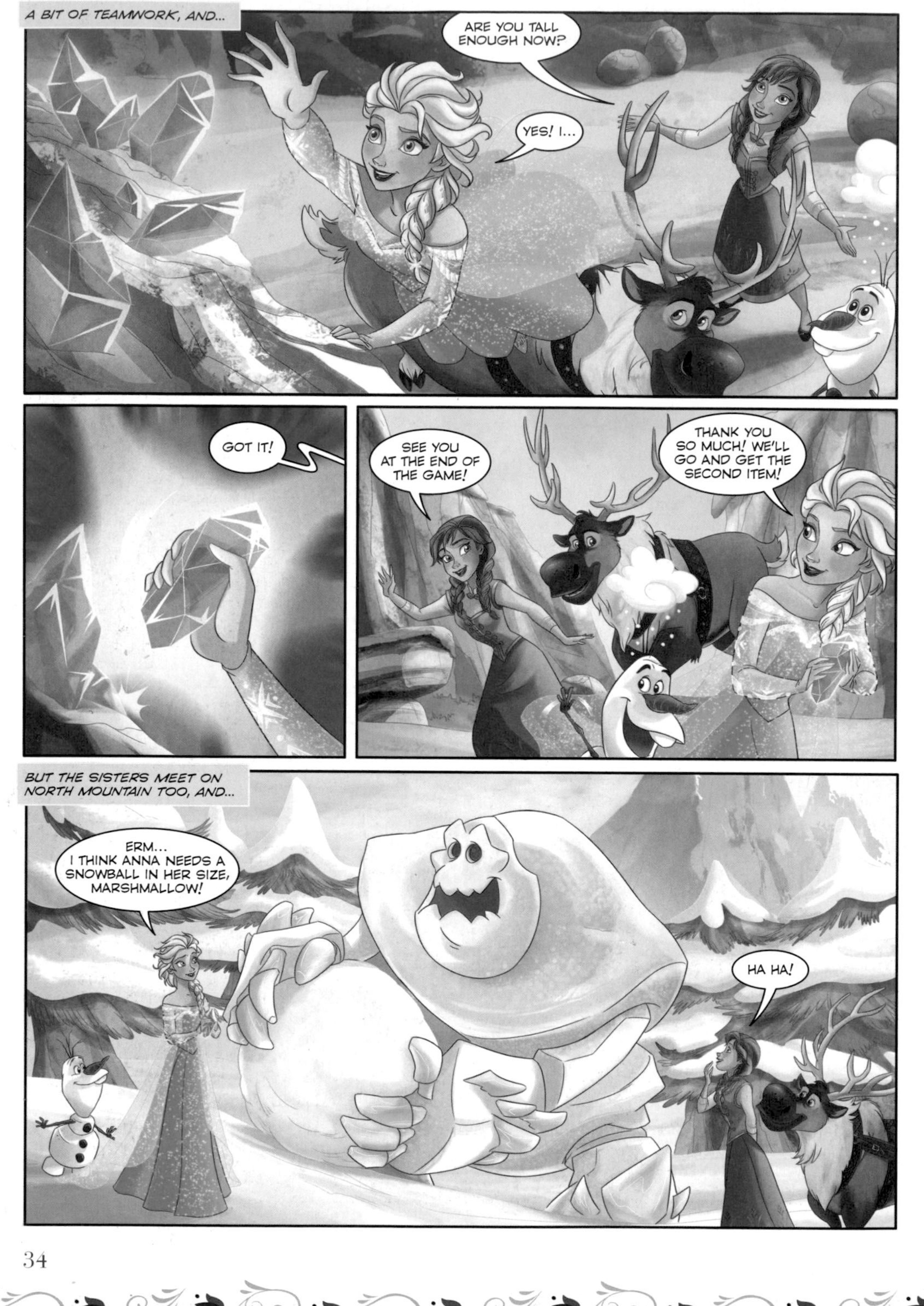
A BIT OF TEAMWORK, AND...
ARE YOU TALL ENOUGH NOW?
YES! I...
GOT IT!
SEE YOU AT THE END OF THE GAME!
THANK YOU SO MUCH! WE'LL GO AND GET THE SECOND ITEM!
BUT THE SISTERS MEET ON NORTH MOUNTAIN TOO, AND...
ERM... I THINK ANNA NEEDS A SNOWBALL IN HER SIZE, MARSHMALLOW!
HA HA!

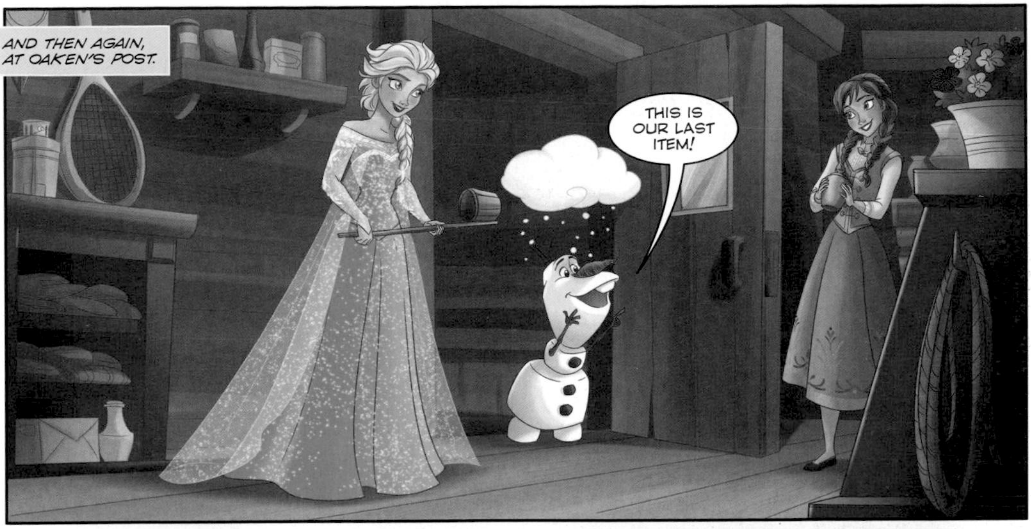
AND THEN AGAIN, AT OAKEN'S POST.
THIS IS OUR LAST ITEM!

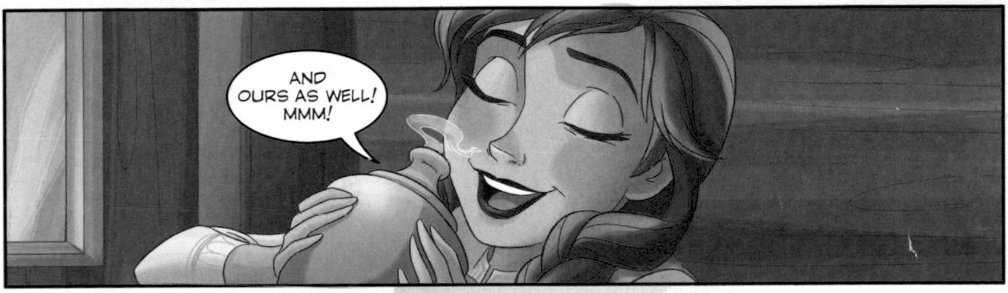
AND OURS AS WELL! MMM!

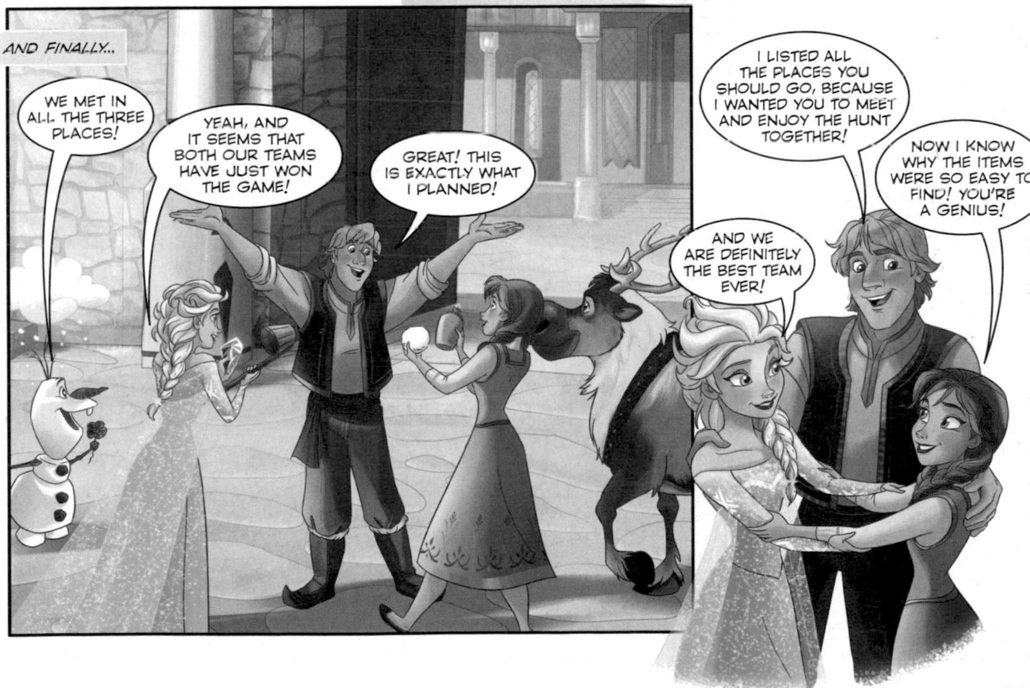
AND FINALLY...
WE MET IN ALL THE THREE PLACES!
YEAH, AND IT SEEMS THAT BOTH OUR TEAMS HAVE JUST WON THE GAME!
GREAT! THIS IS EXACTLY WHAT I PLANNED!
I LISTED ALL THE PLACES YOU SHOULD GO, BECAUSE I WANTED YOU TO MEET AND ENJOY THE HUNT TOGETHER!
NOW I KNOW WHY THE ITEMS WERE SO EASY TO FIND! YOU'RE A GENIUS!
AND WE ARE DEFINITELY THE BEST TEAM EVER!

# A Funny Show

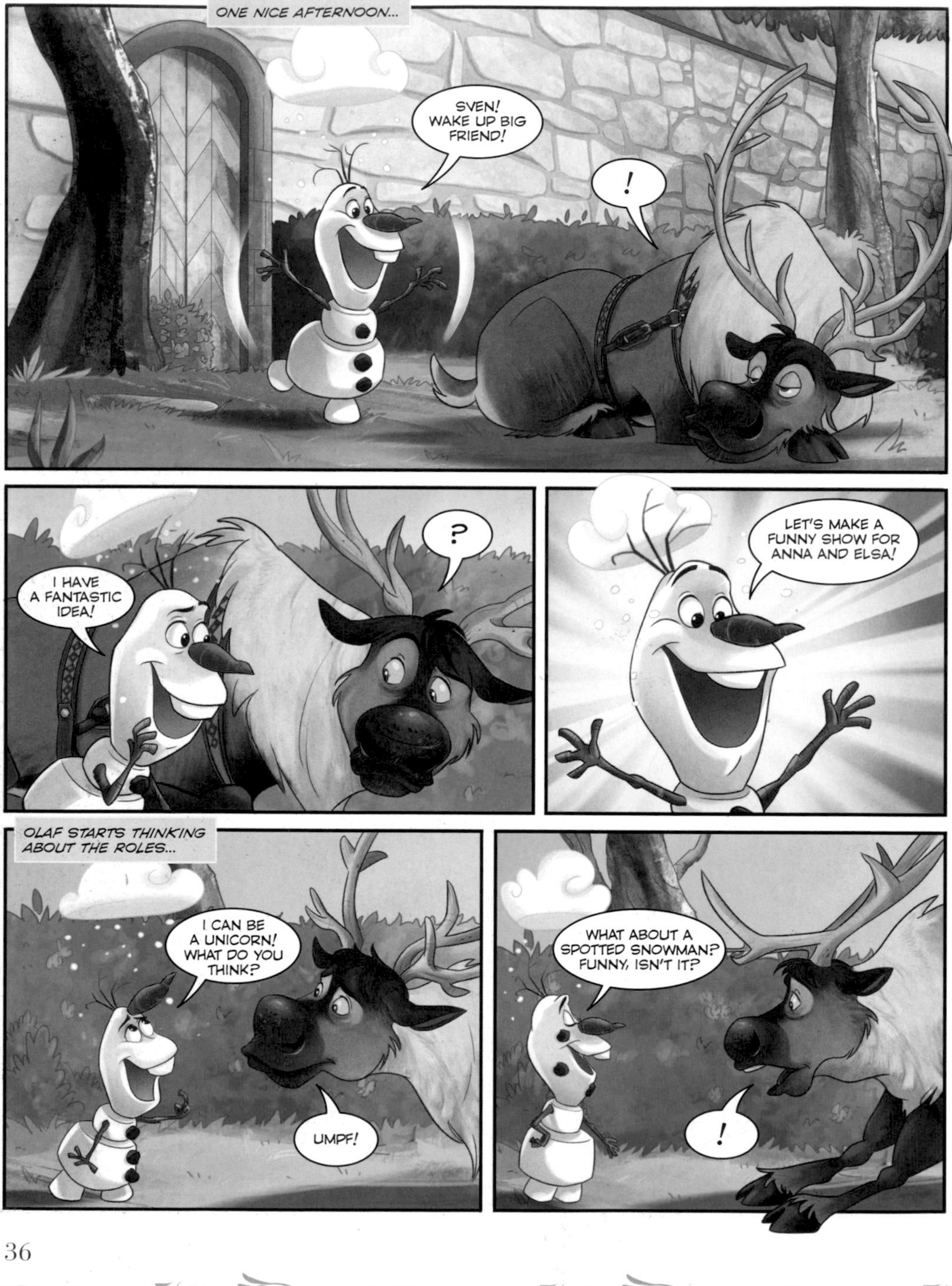
ONE NICE AFTERNOON...
SVEN! WAKE UP BIG FRIEND!
!
I HAVE A FANTASTIC IDEA!
?
LET'S MAKE A FUNNY SHOW FOR ANNA AND ELSA!
OLAF STARTS THINKING ABOUT THE ROLES...
I CAN BE A UNICORN! WHAT DO YOU THINK?
UMPF!
WHAT ABOUT A SPOTTED SNOWMAN? FUNNY, ISN'T IT?
!

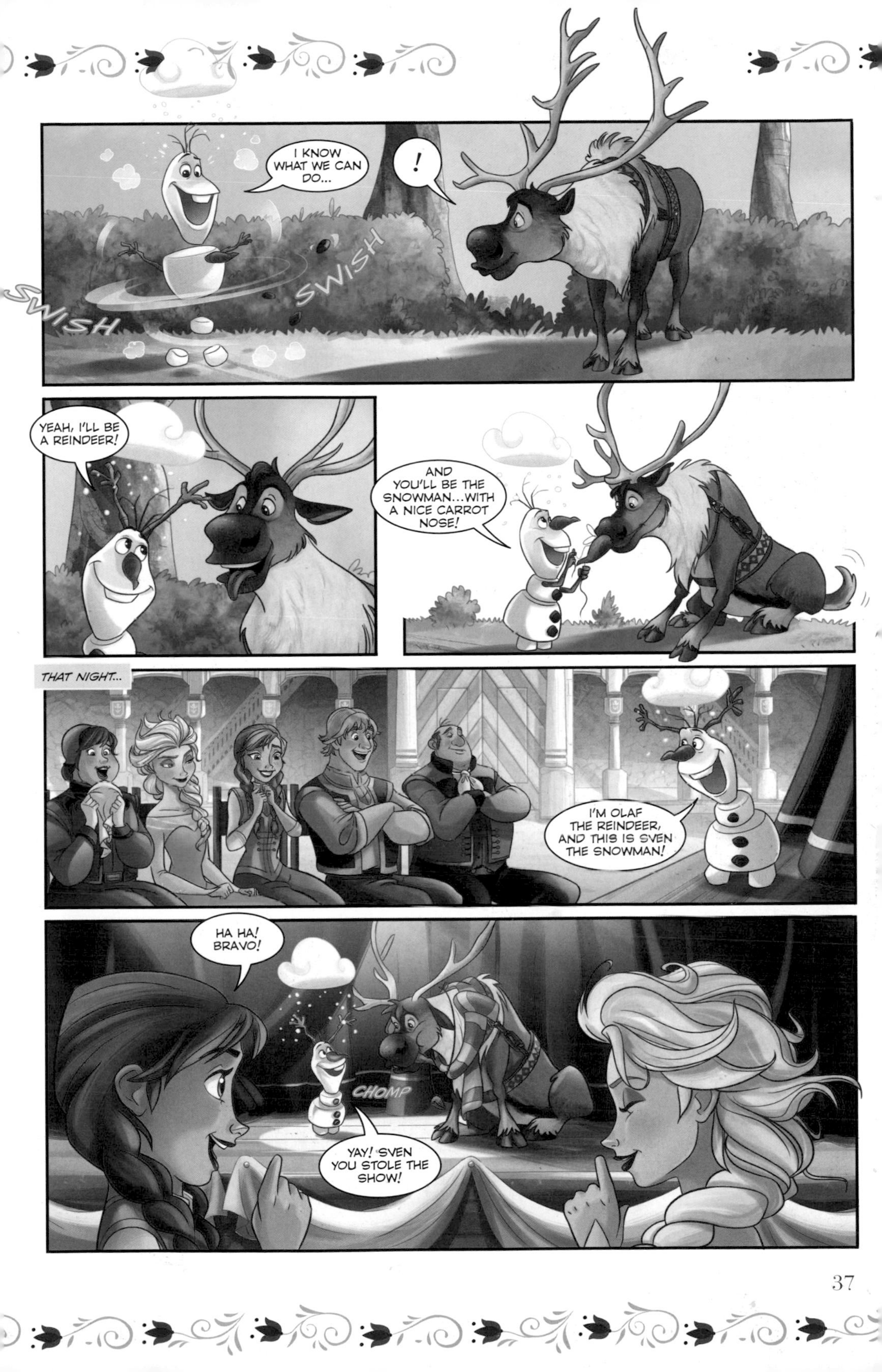
I KNOW WHAT WE CAN DO...
!
SWISH
SWISH
YEAH, I'LL BE A REINDEER!
AND YOU'LL BE THE SNOWMAN...WITH A NICE CARROT NOSE!
THAT NIGHT...
I'M OLAF THE REINDEER, AND THIS IS SVEN THE SNOWMAN!
HA HA! BRAVO!
CHOMP
YAY! SVEN YOU STOLE THE SHOW!

# Heavy Climbing

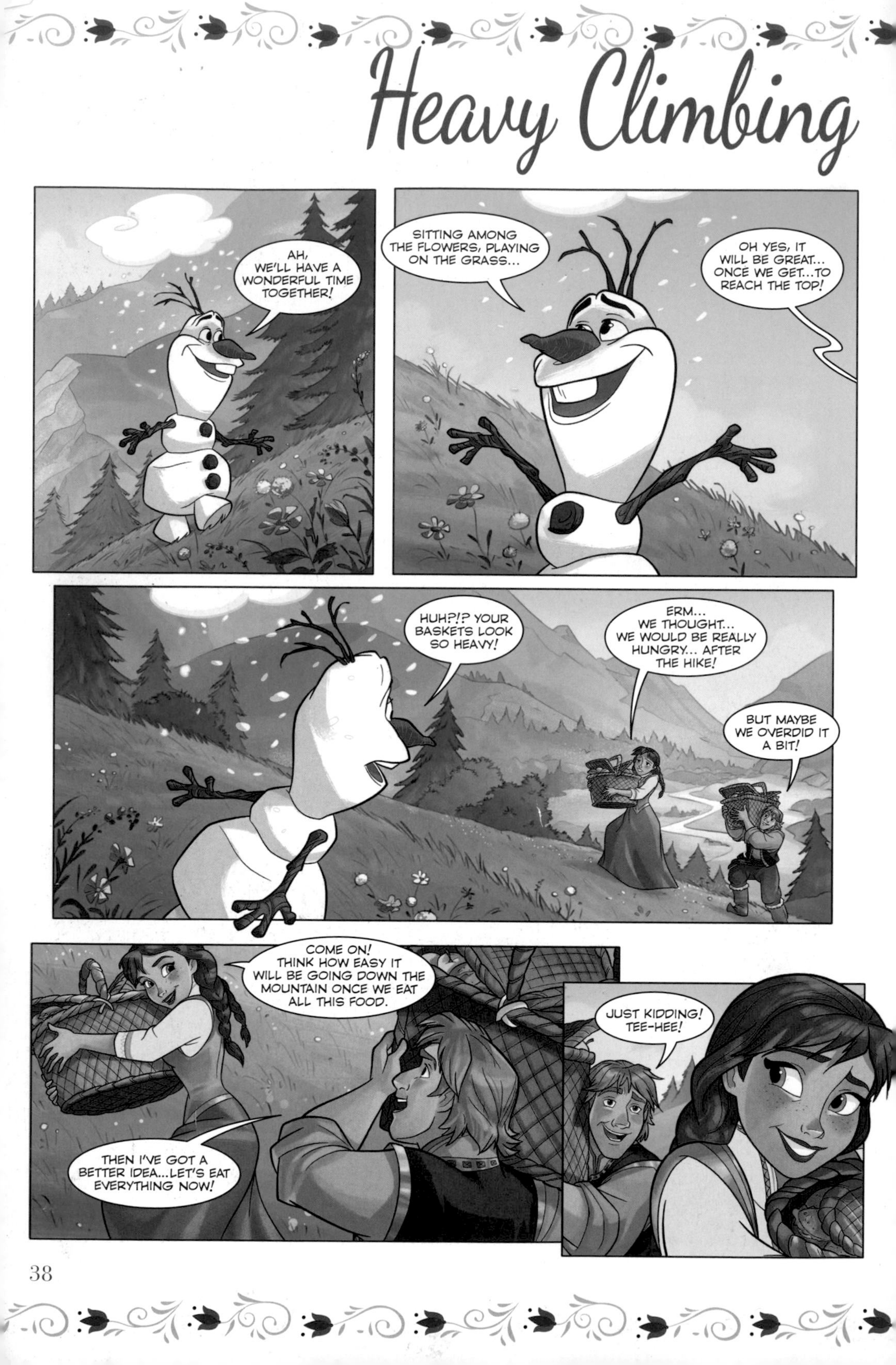
AH, WE'LL HAVE A WONDERFUL TIME TOGETHER!
SITTING AMONG THE FLOWERS, PLAYING ON THE GRASS...
OH YES, IT WILL BE GREAT... ONCE WE GET...TO REACH THE TOP!
HUH?!? YOUR BASKETS LOOK SO HEAVY!
ERM... WE THOUGHT... WE WOULD BE REALLY HUNGRY... AFTER THE HIKE!
BUT MAYBE WE OVERDID IT A BIT!
COME ON! THINK HOW EASY IT WILL BE GOING DOWN THE MOUNTAIN ONCE WE EAT ALL THIS FOOD.
THEN I'VE GOT A BETTER IDEA...LET'S EAT EVERYTHING NOW!
JUST KIDDING! TEE-HEE!

# The Spring Reindeer

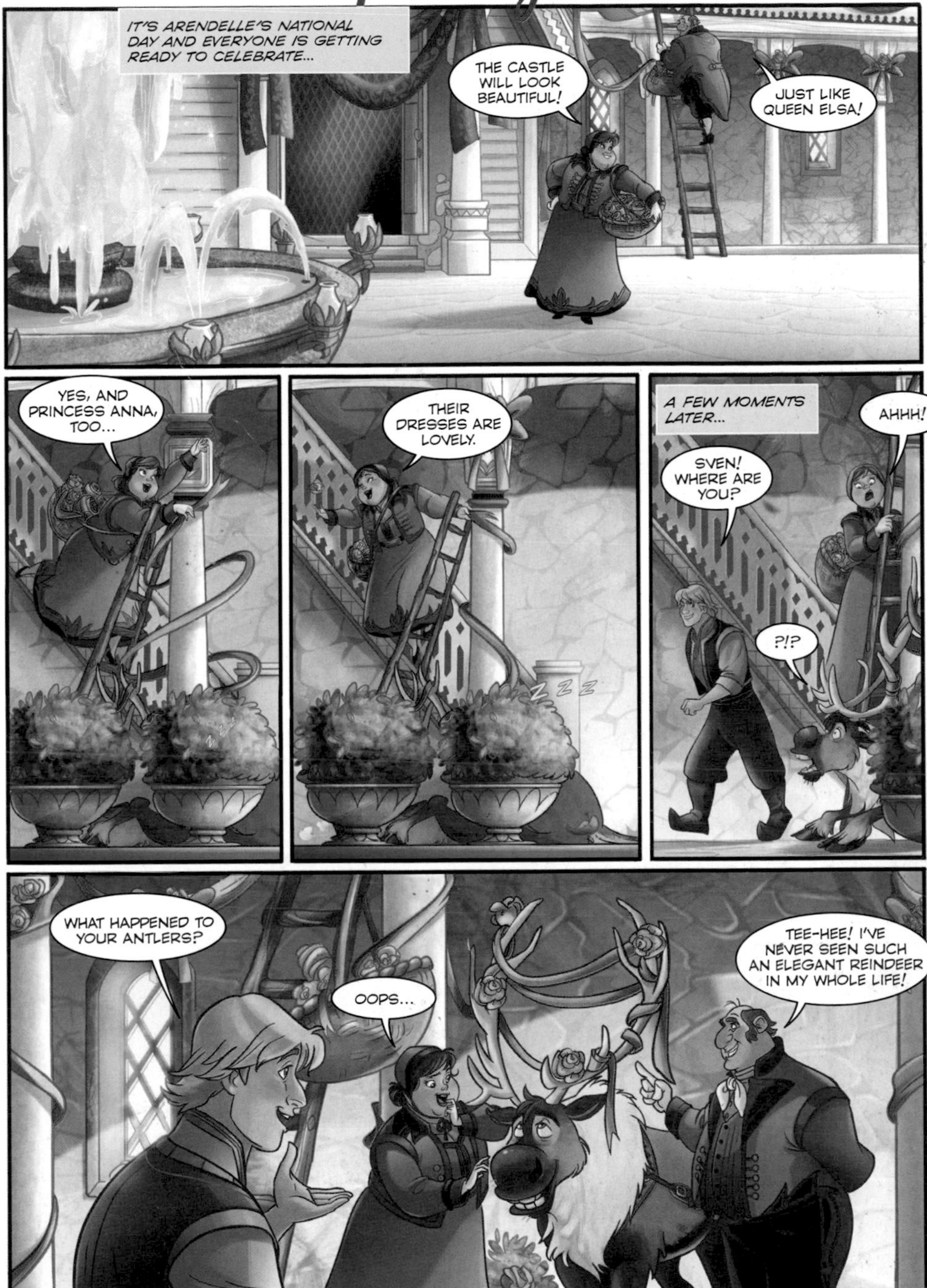

IT'S ARENDELLE'S NATIONAL DAY AND EVERYONE IS GETTING READY TO CELEBRATE...
THE CASTLE WILL LOOK BEAUTIFUL!
JUST LIKE QUEEN ELSA!
YES, AND PRINCESS ANNA, TOO...
THEIR DRESSES ARE LOVELY.
Z Z Z
A FEW MOMENTS LATER...
AHHH!
SVEN! WHERE ARE YOU?
?!?
WHAT HAPPENED TO YOUR ANTLERS?
OOPS...
TEE-HEE! I'VE NEVER SEEN SUCH AN ELEGANT REINDEER IN MY WHOLE LIFE!

# To the Rescue!

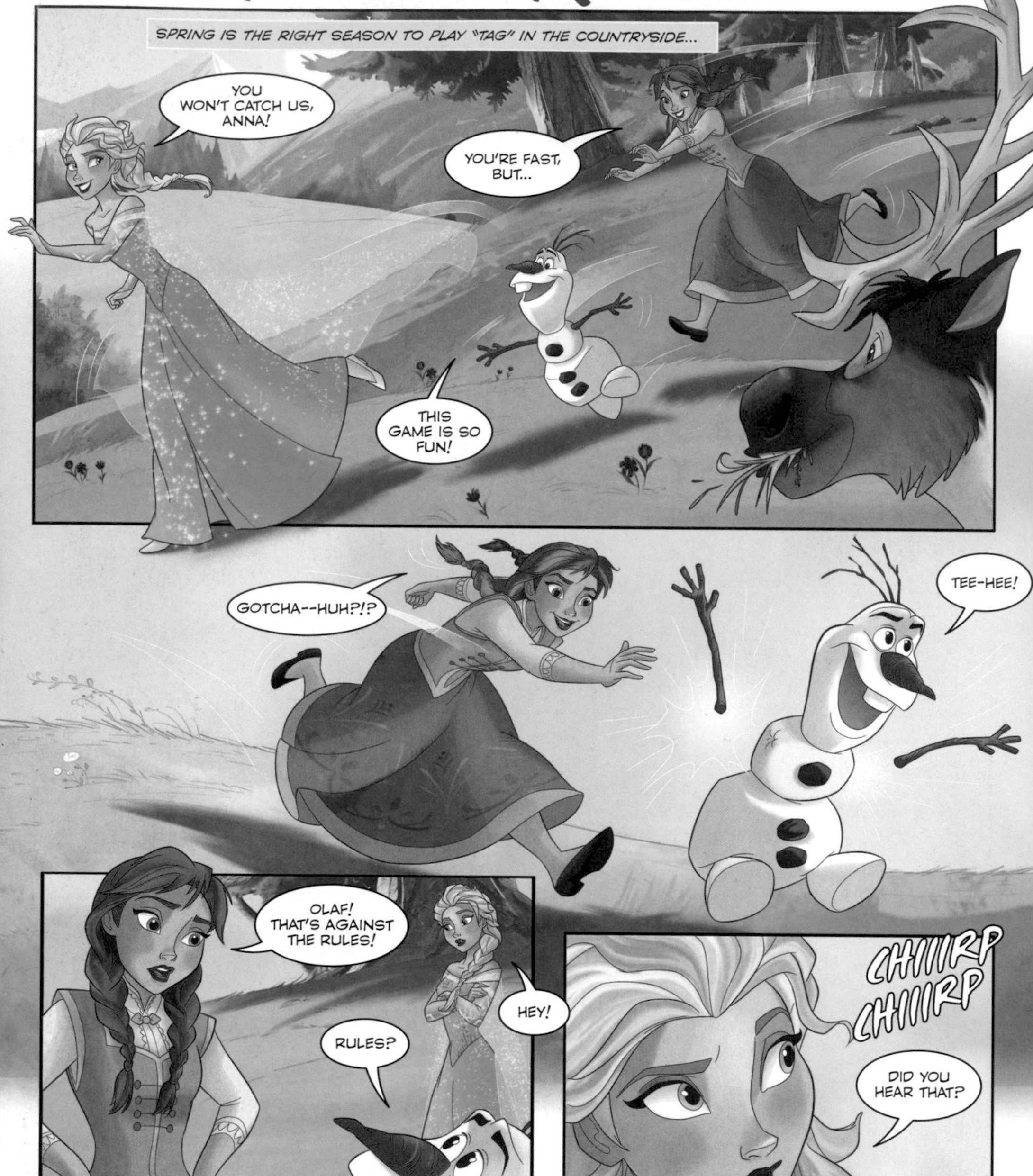
SPRING IS THE RIGHT SEASON TO PLAY "TAG" IN THE COUNTRYSIDE...
YOU WON'T CATCH US, ANNA!
YOU'RE FAST, BUT...
THIS GAME IS SO FUN!
GOTCHA--HUH?!?
TEE-HEE!
OLAF! THAT'S AGAINST THE RULES!
RULES?
HEY!
CHIIIRP CHIIIRP
DID YOU HEAR THAT?

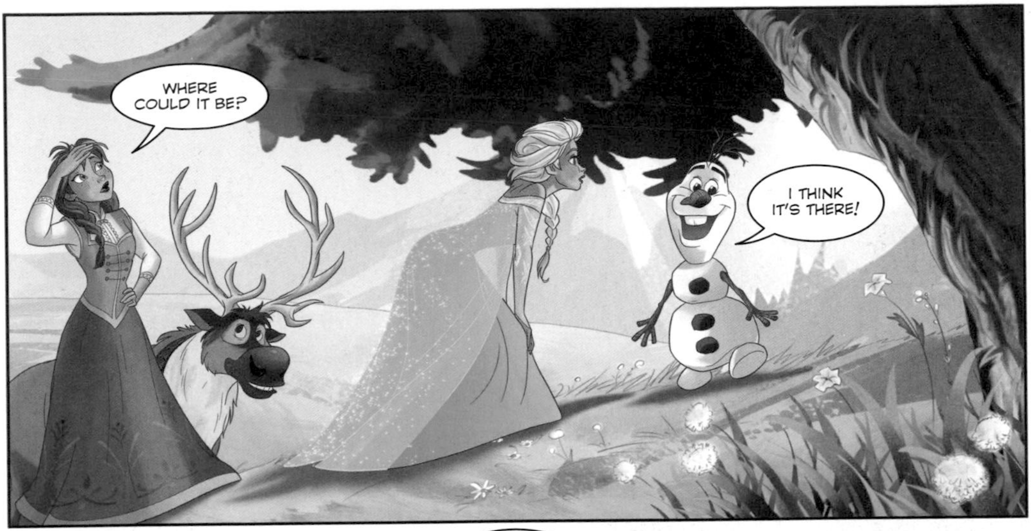
WHERE COULD IT BE?
I THINK IT'S THERE!

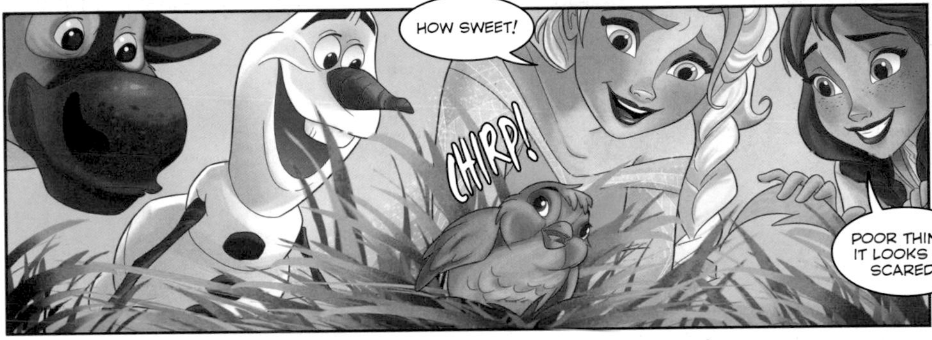
HOW SWEET!
CHIRP!
POOR THING! IT LOOKS SO SCARED!

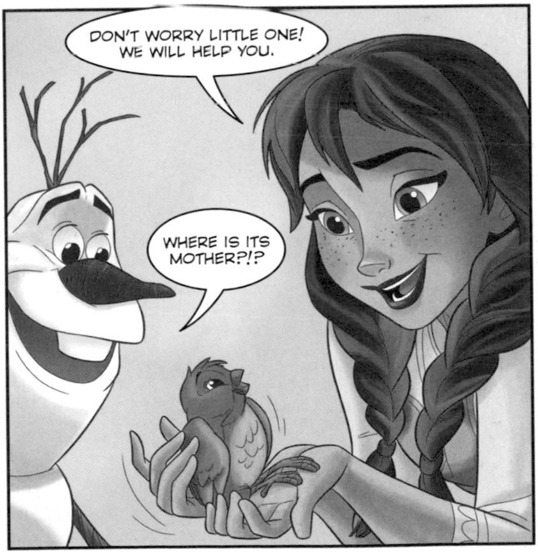
DON'T WORRY LITTLE ONE! WE WILL HELP YOU.
WHERE IS ITS MOTHER?!?

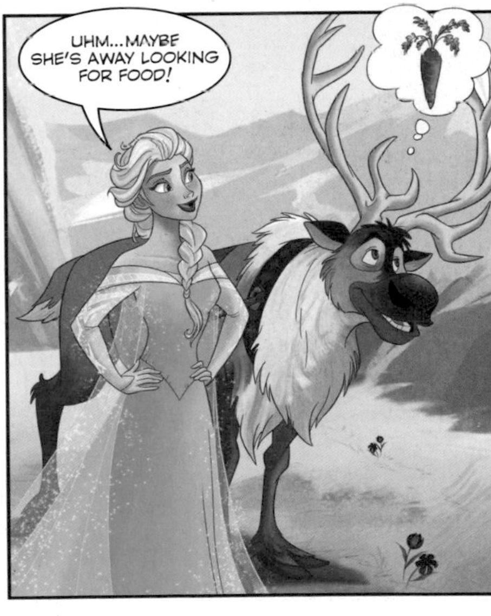
UHM...MAYBE SHE'S AWAY LOOKING FOR FOOD!

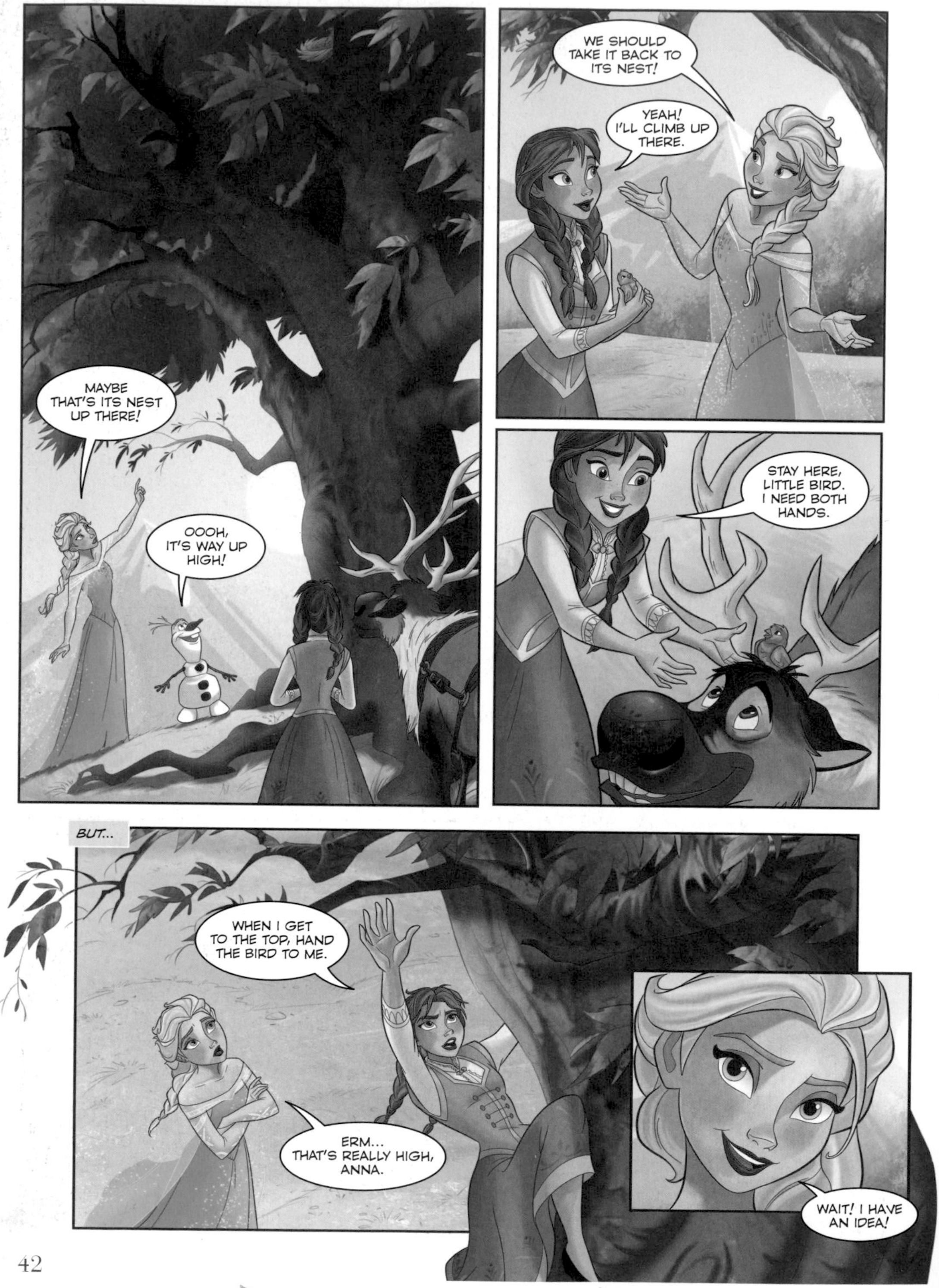
MAYBE THAT'S ITS NEST UP THERE!
OOOH, IT'S WAY UP HIGH!
WE SHOULD TAKE IT BACK TO ITS NEST!
YEAH! I'LL CLIMB UP THERE.
STAY HERE, LITTLE BIRD. I NEED BOTH HANDS.
BUT...
WHEN I GET TO THE TOP, HAND THE BIRD TO ME.
ERM... THAT'S REALLY HIGH, ANNA.
WAIT! I HAVE AN IDEA!

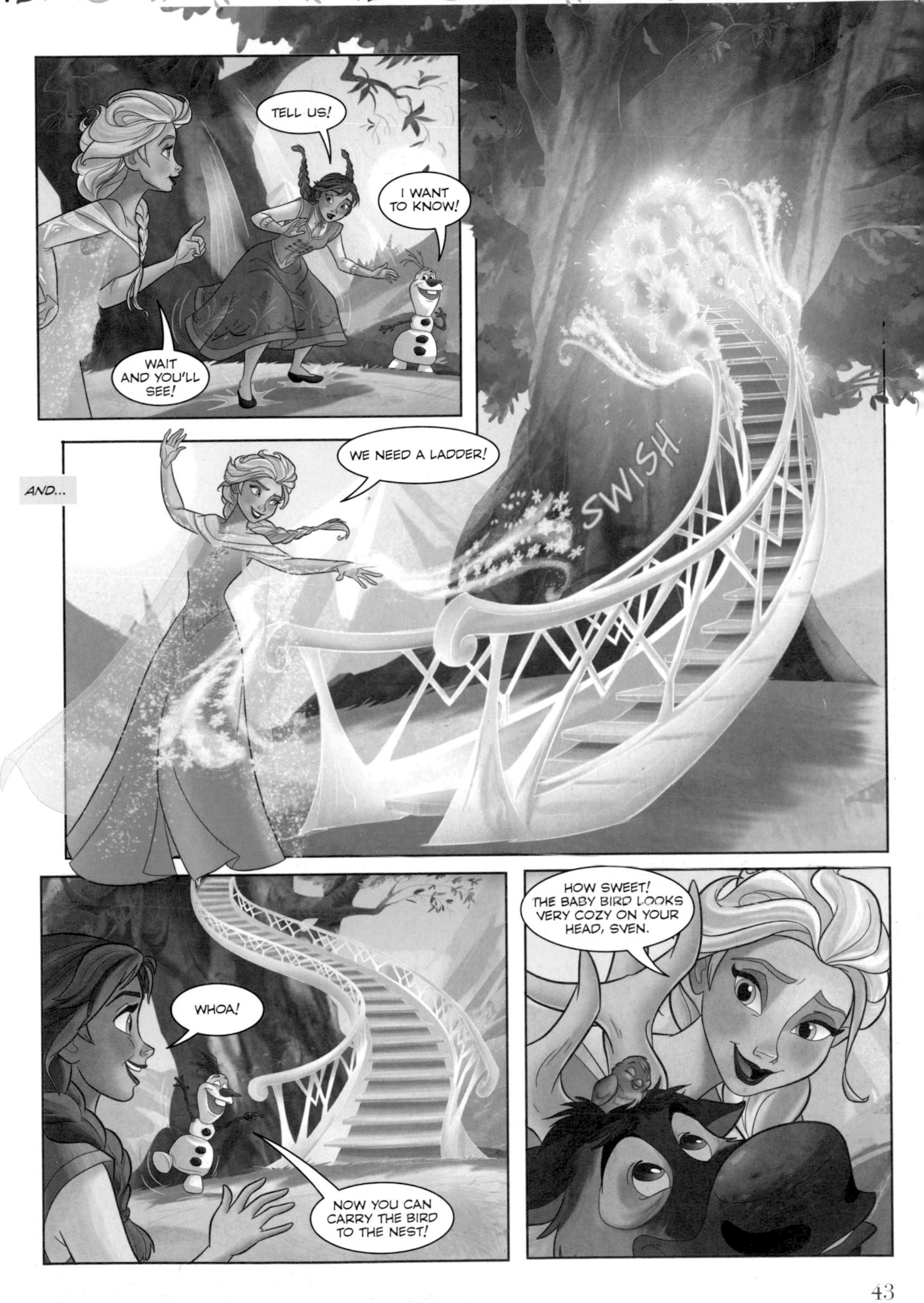
TELL US!
I WANT TO KNOW!
WAIT AND YOU'LL SEE!
AND...
WE NEED A LADDER!
SWISH
WHOA!
NOW YOU CAN CARRY THE BIRD TO THE NEST!
HOW SWEET! THE BABY BIRD LOOKS VERY COZY ON YOUR HEAD, SVEN.

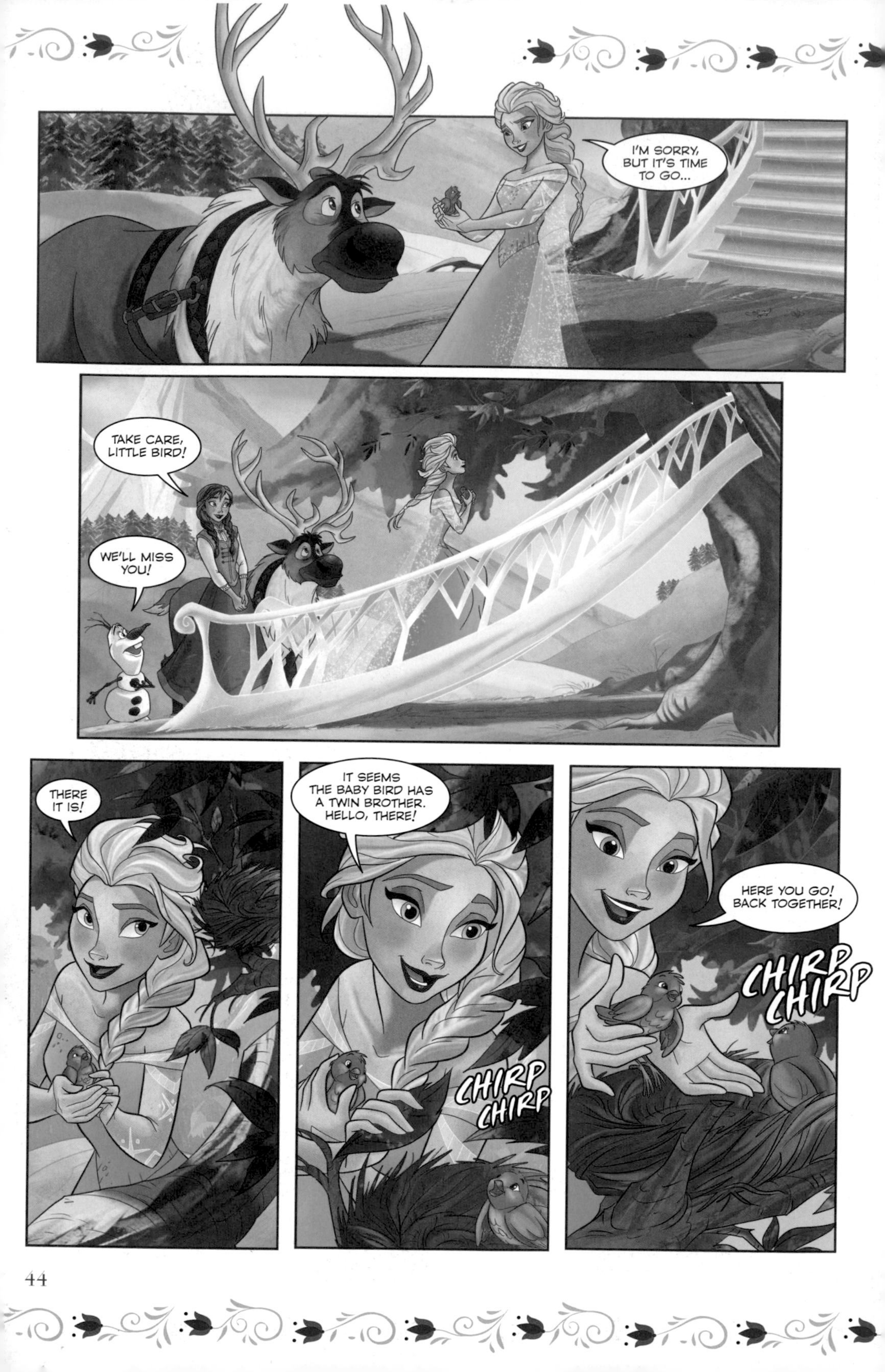

I'M SORRY, BUT IT'S TIME TO GO...
TAKE CARE, LITTLE BIRD!
WE'LL MISS YOU!
THERE IT IS!
IT SEEMS THE BABY BIRD HAS A TWIN BROTHER. HELLO, THERE!
CHIRP CHIRP
HERE YOU GO! BACK TOGETHER!
CHIRP CHIRP

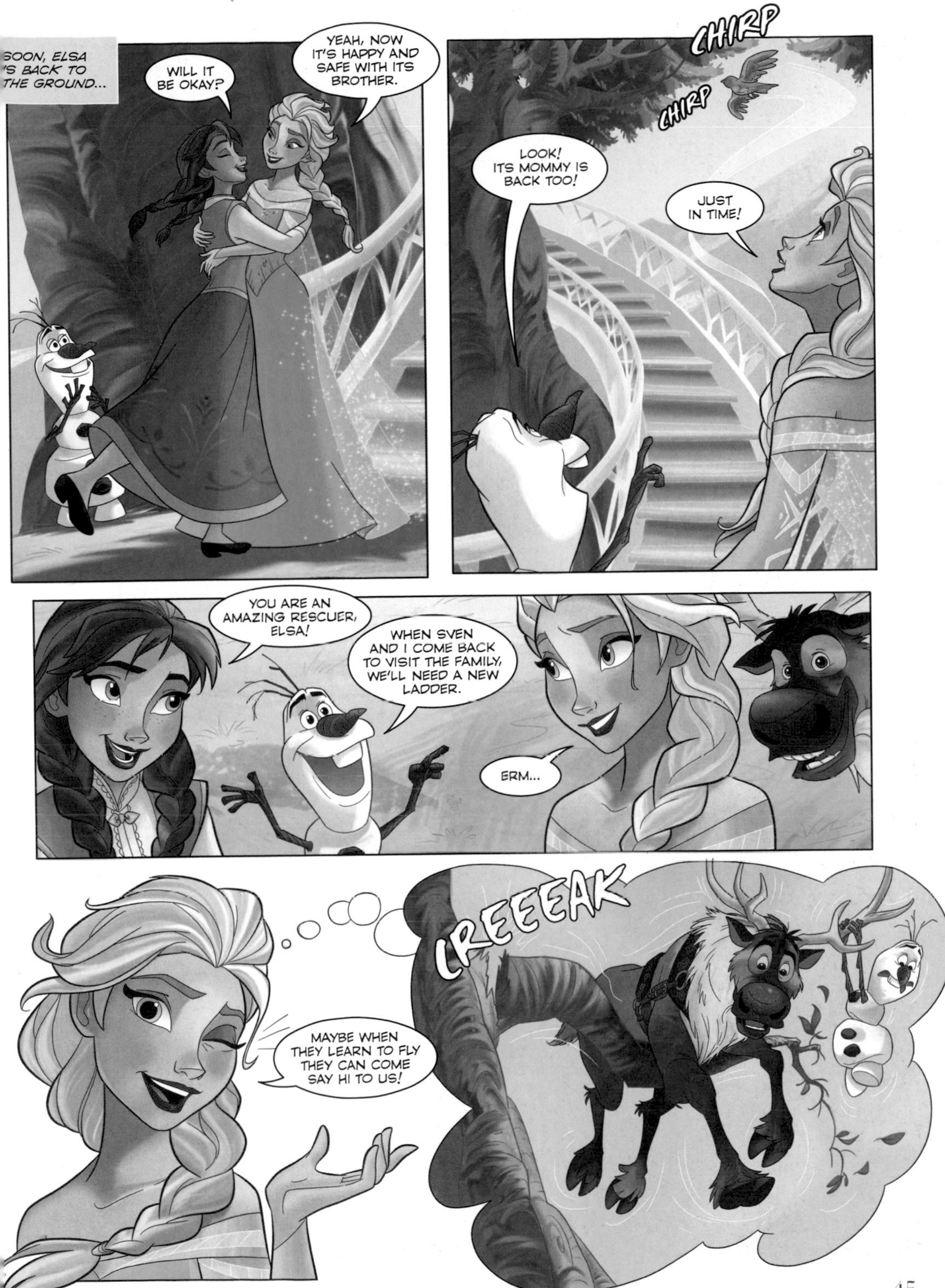
SOON, ELSA
'S BACK TO
THE GROUND...
WILL IT BE OKAY?
YEAH, NOW IT'S HAPPY AND SAFE WITH ITS BROTHER.
CHIRP
CHIRP
LOOK! ITS MOMMY IS BACK TOO!
JUST IN TIME!
YOU ARE AN AMAZING RESCUER, ELSA!
WHEN SVEN AND I COME BACK TO VISIT THE FAMILY, WE'LL NEED A NEW LADDER.
ERM...
MAYBE WHEN THEY LEARN TO FLY THEY CAN COME SAY HI TO US!
CREEEAK

# The Lost Map

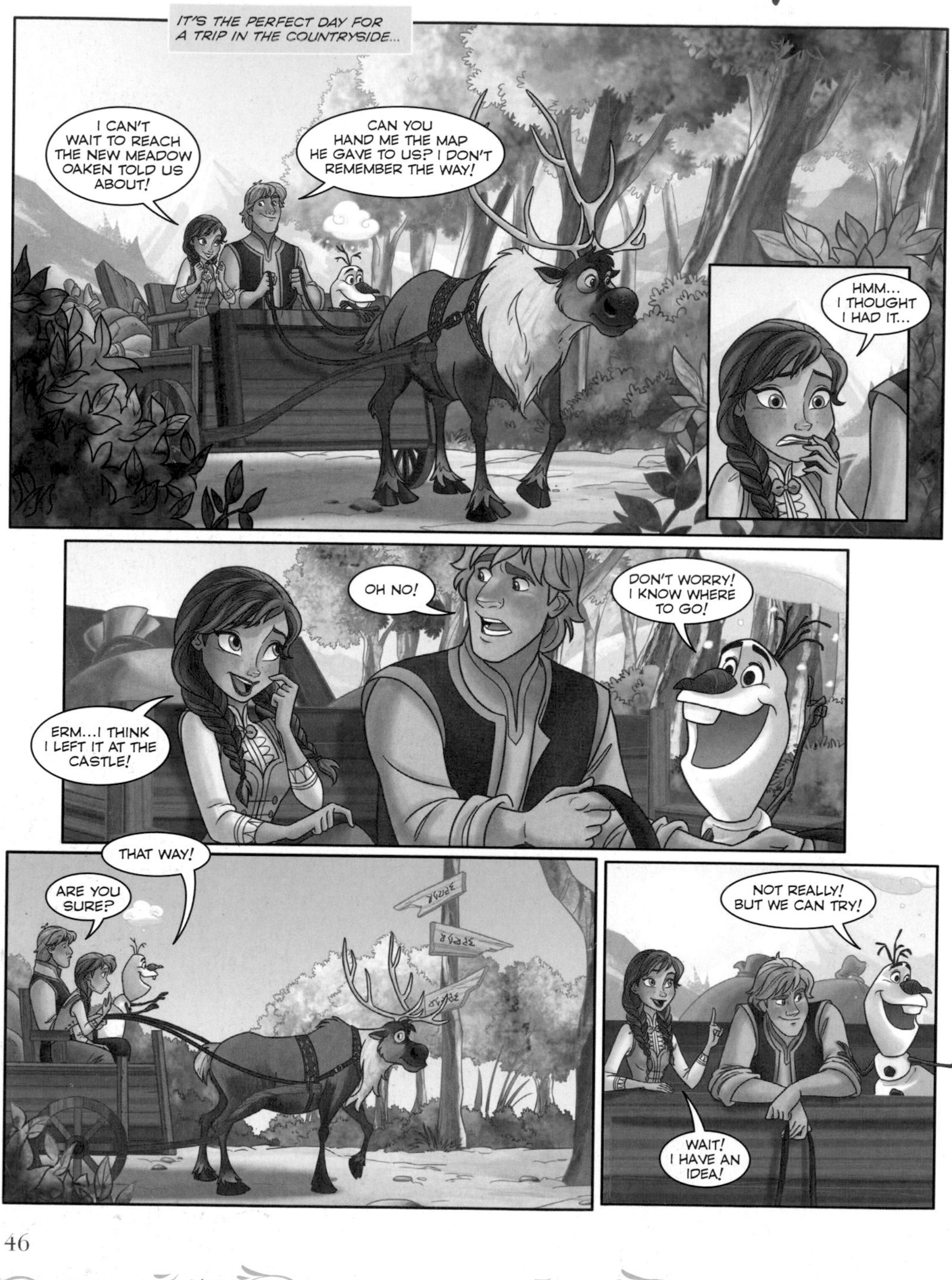

IT'S THE PERFECT DAY FOR A TRIP IN THE COUNTRYSIDE...
I CAN'T WAIT TO REACH THE NEW MEADOW OAKEN TOLD US ABOUT!
CAN YOU HAND ME THE MAP HE GAVE TO US? I DON'T REMEMBER THE WAY!
HMM... I THOUGHT I HAD IT...
ERM...I THINK I LEFT IT AT THE CASTLE!
OH NO!
DON'T WORRY! I KNOW WHERE TO GO!
THAT WAY!
ARE YOU SURE?
NOT REALLY! BUT WE CAN TRY!
WAIT! I HAVE AN IDEA!

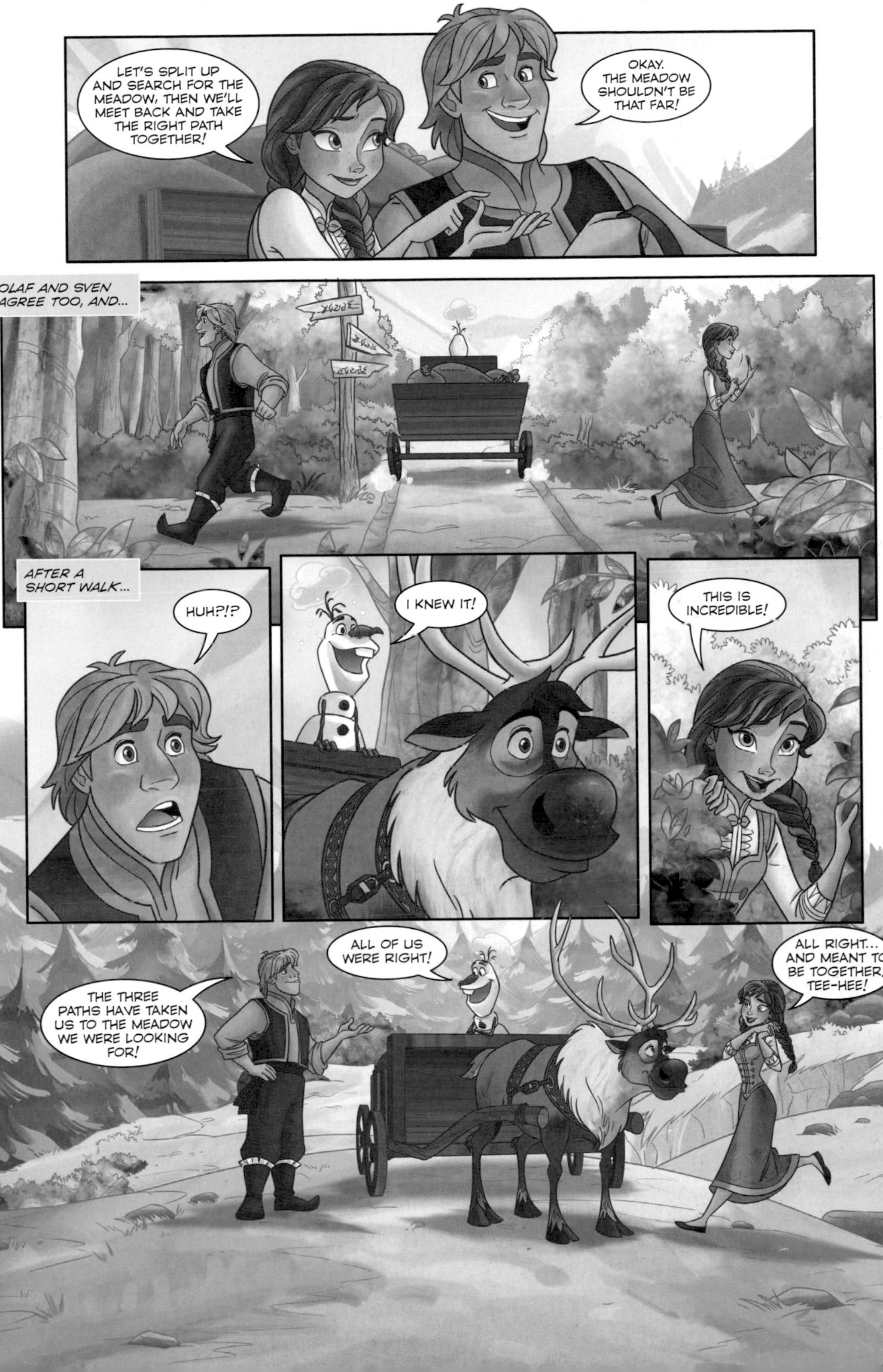
LET'S SPLIT UP AND SEARCH FOR THE MEADOW, THEN WE'LL MEET BACK AND TAKE THE RIGHT PATH TOGETHER!
OKAY. THE MEADOW SHOULDN'T BE THAT FAR!
OLAF AND SVEN AGREE TOO, AND...
AFTER A SHORT WALK...
HUH?!?
I KNEW IT!
THIS IS INCREDIBLE!
THE THREE PATHS HAVE TAKEN US TO THE MEADOW WE WERE LOOKING FOR!
ALL OF US WERE RIGHT!
ALL RIGHT... AND MEANT TO BE TOGETHER! TEE-HEE!

# The Best Drink Ever

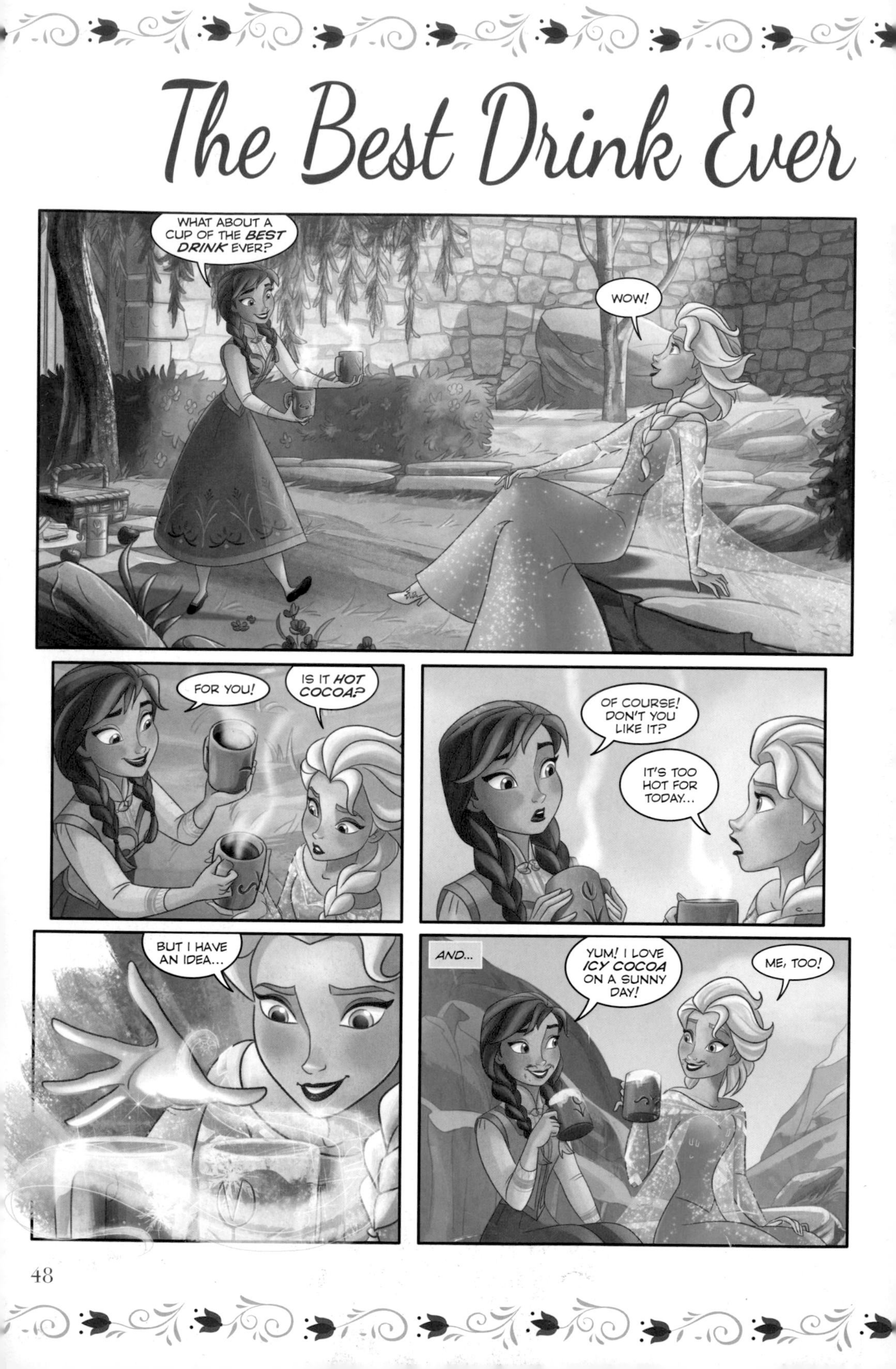
WHAT ABOUT A CUP OF THE *BEST DRINK* EVER?
WOW!
FOR YOU!
IS IT *HOT COCOA?*
OF COURSE! DON'T YOU LIKE IT?
IT'S TOO HOT FOR TODAY...
BUT I HAVE AN IDEA...
AND...
YUM! I LOVE *ICY COCOA* ON A SUNNY DAY!
ME, TOO!

# A Fuzzy Rest

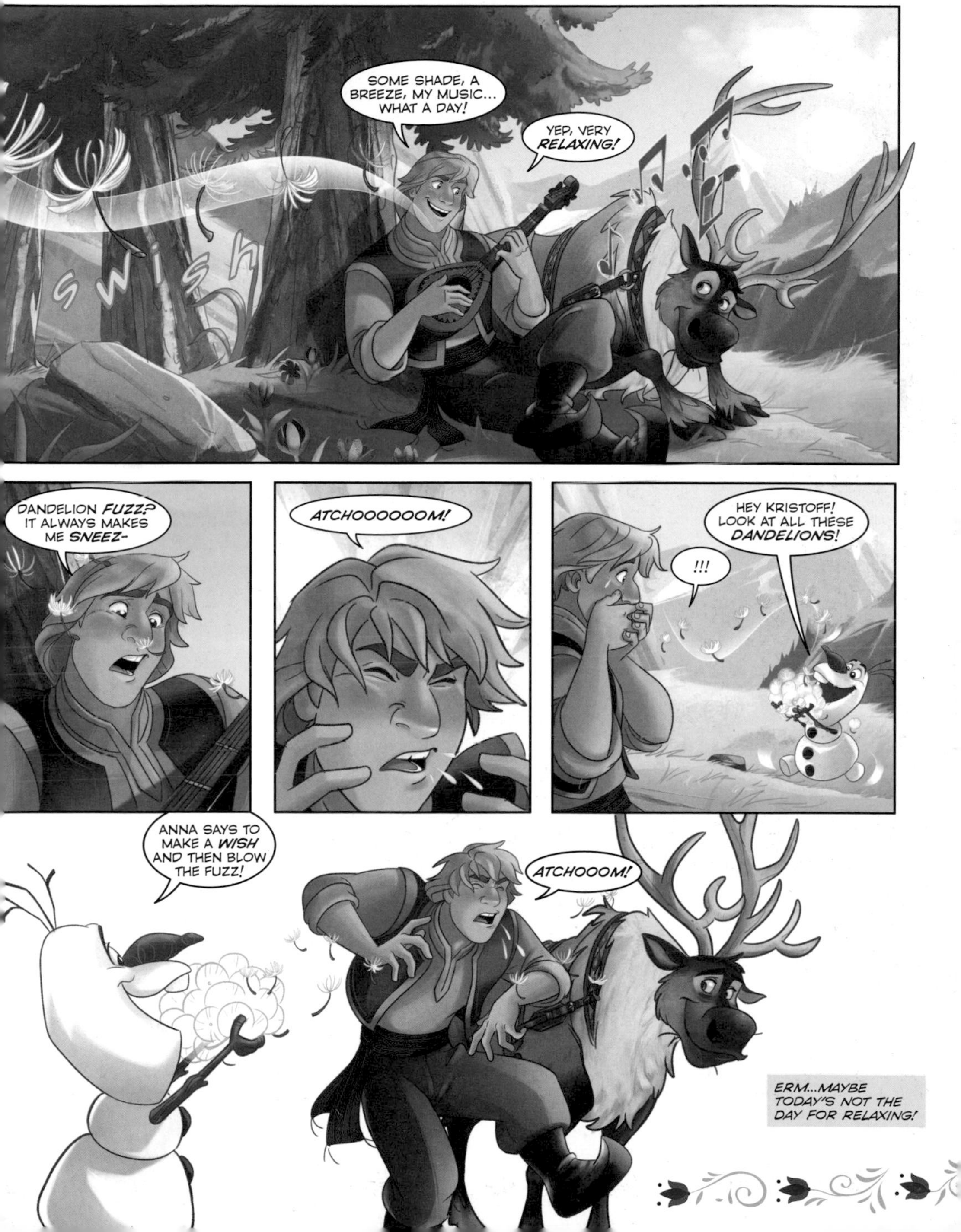
SOME SHADE, A BREEZE, MY MUSIC... WHAT A DAY!
YEP, VERY RELAXING!
swish
DANDELION FUZZ? IT ALWAYS MAKES ME SNEEZ-
ATCHOOOOOOM!
HEY KRISTOFF! LOOK AT ALL THESE DANDELIONS!
!!!
ANNA SAYS TO MAKE A WISH AND THEN BLOW THE FUZZ!
ATCHOOOM!
ERM...MAYBE TODAY'S NOT THE DAY FOR RELAXING!

# Sailing Sisters

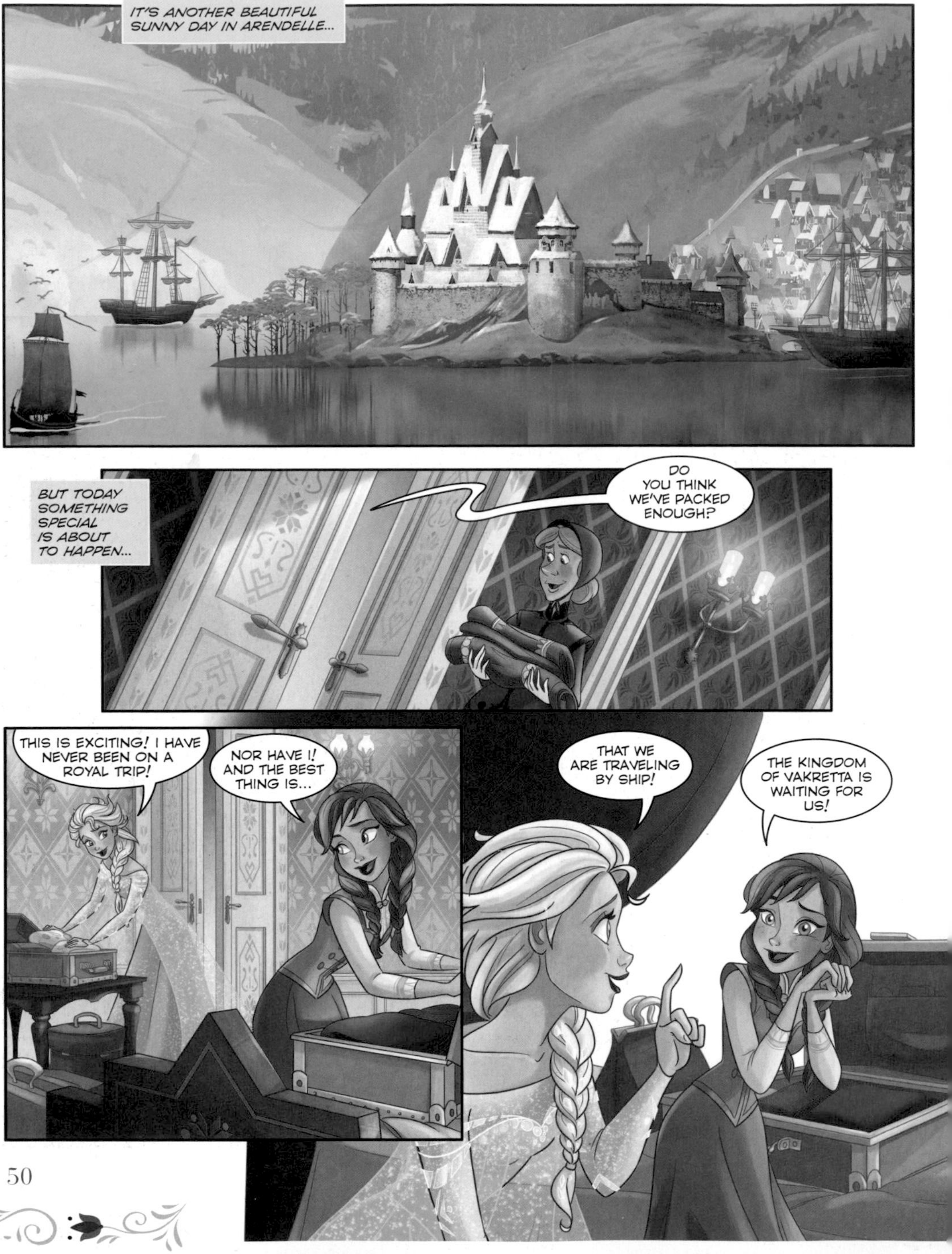
IT'S ANOTHER BEAUTIFUL SUNNY DAY IN ARENDELLE...
BUT TODAY SOMETHING SPECIAL IS ABOUT TO HAPPEN...
DO YOU THINK WE'VE PACKED ENOUGH?
THIS IS EXCITING! I HAVE NEVER BEEN ON A ROYAL TRIP!
NOR HAVE I! AND THE BEST THING IS...
THAT WE ARE TRAVELING BY SHIP!
THE KINGDOM OF VAKRETTA IS WAITING FOR US!

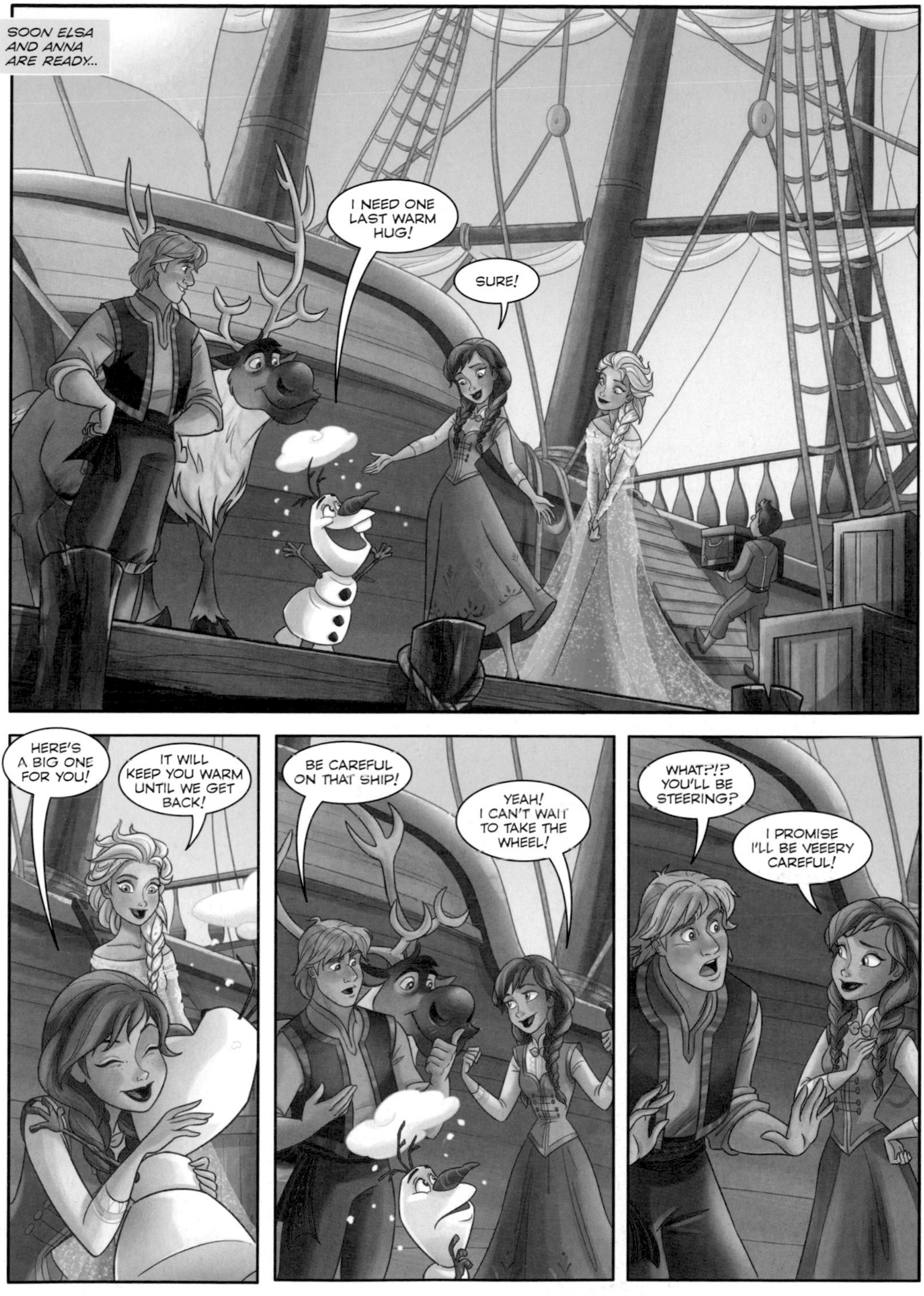
SOON ELSA AND ANNA ARE READY...
I NEED ONE LAST WARM HUG!
SURE!
HERE'S A BIG ONE FOR YOU!
IT WILL KEEP YOU WARM UNTIL WE GET BACK!
BE CAREFUL ON THAT SHIP!
YEAH! I CAN'T WAIT TO TAKE THE WHEEL!
WHAT?!? YOU'LL BE STEERING?
I PROMISE I'LL BE VEEERY CAREFUL!

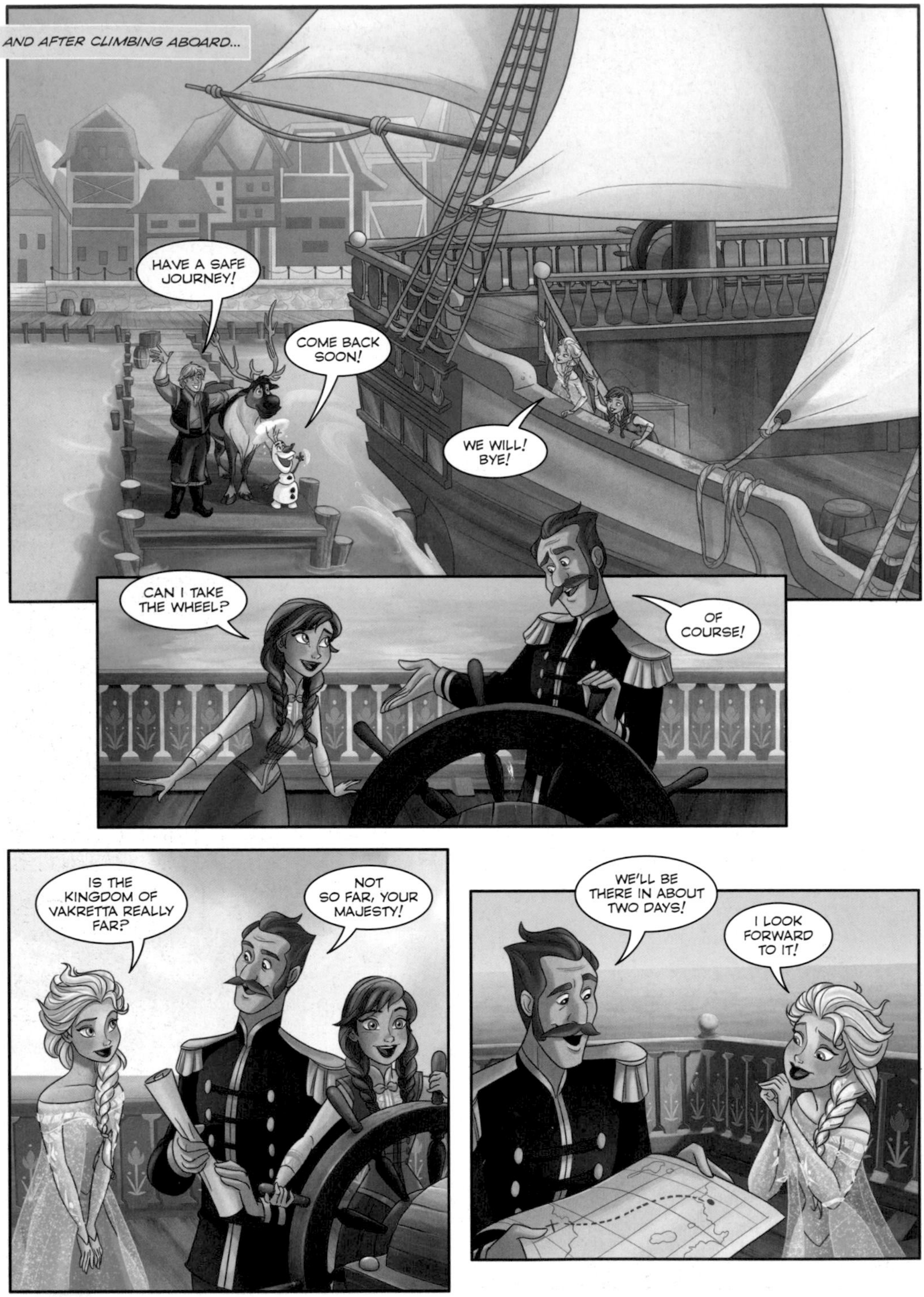
AND AFTER CLIMBING ABOARD...
HAVE A SAFE JOURNEY!
COME BACK SOON!
WE WILL! BYE!
CAN I TAKE THE WHEEL?
OF COURSE!
IS THE KINGDOM OF VAKRETTA REALLY FAR?
NOT SO FAR, YOUR MAJESTY!
WE'LL BE THERE IN ABOUT TWO DAYS!
I LOOK FORWARD TO IT!

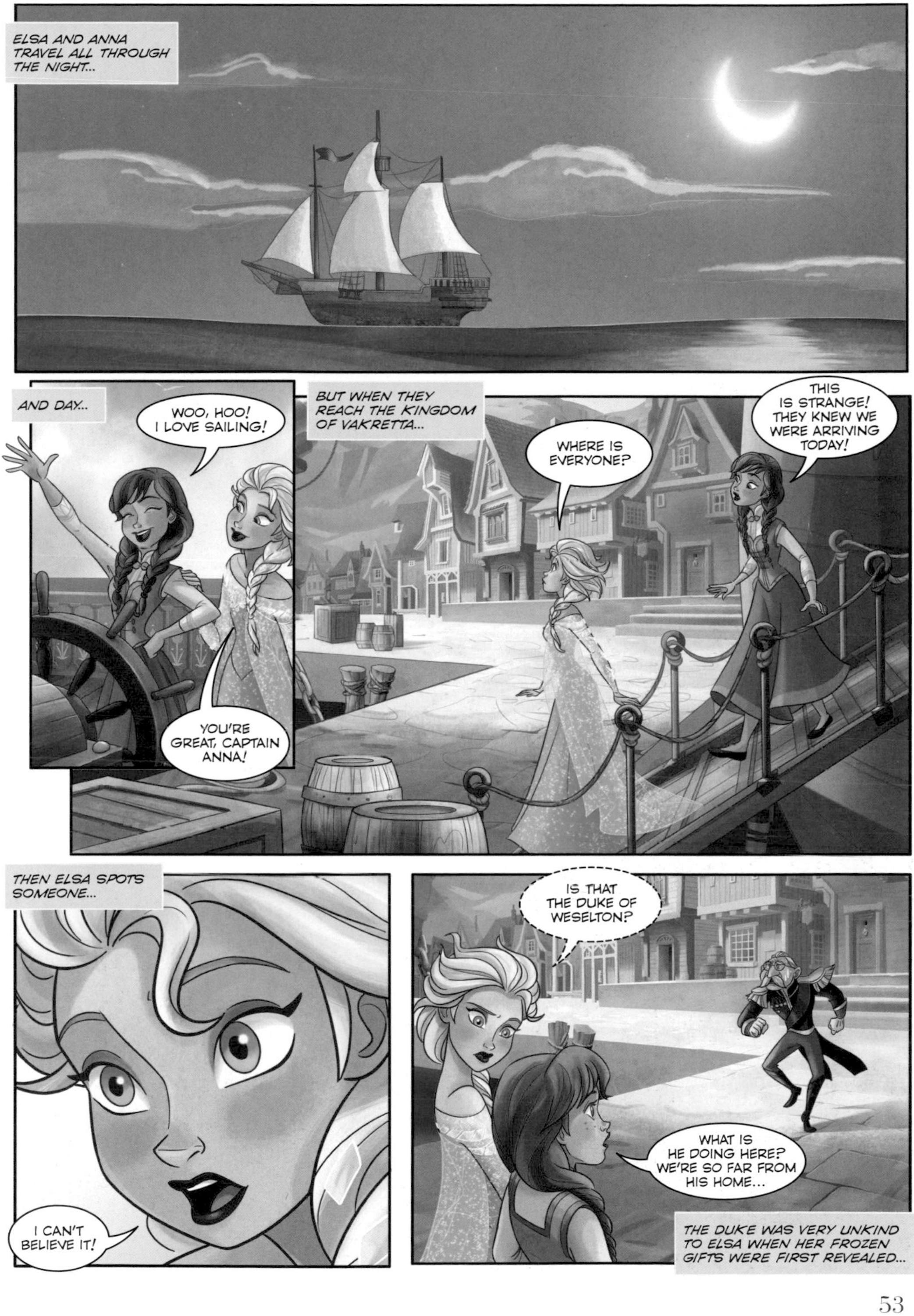
ELSA AND ANNA TRAVEL ALL THROUGH THE NIGHT...
AND DAY...
WOO, HOO! I LOVE SAILING!
YOU'RE GREAT, CAPTAIN ANNA!
BUT WHEN THEY REACH THE KINGDOM OF VAKRETTA...
WHERE IS EVERYONE?
THIS IS STRANGE! THEY KNEW WE WERE ARRIVING TODAY!
THEN ELSA SPOTS SOMEONE...
I CAN'T BELIEVE IT!
IS THAT THE DUKE OF WESELTON?
WHAT IS HE DOING HERE? WE'RE SO FAR FROM HIS HOME...
THE DUKE WAS VERY UNKIND TO ELSA WHEN HER FROZEN GIFTS WERE FIRST REVEALED...

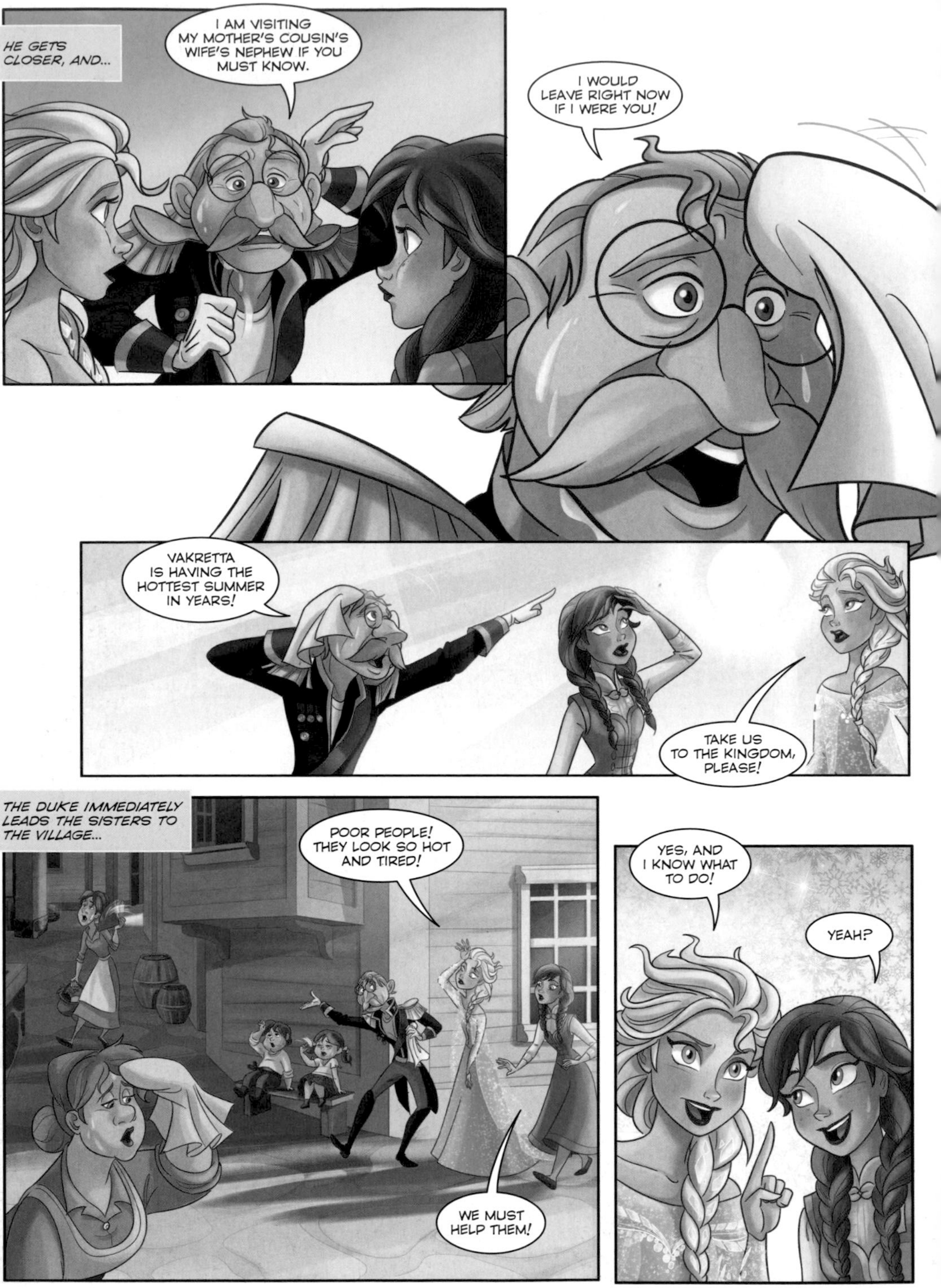
HE GETS CLOSER, AND...
I AM VISITING MY MOTHER'S COUSIN'S WIFE'S NEPHEW IF YOU MUST KNOW.
I WOULD LEAVE RIGHT NOW IF I WERE YOU!
VAKRETTA IS HAVING THE HOTTEST SUMMER IN YEARS!
TAKE US TO THE KINGDOM, PLEASE!
THE DUKE IMMEDIATELY LEADS THE SISTERS TO THE VILLAGE...
POOR PEOPLE! THEY LOOK SO HOT AND TIRED!
WE MUST HELP THEM!
YES, AND I KNOW WHAT TO DO!
YEAH?

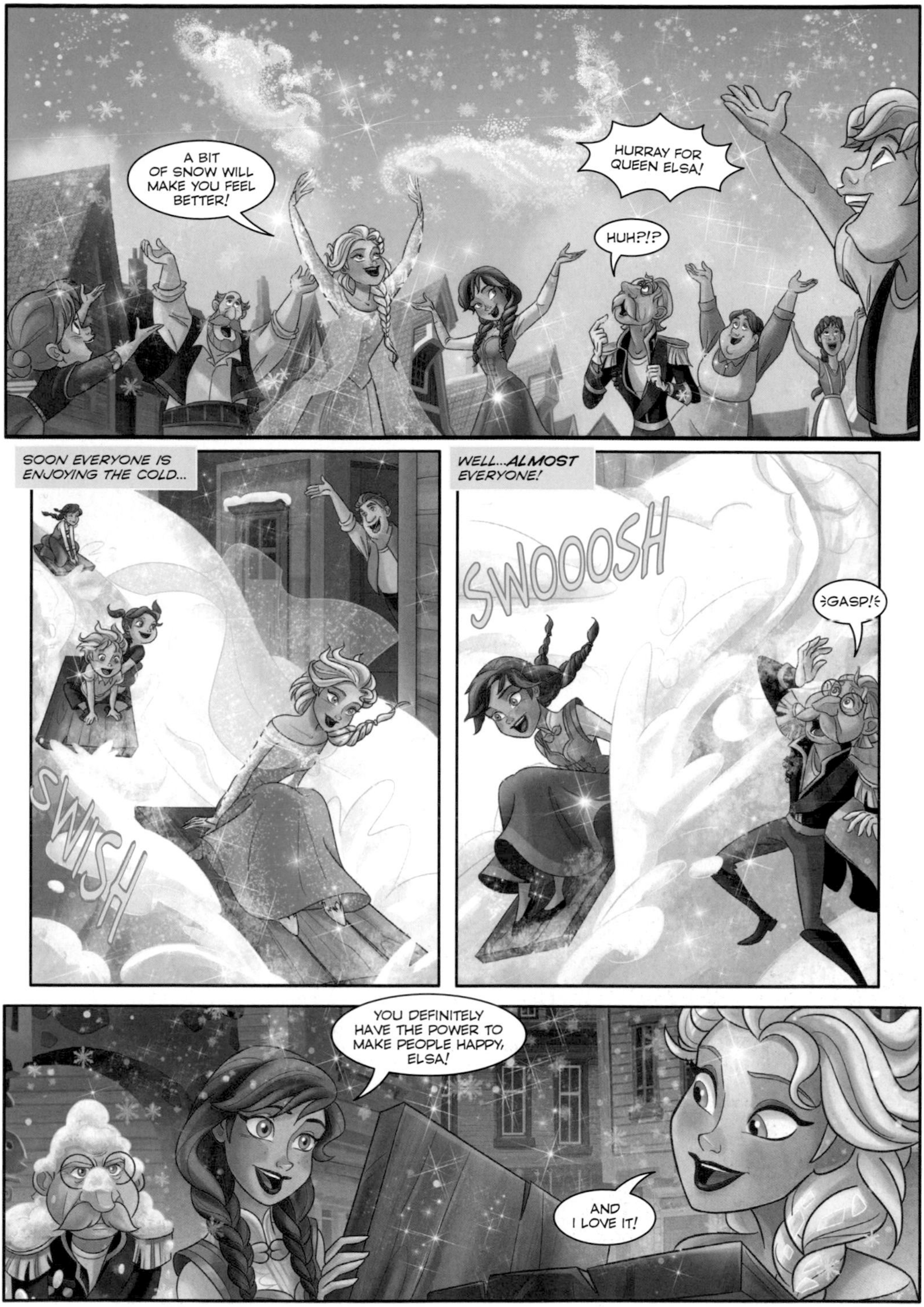
A BIT OF SNOW WILL MAKE YOU FEEL BETTER!
HURRAY FOR QUEEN ELSA!
HUH?!?
SOON EVERYONE IS ENJOYING THE COLD...
SWISH
WELL...ALMOST EVERYONE!
SWOOOSH
GASP!
YOU DEFINITELY HAVE THE POWER TO MAKE PEOPLE HAPPY, ELSA!
AND I LOVE IT!

# Scary Noise

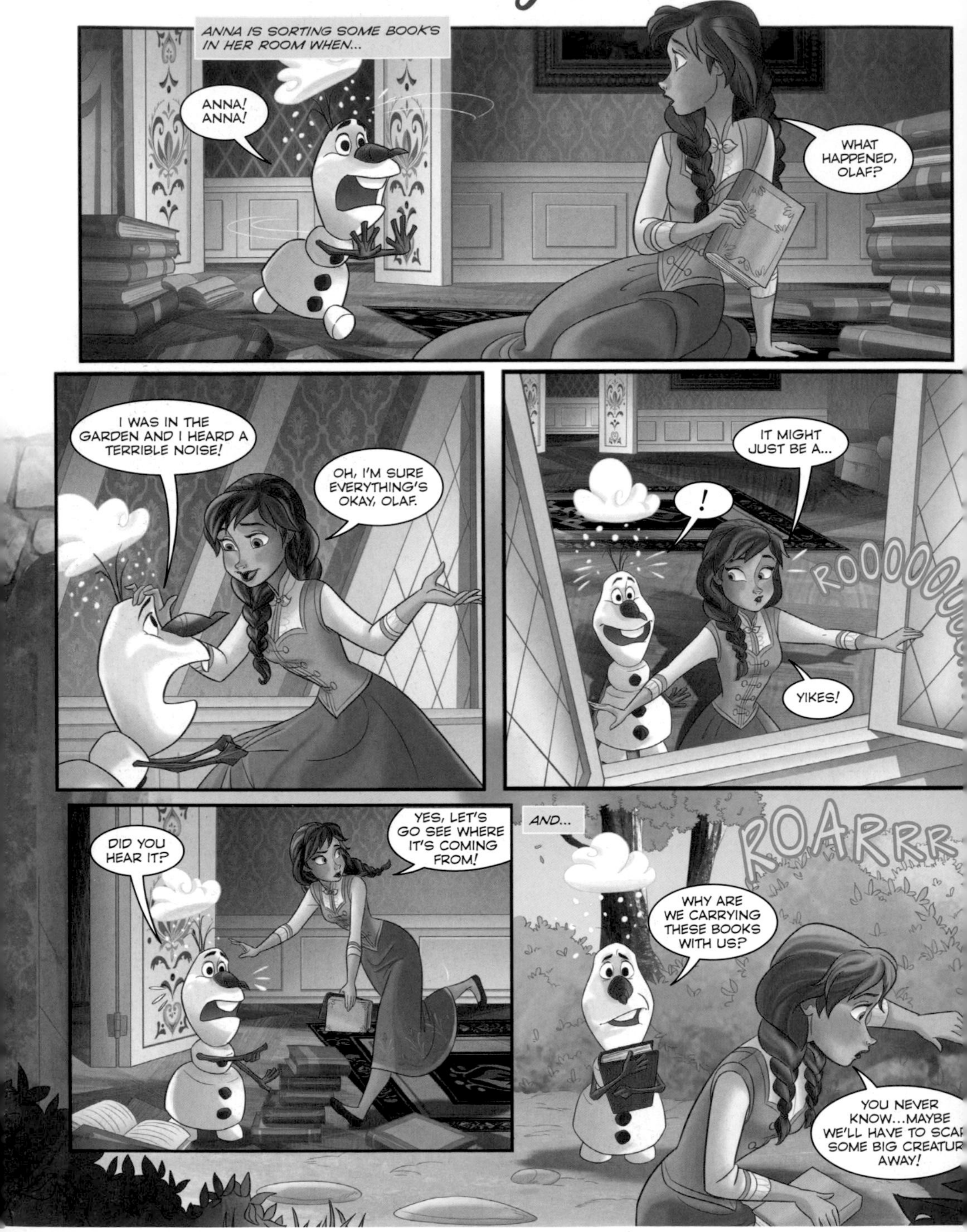
ANNA IS SORTING SOME BOOKS IN HER ROOM WHEN...
ANNA! ANNA!
WHAT HAPPENED, OLAF?
I WAS IN THE GARDEN AND I HEARD A TERRIBLE NOISE!
OH, I'M SURE EVERYTHING'S OKAY, OLAF.
IT MIGHT JUST BE A...
!
ROOOOOU
YIKES!
DID YOU HEAR IT?
YES, LET'S GO SEE WHERE IT'S COMING FROM!
AND...
ROARRR
WHY ARE WE CARRYING THESE BOOKS WITH US?
YOU NEVER KNOW...MAYBE WE'LL HAVE TO SCAR SOME BIG CREATUR AWAY!

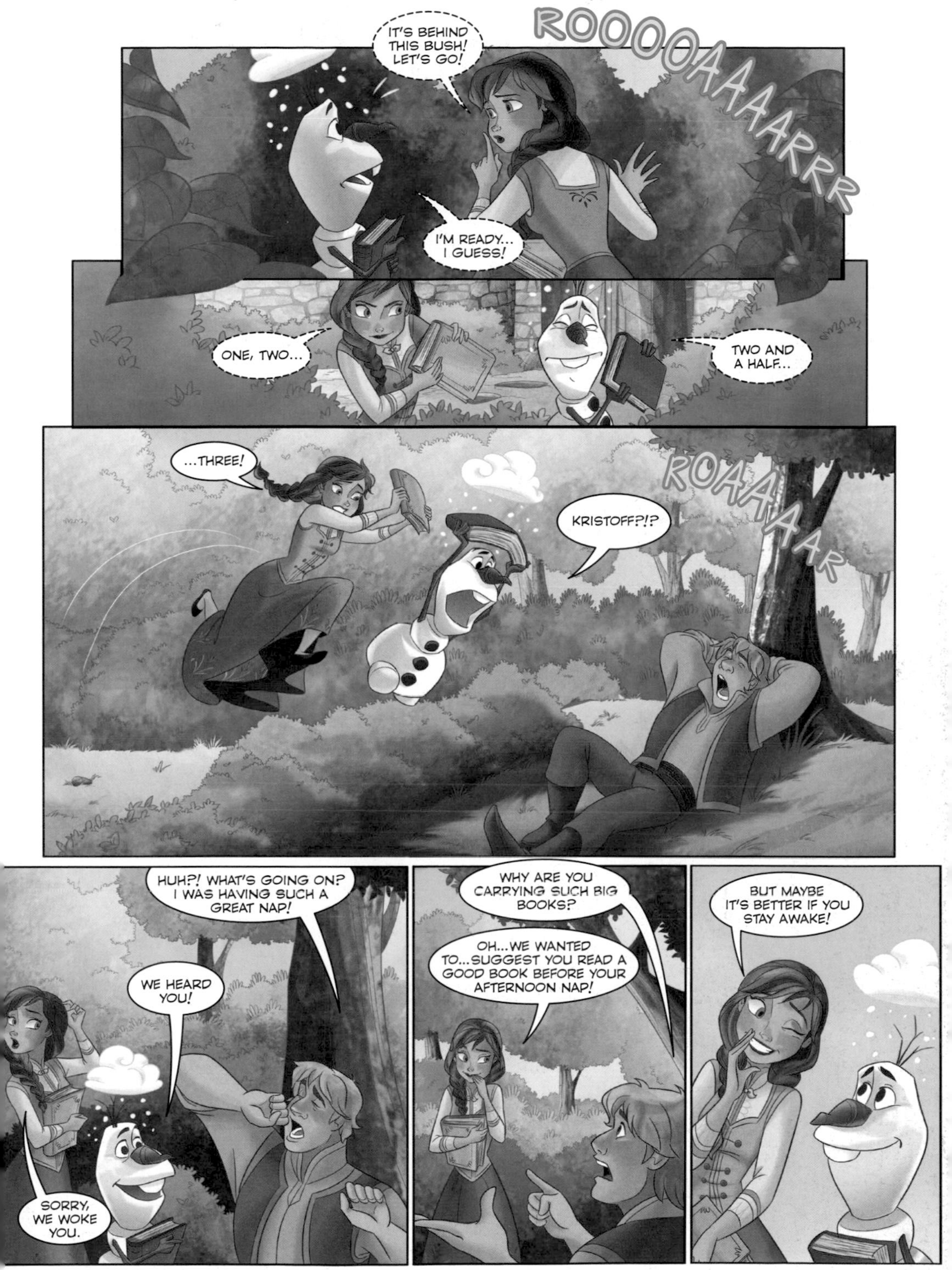
IT'S BEHIND THIS BUSH! LET'S GO!
ROOOOOAAAAARRR
I'M READY... I GUESS!
ONE, TWO...
TWO AND A HALF...
...THREE!
ROAAAAAR
KRISTOFF?!?
HUH?! WHAT'S GOING ON? I WAS HAVING SUCH A GREAT NAP!
WE HEARD YOU!
SORRY, WE WOKE YOU.
WHY ARE YOU CARRYING SUCH BIG BOOKS?
OH...WE WANTED TO...SUGGEST YOU READ A GOOD BOOK BEFORE YOUR AFTERNOON NAP!
BUT MAYBE IT'S BETTER IF YOU STAY AWAKE!

# A Day On The Beach

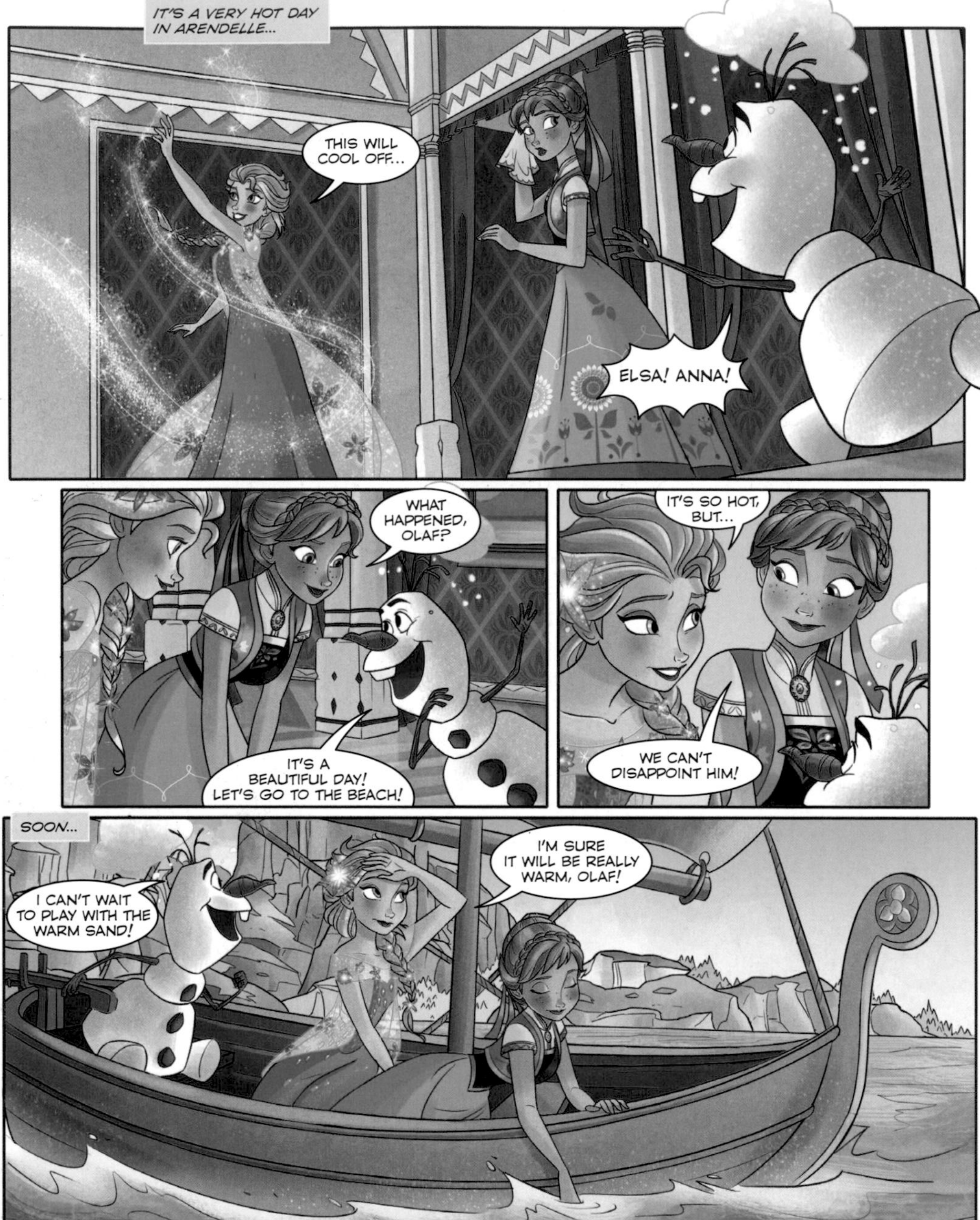
IT'S A VERY HOT DAY IN ARENDELLE...
THIS WILL COOL OFF...
ELSA! ANNA!
WHAT HAPPENED, OLAF?
IT'S A BEAUTIFUL DAY! LET'S GO TO THE BEACH!
IT'S SO HOT, BUT...
WE CAN'T DISAPPOINT HIM!
SOON...
I'M SURE IT WILL BE REALLY WARM, OLAF!
I CAN'T WAIT TO PLAY WITH THE WARM SAND!

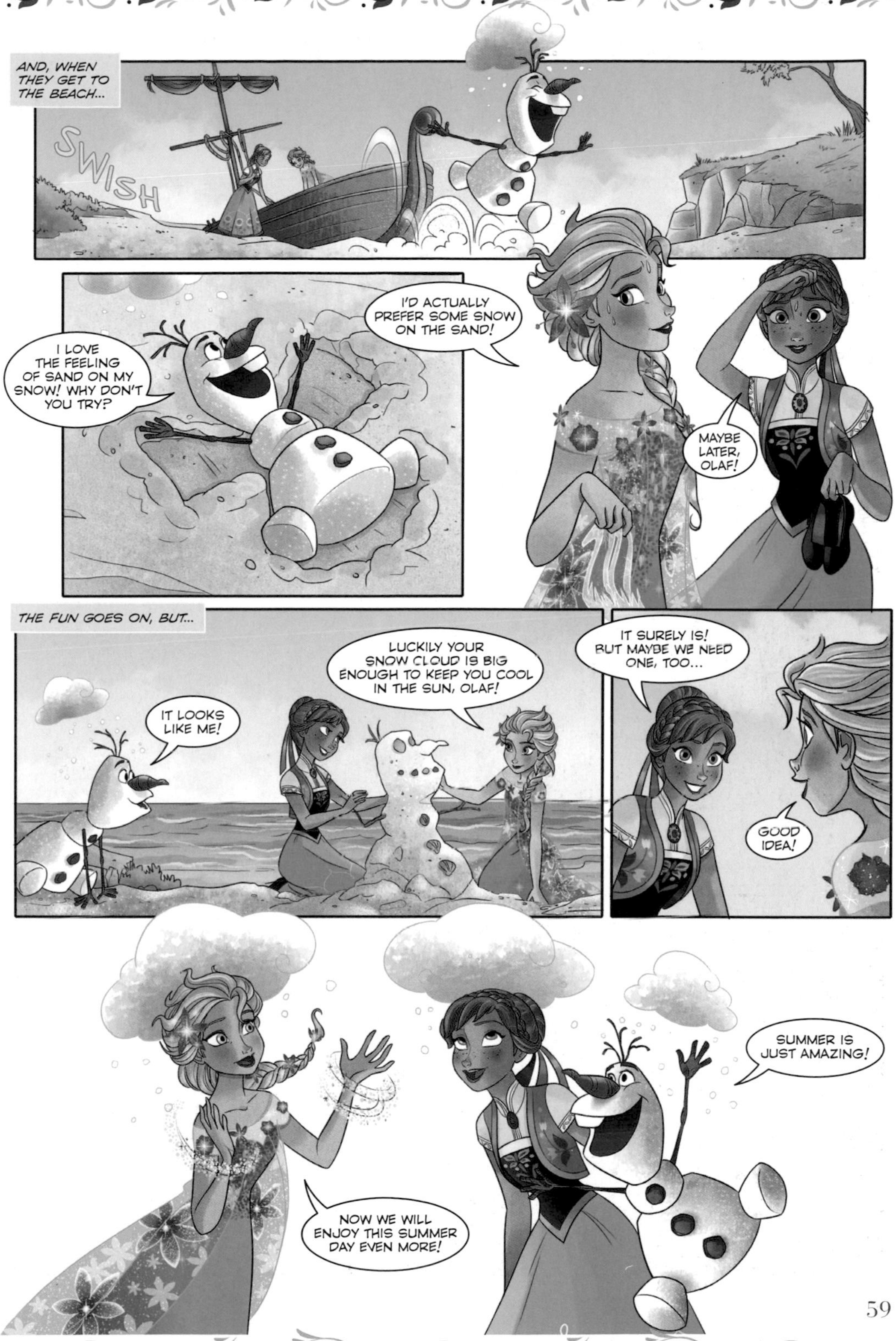
AND, WHEN THEY GET TO THE BEACH...
SWISH
I LOVE THE FEELING OF SAND ON MY SNOW! WHY DON'T YOU TRY?
I'D ACTUALLY PREFER SOME SNOW ON THE SAND!
MAYBE LATER, OLAF!
THE FUN GOES ON, BUT...
IT LOOKS LIKE ME!
LUCKILY YOUR SNOW CLOUD IS BIG ENOUGH TO KEEP YOU COOL IN THE SUN, OLAF!
IT SURELY IS! BUT MAYBE WE NEED ONE, TOO...
GOOD IDEA!
NOW WE WILL ENJOY THIS SUMMER DAY EVEN MORE!
SUMMER IS JUST AMAZING!

# Let's Help Oaken!

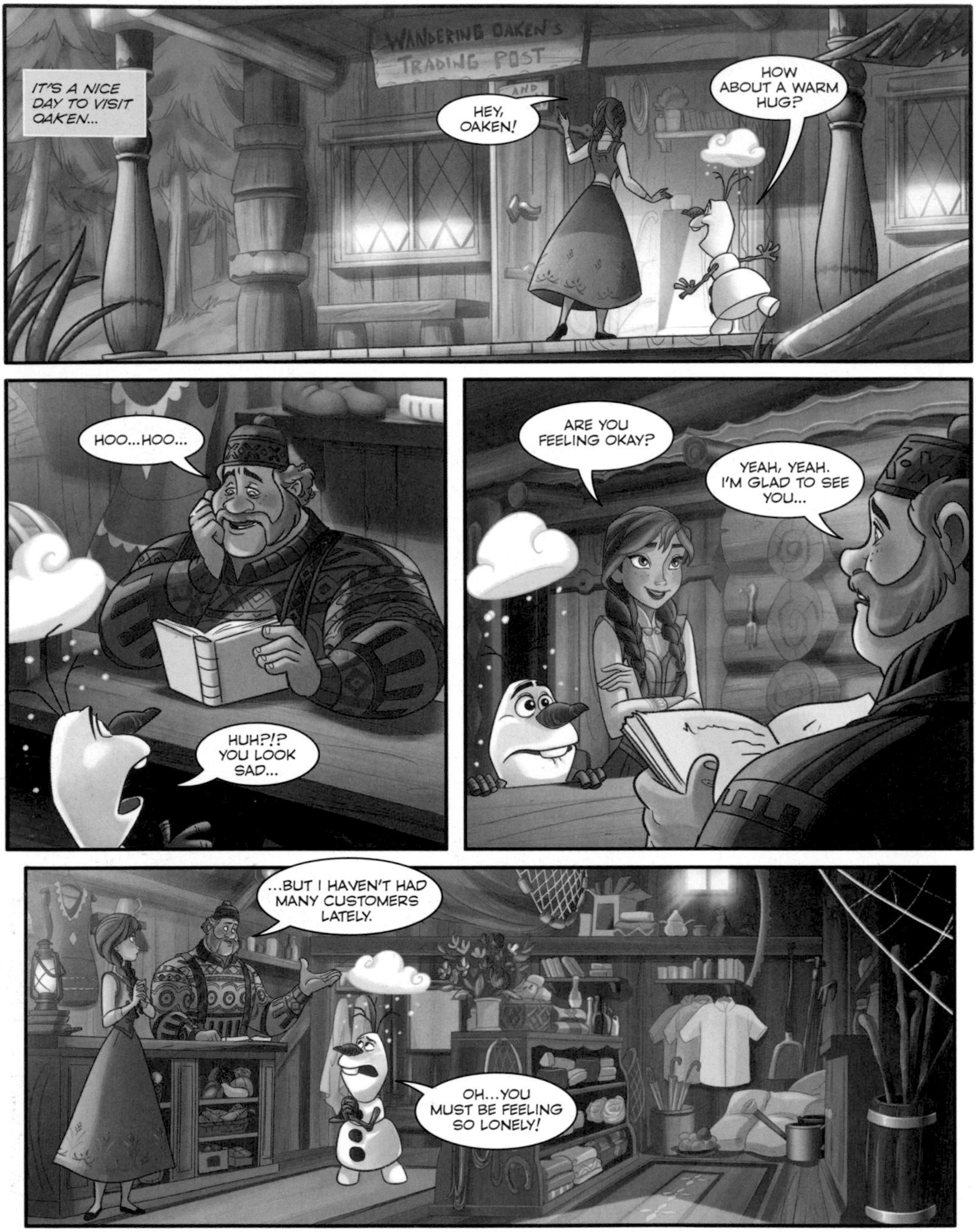

WANDERING OAKEN'S TRADING POST
IT'S A NICE DAY TO VISIT OAKEN...
HEY, OAKEN!
HOW ABOUT A WARM HUG?
HOO...HOO...
HUH?!? YOU LOOK SAD...
ARE YOU FEELING OKAY?
YEAH, YEAH. I'M GLAD TO SEE YOU...
...BUT I HAVEN'T HAD MANY CUSTOMERS LATELY.
OH...YOU MUST BE FEELING SO LONELY!

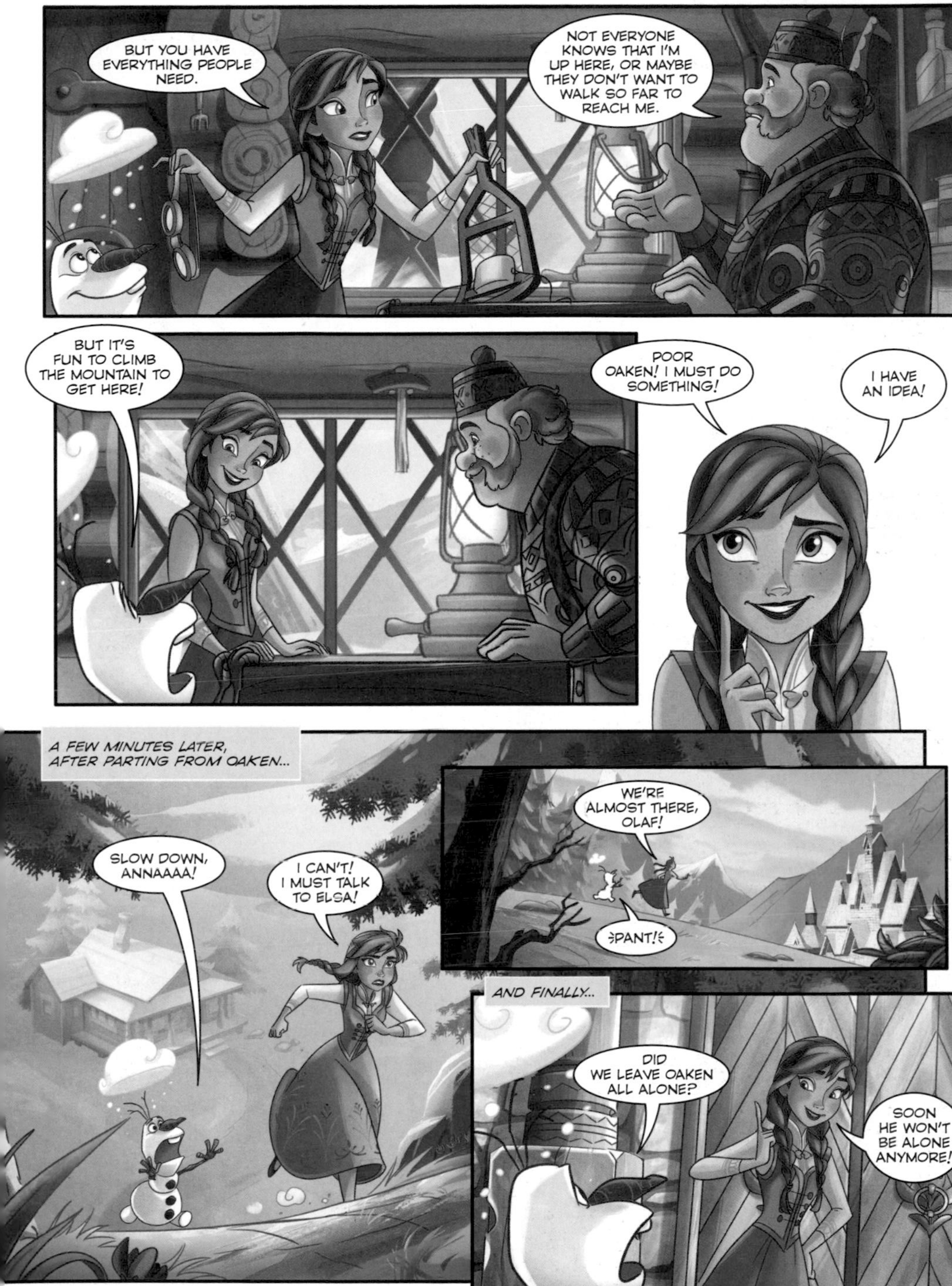
BUT YOU HAVE EVERYTHING PEOPLE NEED.
NOT EVERYONE KNOWS THAT I'M UP HERE, OR MAYBE THEY DON'T WANT TO WALK SO FAR TO REACH ME.
BUT IT'S FUN TO CLIMB THE MOUNTAIN TO GET HERE!
POOR OAKEN! I MUST DO SOMETHING!
I HAVE AN IDEA!
A FEW MINUTES LATER, AFTER PARTING FROM OAKEN...
SLOW DOWN, ANNAAAA!
I CAN'T! I MUST TALK TO ELSA!
WE'RE ALMOST THERE, OLAF!
PANT!
AND FINALLY...
DID WE LEAVE OAKEN ALL ALONE?
SOON HE WON'T BE ALONE ANYMORE!

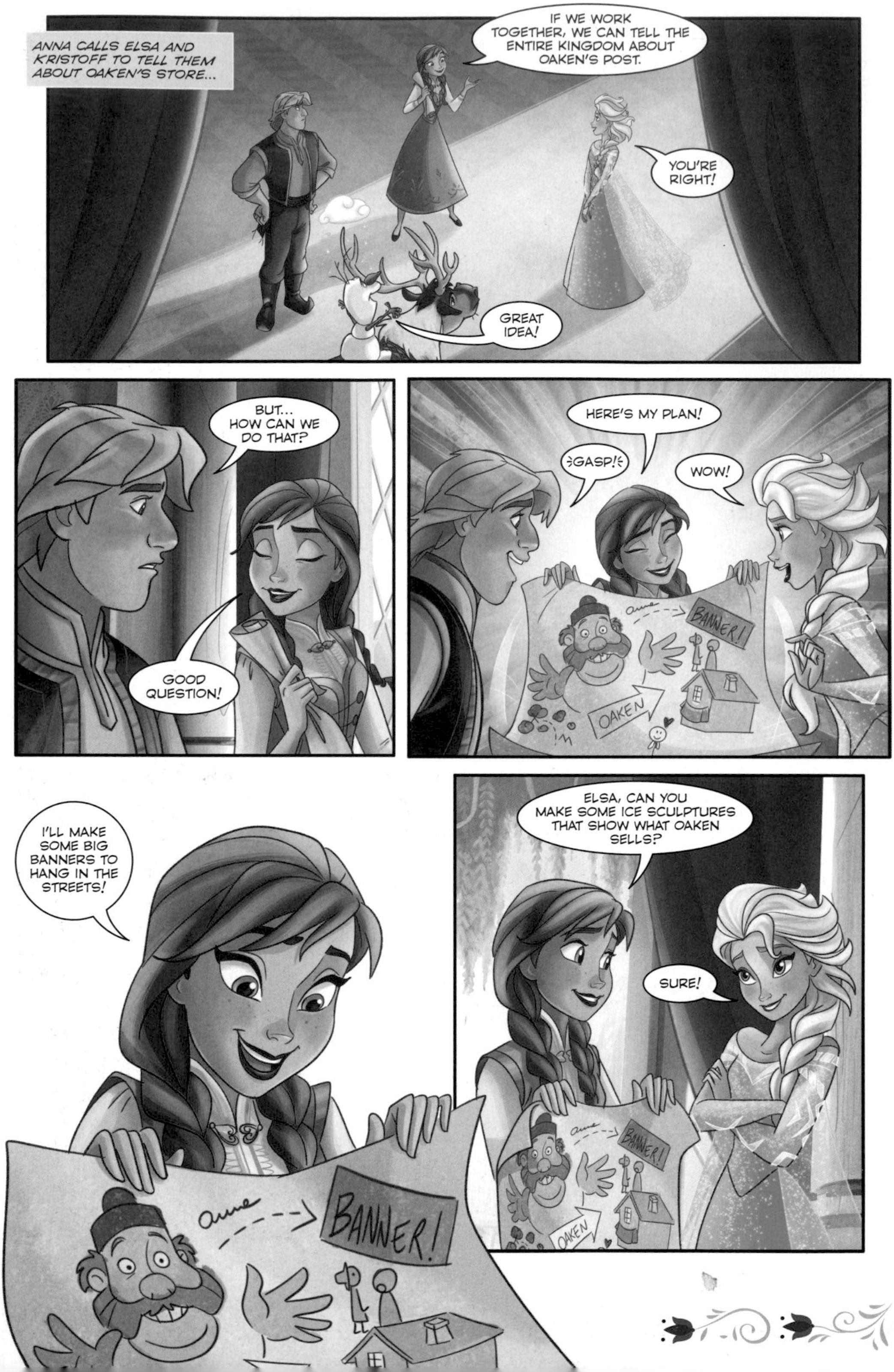
ANNA CALLS ELSA AND KRISTOFF TO TELL THEM ABOUT OAKEN'S STORE...
IF WE WORK TOGETHER, WE CAN TELL THE ENTIRE KINGDOM ABOUT OAKEN'S POST.
YOU'RE RIGHT!
GREAT IDEA!
BUT... HOW CAN WE DO THAT?
GOOD QUESTION!
HERE'S MY PLAN!
GASP!
WOW!
BANNER!
OAKEN
I'LL MAKE SOME BIG BANNERS TO HANG IN THE STREETS!
BANNER!
ELSA, CAN YOU MAKE SOME ICE SCULPTURES THAT SHOW WHAT OAKEN SELLS?
SURE!
BANNER!
OAKEN

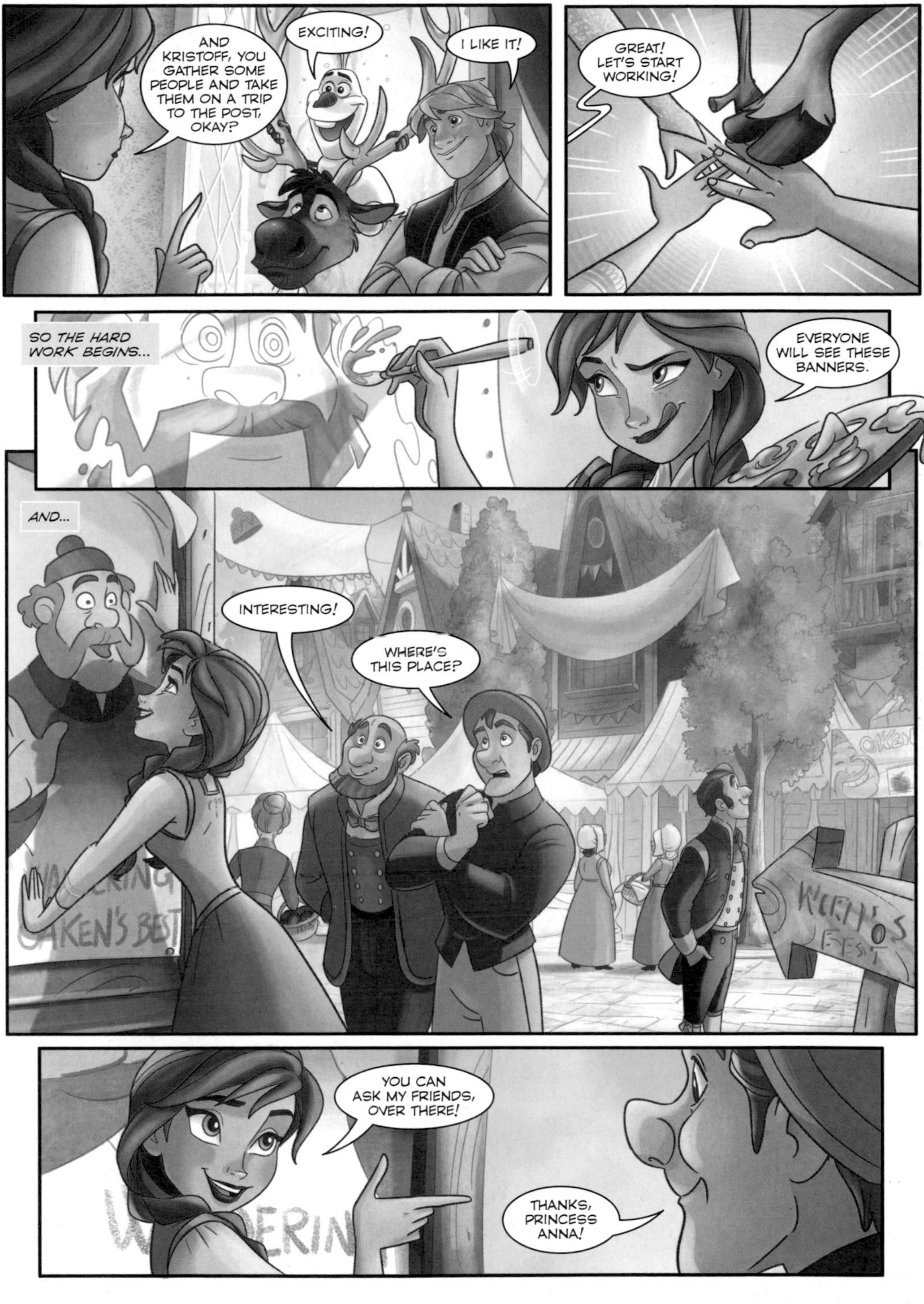
AND KRISTOFF, YOU GATHER SOME PEOPLE AND TAKE THEM ON A TRIP TO THE POST, OKAY?
EXCITING!
I LIKE IT!
GREAT! LET'S START WORKING!
SO THE HARD WORK BEGINS...
EVERYONE WILL SEE THESE BANNERS.
AND...
INTERESTING!
WHERE'S THIS PLACE?
OAKEN'S
WANDERING OAKEN'S BEST
YOU CAN ASK MY FRIENDS, OVER THERE!
THANKS, PRINCESS ANNA!

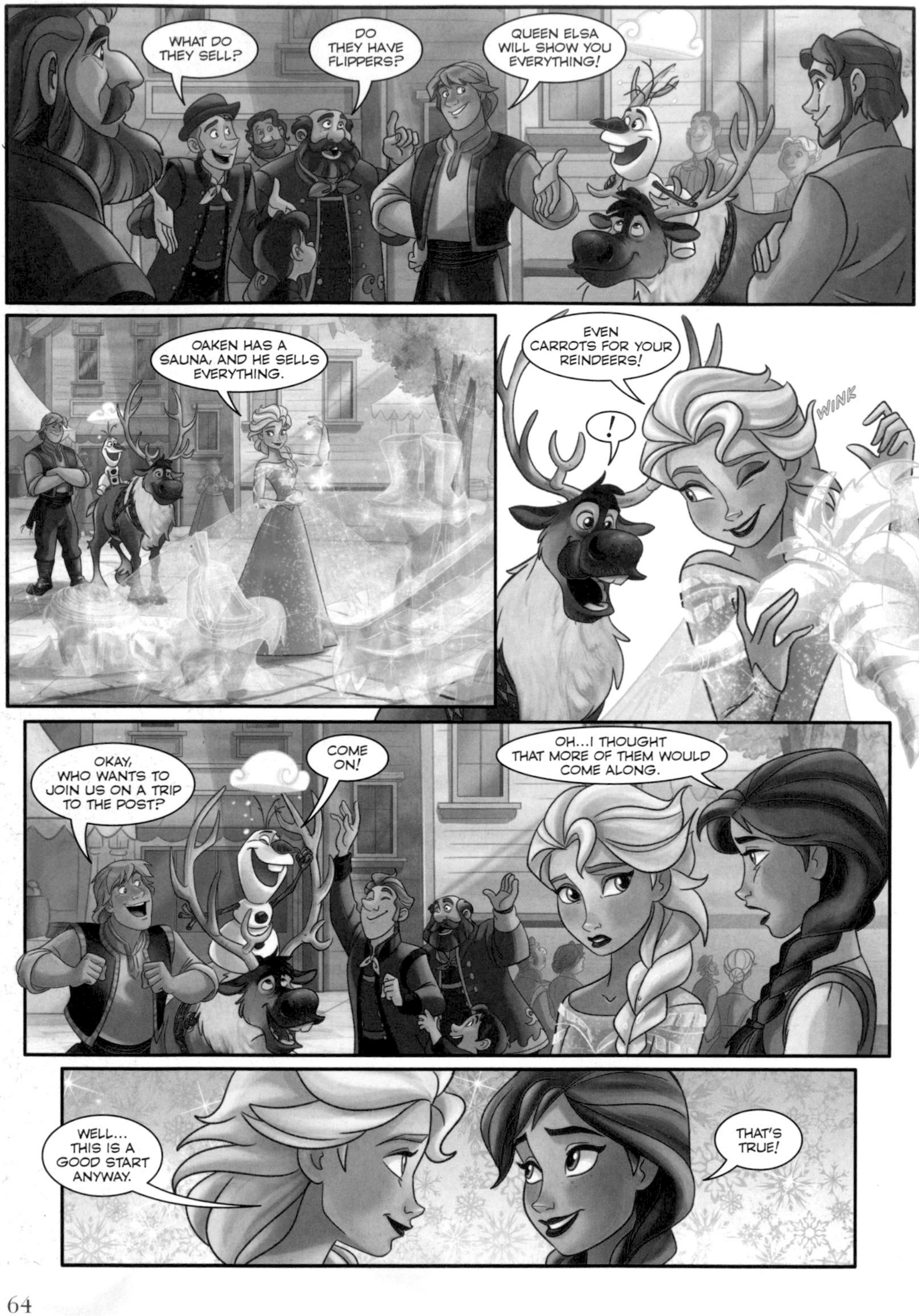
WHAT DO THEY SELL?
DO THEY HAVE FLIPPERS?
QUEEN ELSA WILL SHOW YOU EVERYTHING!
OAKEN HAS A SAUNA, AND HE SELLS EVERYTHING.
EVEN CARROTS FOR YOUR REINDEERS!
!
WINK
OKAY, WHO WANTS TO JOIN US ON A TRIP TO THE POST?
COME ON!
OH...I THOUGHT THAT MORE OF THEM WOULD COME ALONG.
WELL... THIS IS A GOOD START ANYWAY.
THAT'S TRUE!

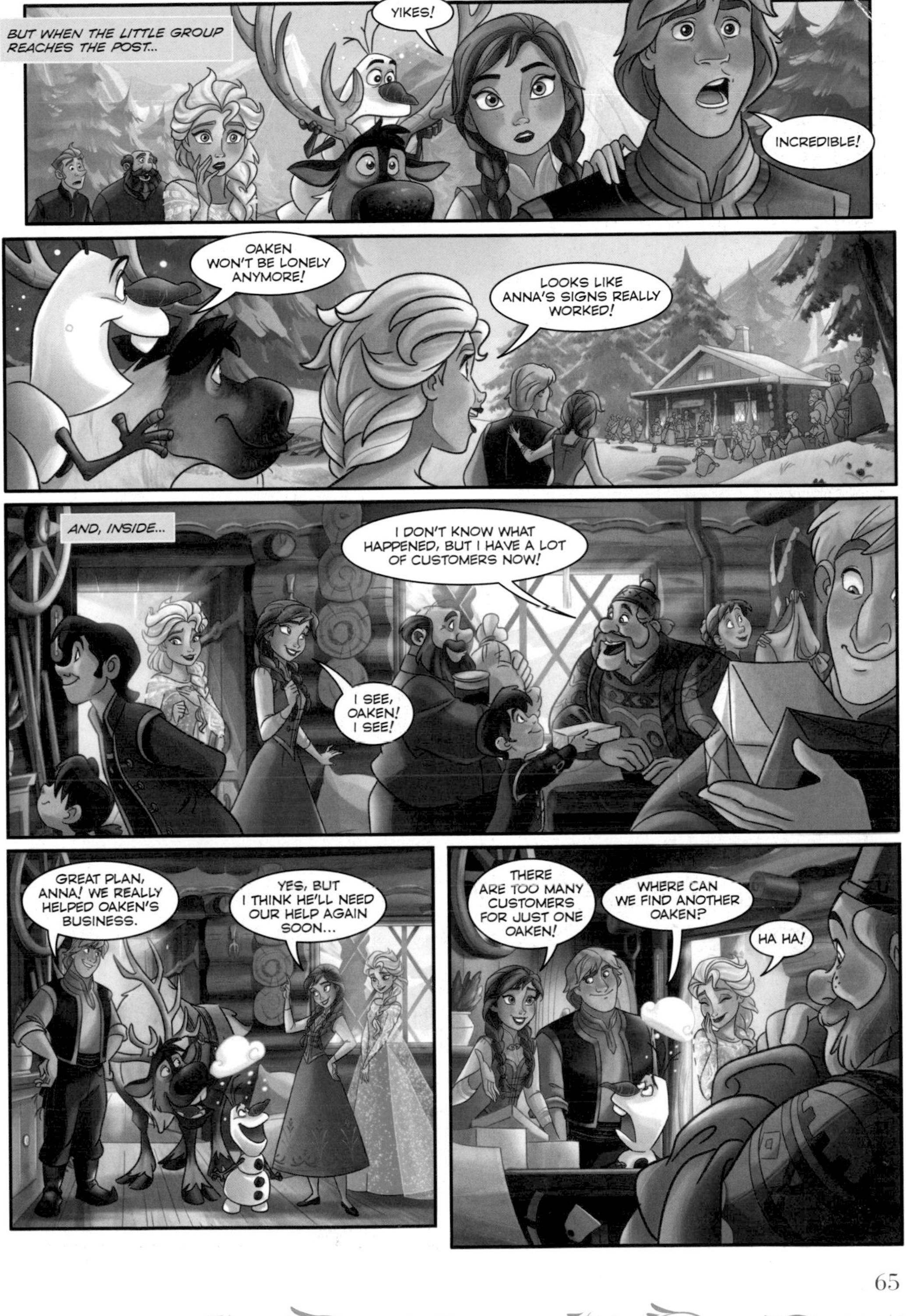
BUT WHEN THE LITTLE GROUP REACHES THE POST...
YIKES!
INCREDIBLE!
OAKEN WON'T BE LONELY ANYMORE!
LOOKS LIKE ANNA'S SIGNS REALLY WORKED!
AND, INSIDE...
I DON'T KNOW WHAT HAPPENED, BUT I HAVE A LOT OF CUSTOMERS NOW!
I SEE, OAKEN! I SEE!
GREAT PLAN, ANNA! WE REALLY HELPED OAKEN'S BUSINESS.
YES, BUT I THINK HE'LL NEED OUR HELP AGAIN SOON...
THERE ARE TOO MANY CUSTOMERS FOR JUST ONE OAKEN!
WHERE CAN WE FIND ANOTHER OAKEN?
HA HA!

# A Very Hot Day

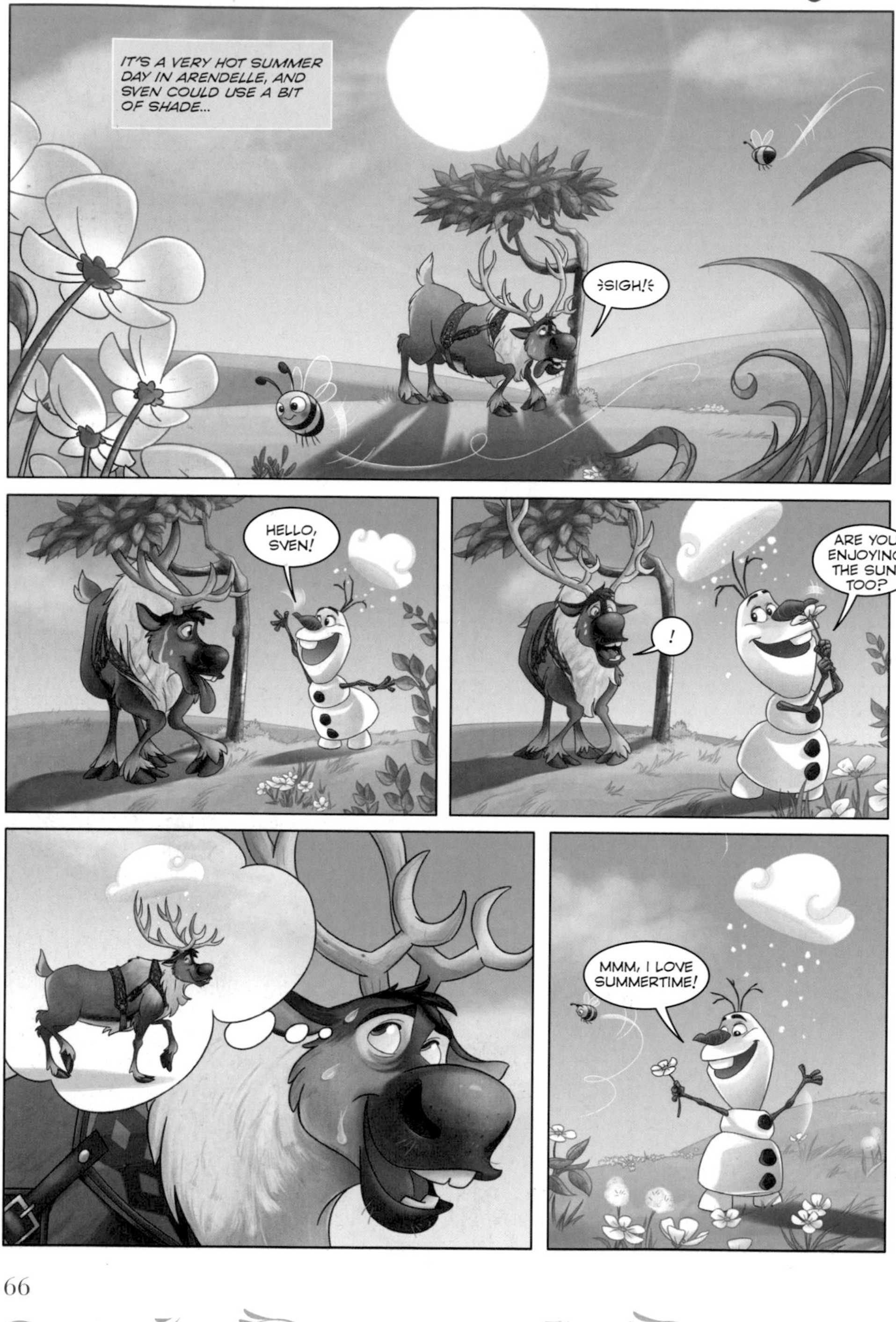
IT'S A VERY HOT SUMMER DAY IN ARENDELLE, AND SVEN COULD USE A BIT OF SHADE...
SIGH!
HELLO, SVEN!
ARE YOU ENJOYING THE SUN, TOO?
!
MMM, I LOVE SUMMERTIME!

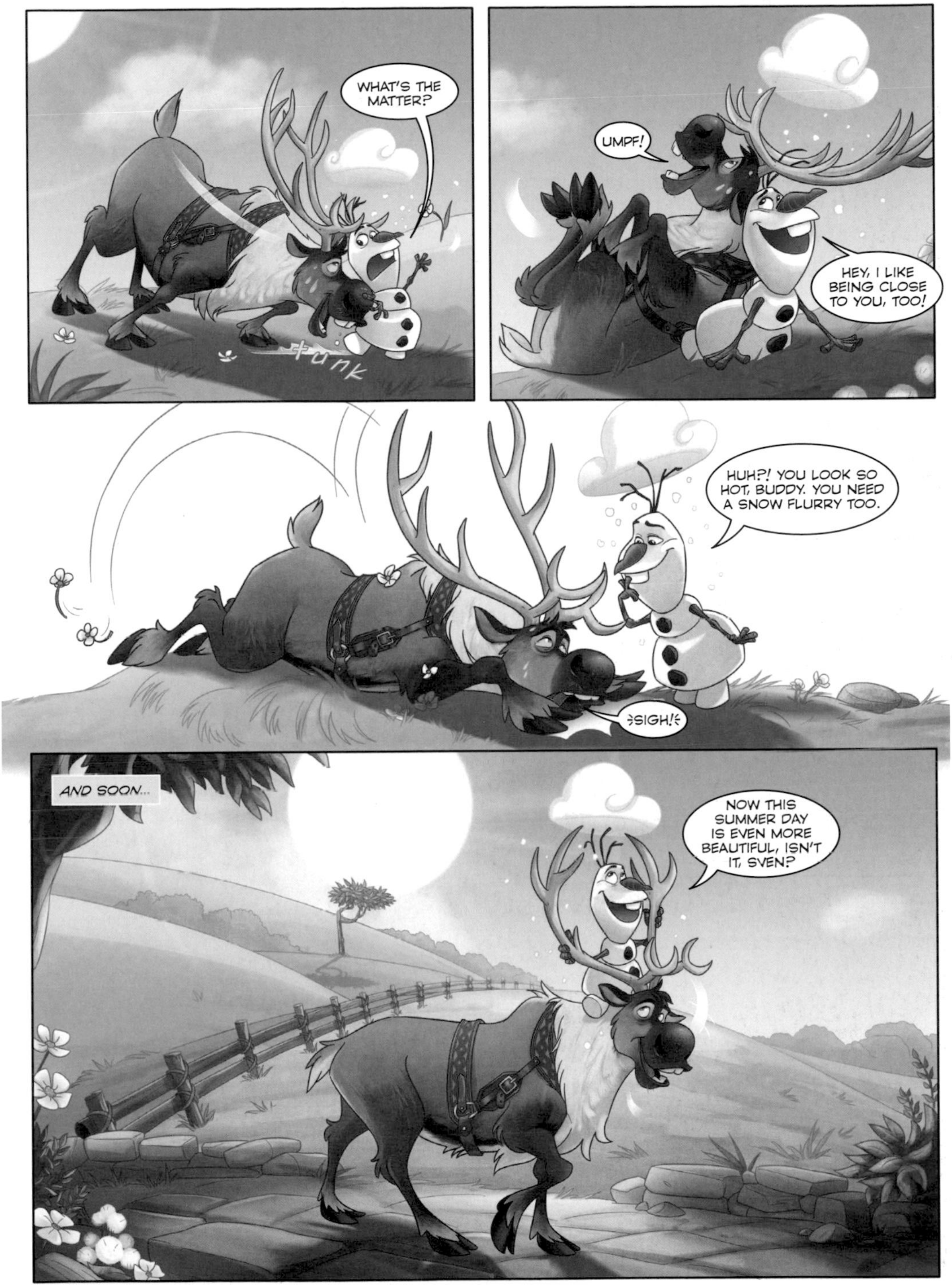
WHAT'S THE MATTER?
THUNK
UMPF!
HEY, I LIKE BEING CLOSE TO YOU, TOO!
HUH?! YOU LOOK SO HOT, BUDDY. YOU NEED A SNOW FLURRY TOO.
SIGH!
AND SOON...
NOW THIS SUMMER DAY IS EVEN MORE BEAUTIFUL, ISN'T IT, SVEN?

# A Snowflakes Surprise

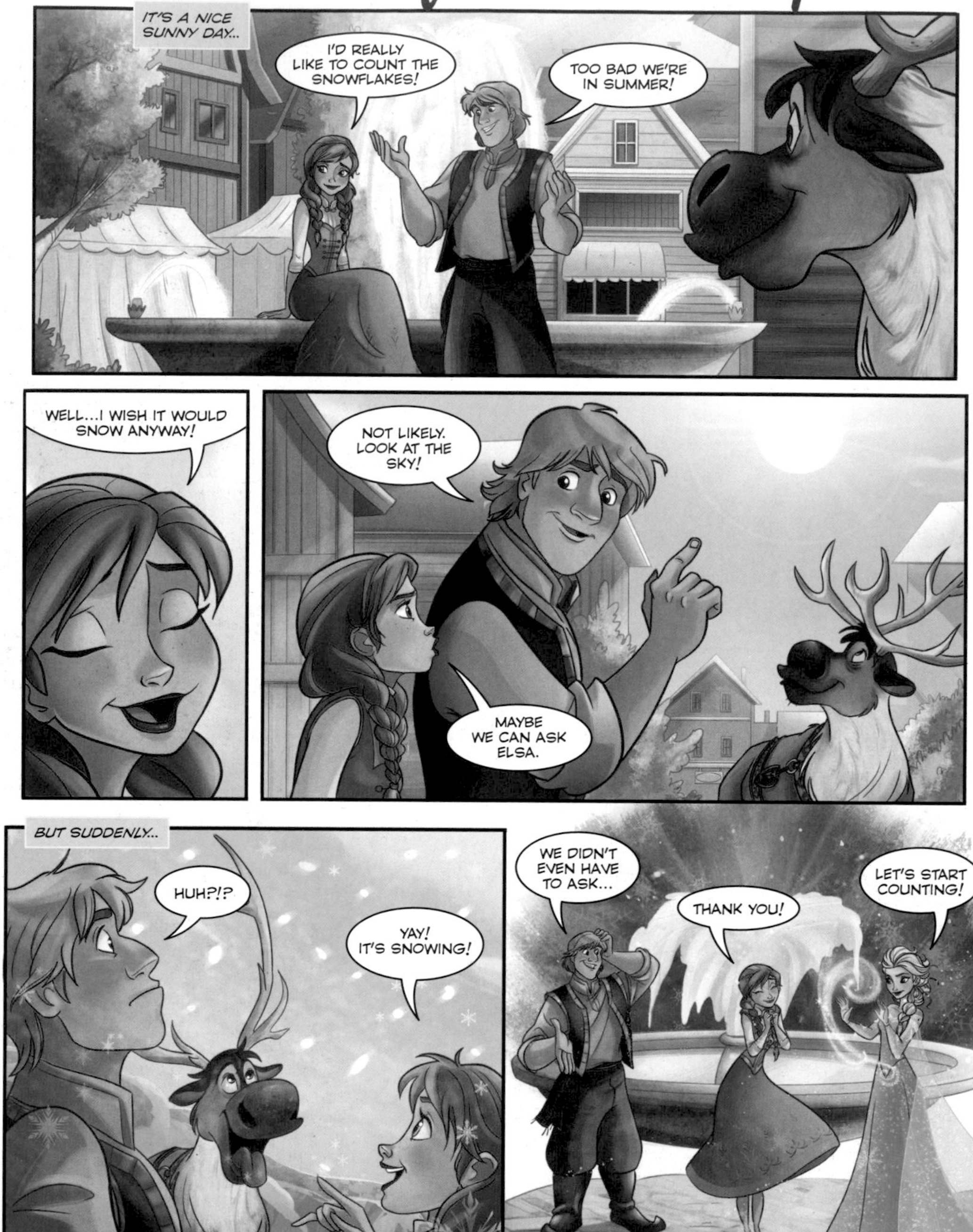
IT'S A NICE SUNNY DAY...
I'D REALLY LIKE TO COUNT THE SNOWFLAKES!
TOO BAD WE'RE IN SUMMER!
WELL...I WISH IT WOULD SNOW ANYWAY!
NOT LIKELY. LOOK AT THE SKY!
MAYBE WE CAN ASK ELSA.
BUT SUDDENLY...
HUH?!?
YAY! IT'S SNOWING!
WE DIDN'T EVEN HAVE TO ASK...
THANK YOU!
LET'S START COUNTING!

# A Great Song

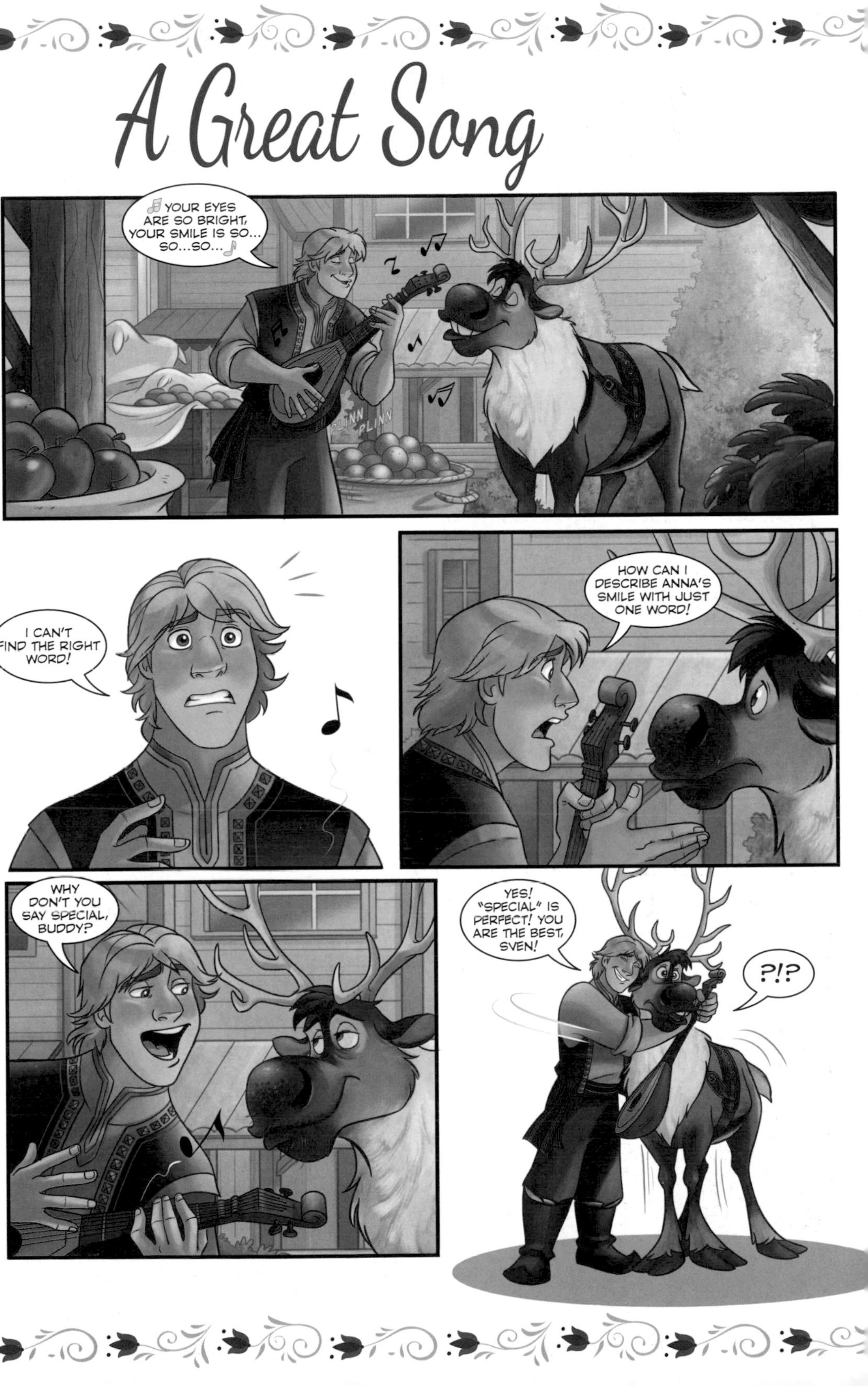

YOUR EYES ARE SO BRIGHT, YOUR SMILE IS SO... SO...SO...
PLINN PLINN
I CAN'T FIND THE RIGHT WORD!
HOW CAN I DESCRIBE ANNA'S SMILE WITH JUST ONE WORD!
WHY DON'T YOU SAY SPECIAL, BUDDY?
YES! "SPECIAL" IS PERFECT! YOU ARE THE BEST, SVEN!
?!?

# The Para-Snow

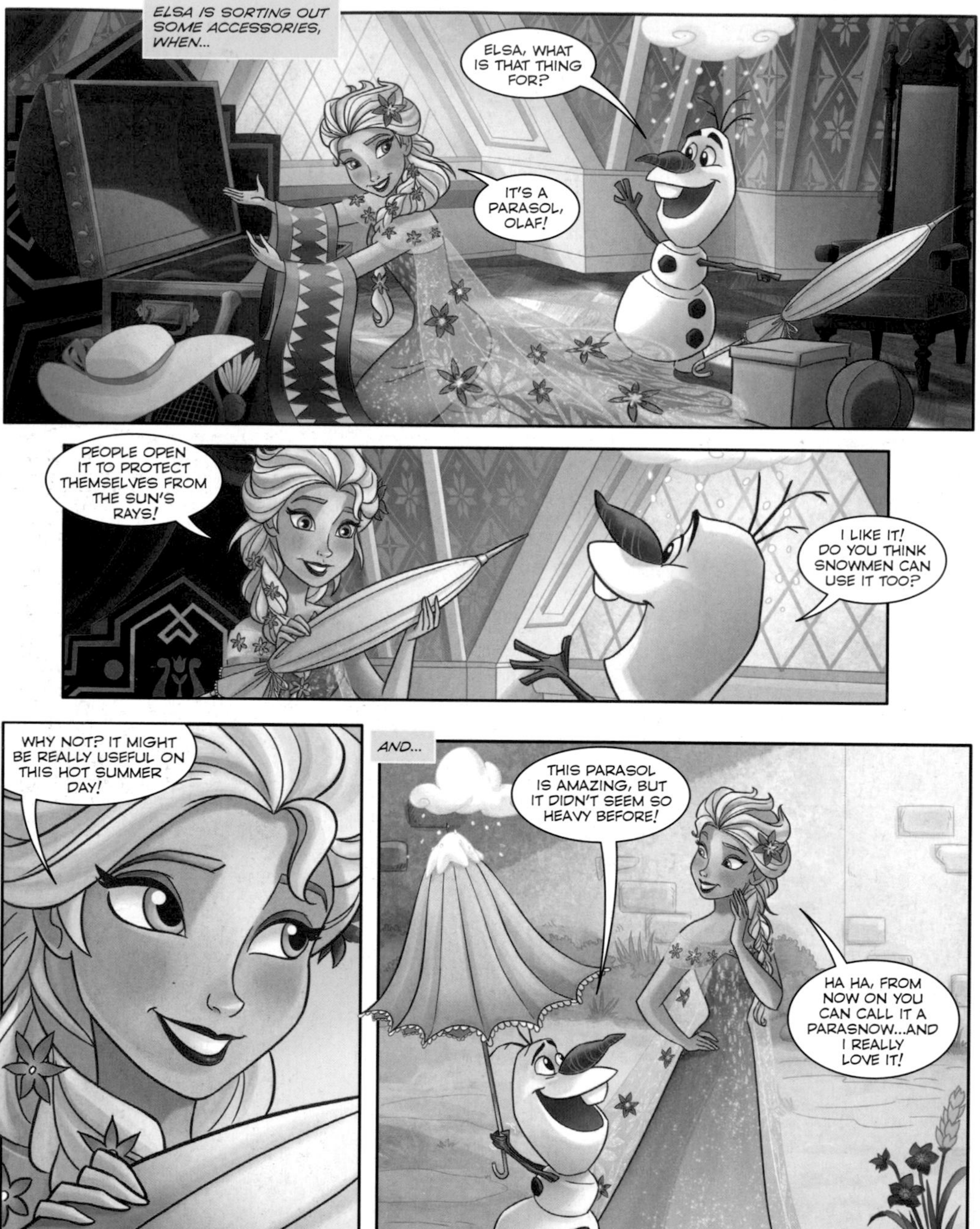
ELSA IS SORTING OUT SOME ACCESSORIES, WHEN...
ELSA, WHAT IS THAT THING FOR?
IT'S A PARASOL, OLAF!
PEOPLE OPEN IT TO PROTECT THEMSELVES FROM THE SUN'S RAYS!
I LIKE IT! DO YOU THINK SNOWMEN CAN USE IT TOO?
WHY NOT? IT MIGHT BE REALLY USEFUL ON THIS HOT SUMMER DAY!
AND...
THIS PARASOL IS AMAZING, BUT IT DIDN'T SEEM SO HEAVY BEFORE!
HA HA, FROM NOW ON YOU CAN CALL IT A PARASNOW...AND I REALLY LOVE IT!

# Oaken's Mystery Box

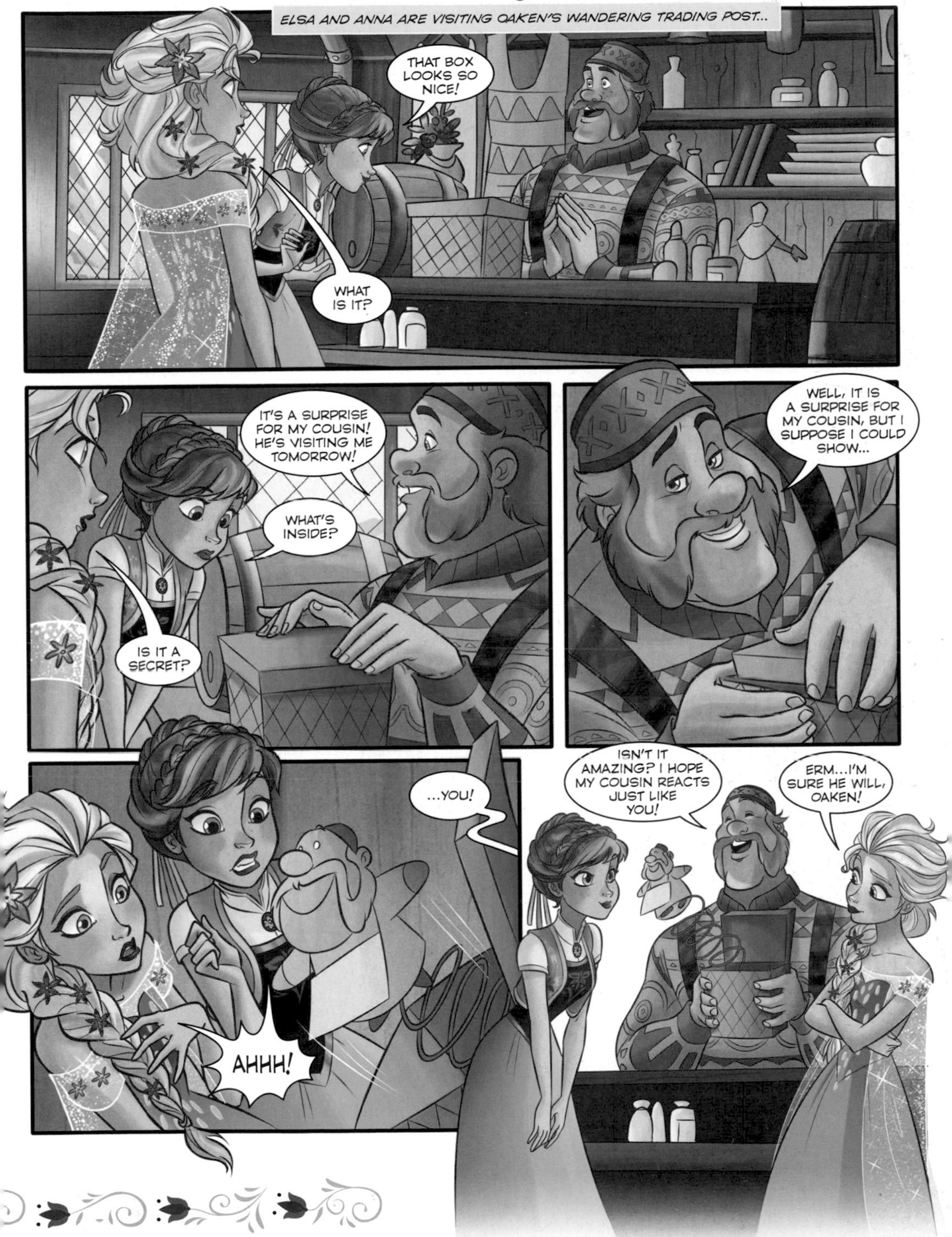
ELSA AND ANNA ARE VISITING OAKEN'S WANDERING TRADING POST...
THAT BOX LOOKS SO NICE!
WHAT IS IT?
IT'S A SURPRISE FOR MY COUSIN! HE'S VISITING ME TOMORROW!
WHAT'S INSIDE?
IS IT A SECRET?
WELL, IT IS A SURPRISE FOR MY COUSIN, BUT I SUPPOSE I COULD SHOW...
...YOU!
AHHH!
ISN'T IT AMAZING? I HOPE MY COUSIN REACTS JUST LIKE YOU!
ERM...I'M SURE HE WILL, OAKEN!

# Through the Wall

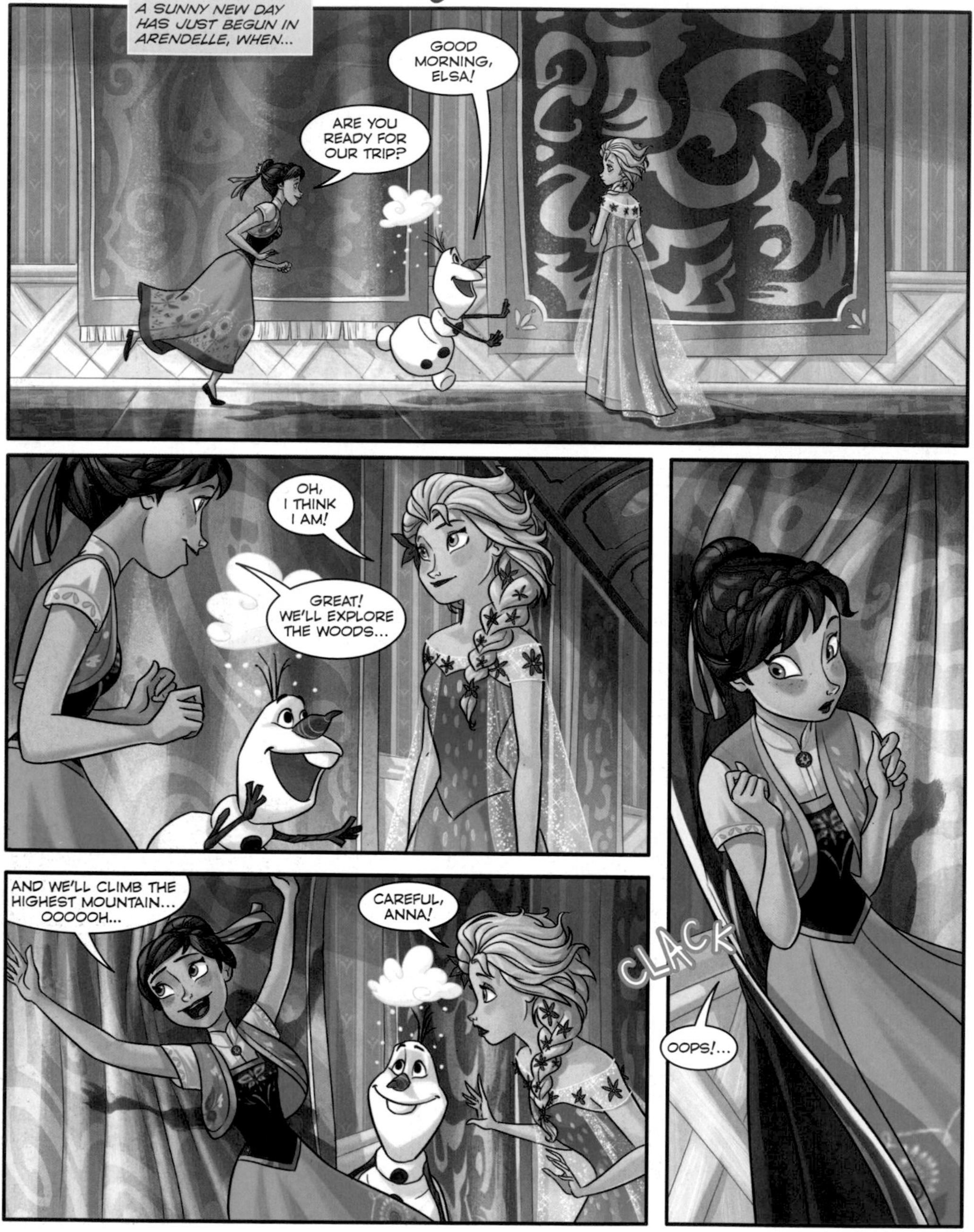
A SUNNY NEW DAY HAS JUST BEGUN IN ARENDELLE, WHEN...
GOOD MORNING, ELSA!
ARE YOU READY FOR OUR TRIP?
OH, I THINK I AM!
GREAT! WE'LL EXPLORE THE WOODS...
AND WE'LL CLIMB THE HIGHEST MOUNTAIN... OOOOOH...
CAREFUL, ANNA!
CLACK
OOPS!...

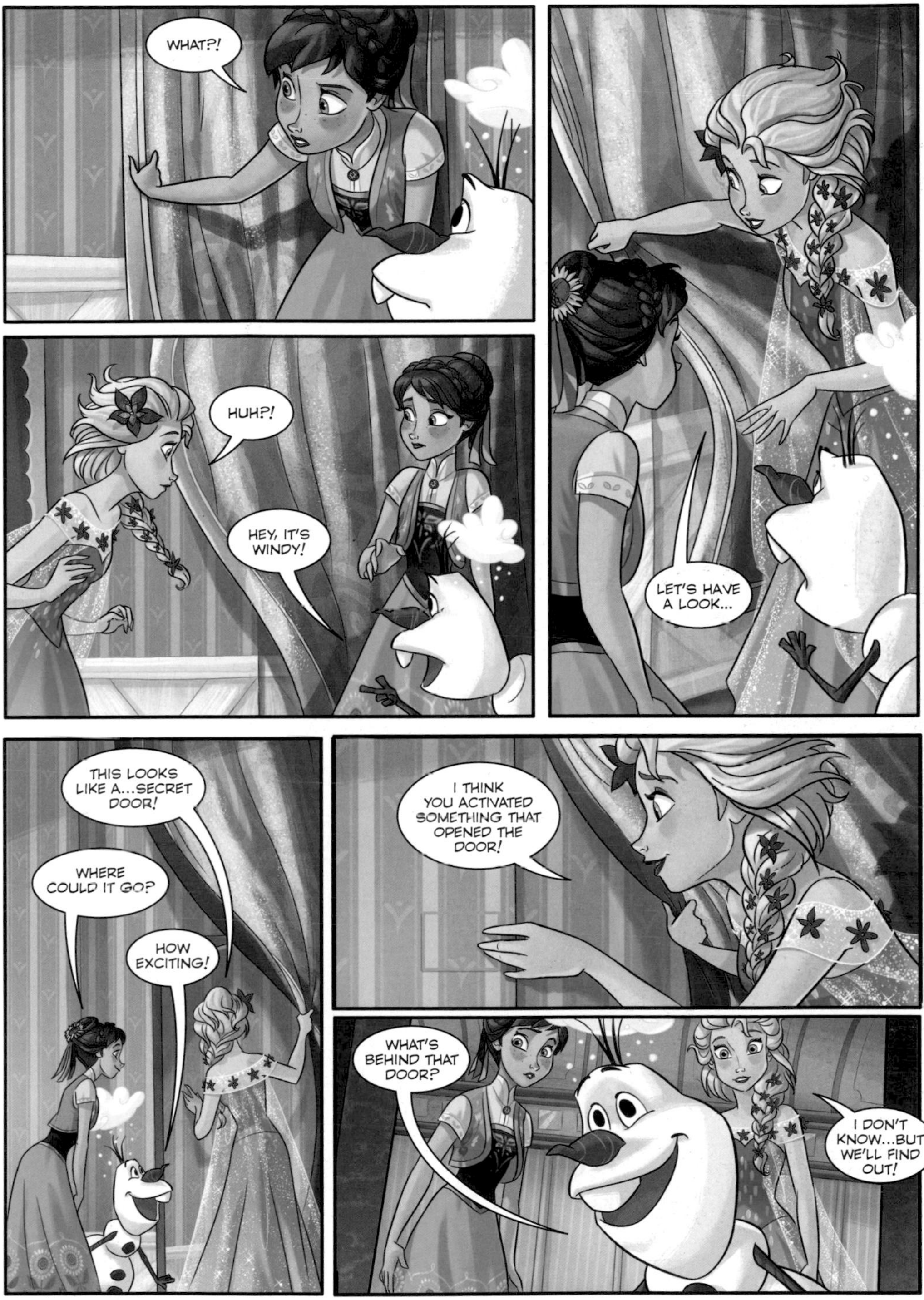
WHAT?!
HUH?!
HEY, IT'S WINDY!
LET'S HAVE A LOOK...
THIS LOOKS LIKE A...SECRET DOOR!
WHERE COULD IT GO?
HOW EXCITING!
I THINK YOU ACTIVATED SOMETHING THAT OPENED THE DOOR!
WHAT'S BEHIND THAT DOOR?
I DON'T KNOW...BUT WE'LL FIND OUT!

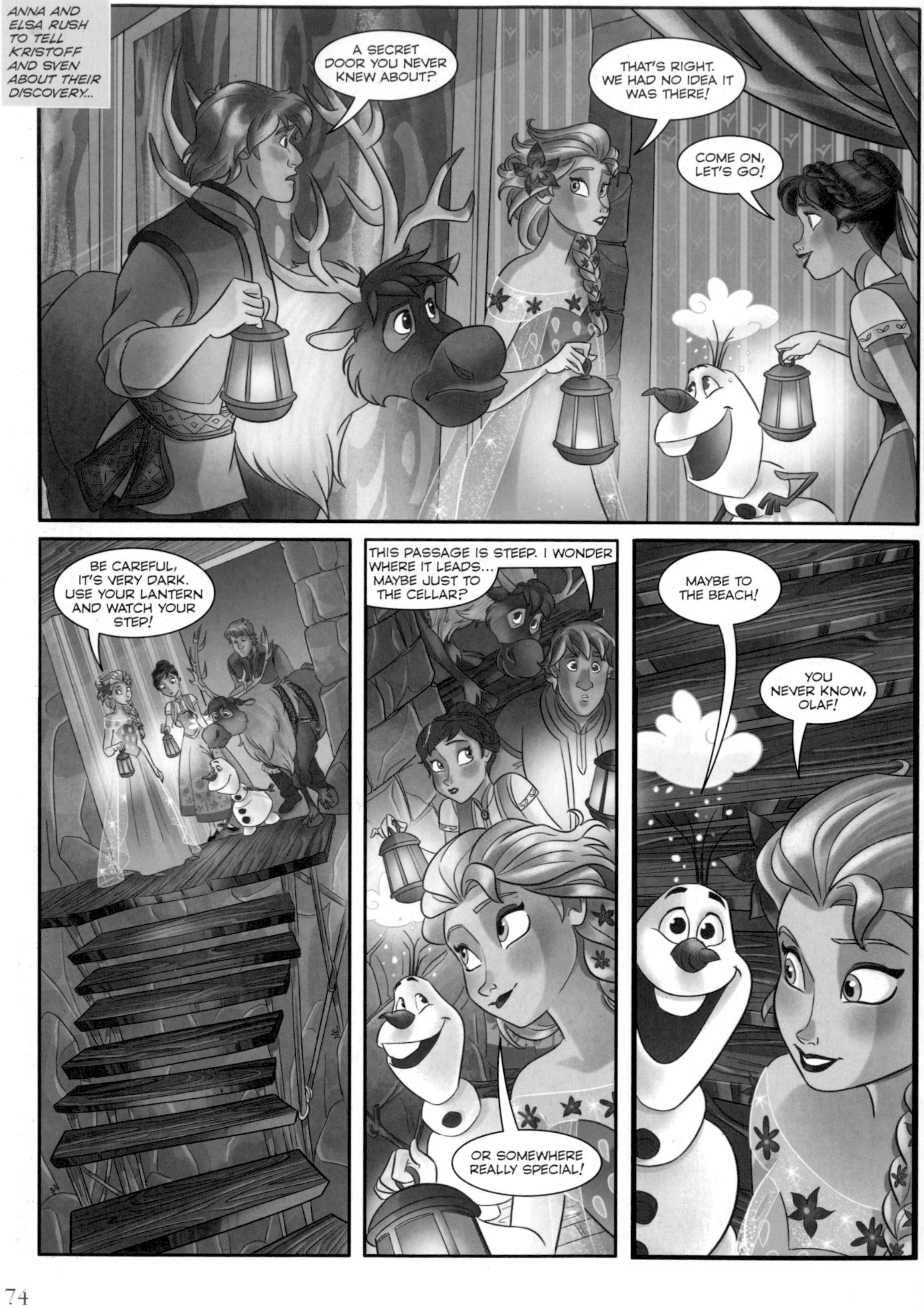
ANNA AND ELSA RUSH TO TELL KRISTOFF AND SVEN ABOUT THEIR DISCOVERY...
A SECRET DOOR YOU NEVER KNEW ABOUT?
THAT'S RIGHT. WE HAD NO IDEA IT WAS THERE!
COME ON, LET'S GO!
BE CAREFUL, IT'S VERY DARK. USE YOUR LANTERN AND WATCH YOUR STEP!
THIS PASSAGE IS STEEP. I WONDER WHERE IT LEADS... MAYBE JUST TO THE CELLAR?
OR SOMEWHERE REALLY SPECIAL!
MAYBE TO THE BEACH!
YOU NEVER KNOW, OLAF!

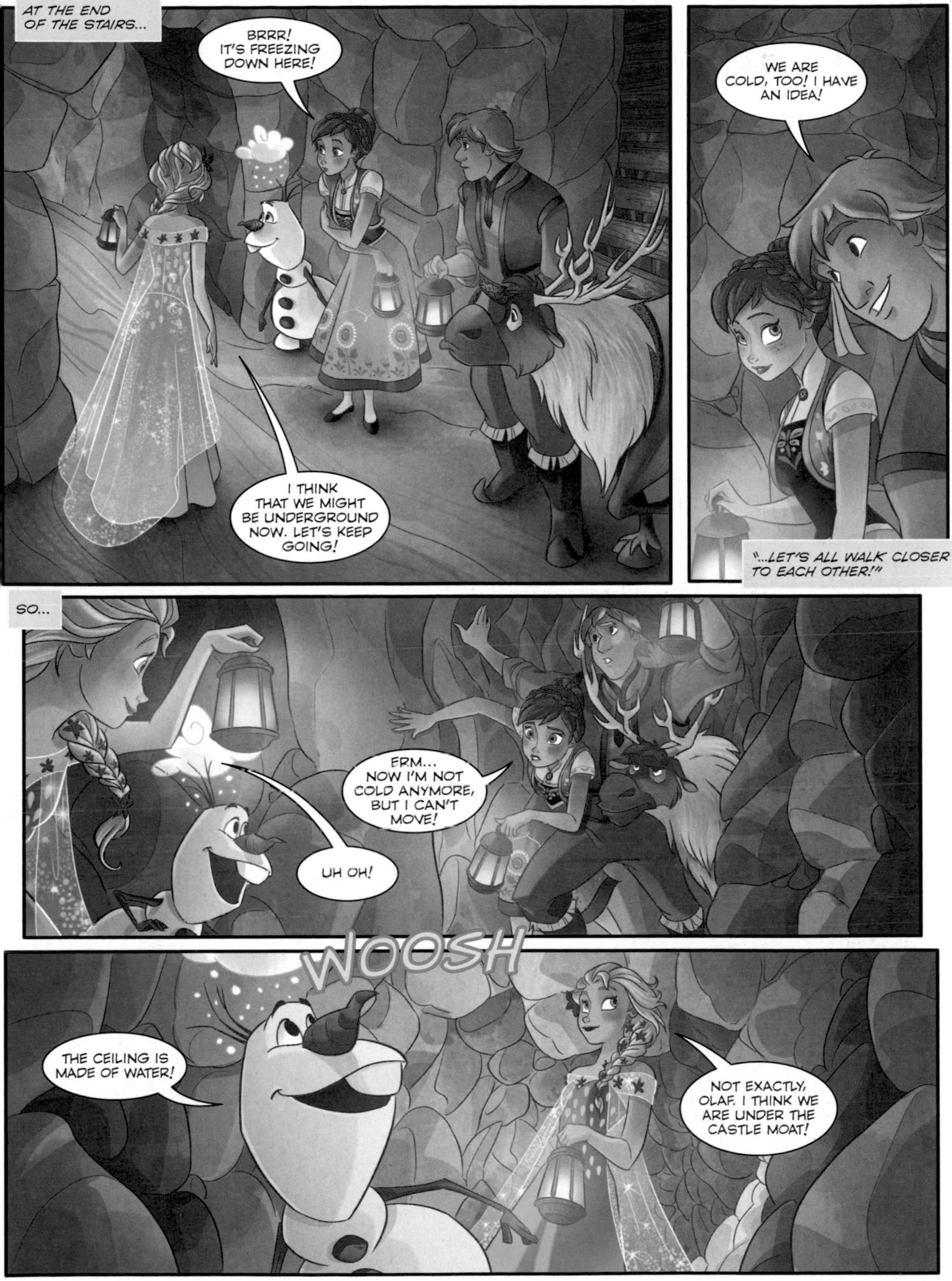
AT THE END OF THE STAIRS...
BRRR! IT'S FREEZING DOWN HERE!
I THINK THAT WE MIGHT BE UNDERGROUND NOW. LET'S KEEP GOING!
WE ARE COLD, TOO! I HAVE AN IDEA!
"...LET'S ALL WALK CLOSER TO EACH OTHER!"
SO...
ERM... NOW I'M NOT COLD ANYMORE, BUT I CAN'T MOVE!
UH OH!
WOOSH
THE CEILING IS MADE OF WATER!
NOT EXACTLY, OLAF. I THINK WE ARE UNDER THE CASTLE MOAT!

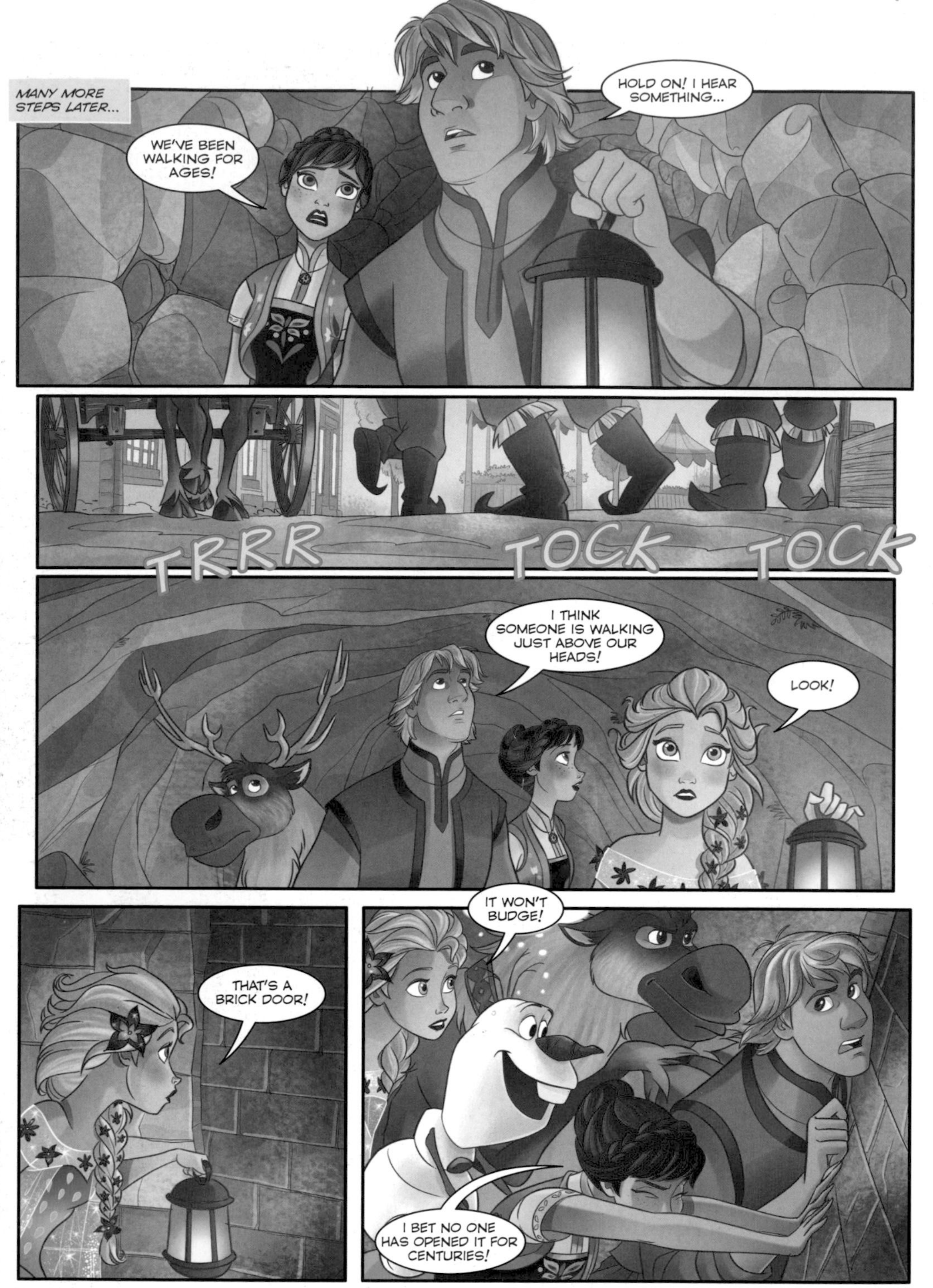
MANY MORE STEPS LATER...
WE'VE BEEN WALKING FOR AGES!
HOLD ON! I HEAR SOMETHING...
TRRR
TOCK
TOCK
I THINK SOMEONE IS WALKING JUST ABOVE OUR HEADS!
LOOK!
THAT'S A BRICK DOOR!
IT WON'T BUDGE!
I BET NO ONE HAS OPENED IT FOR CENTURIES!

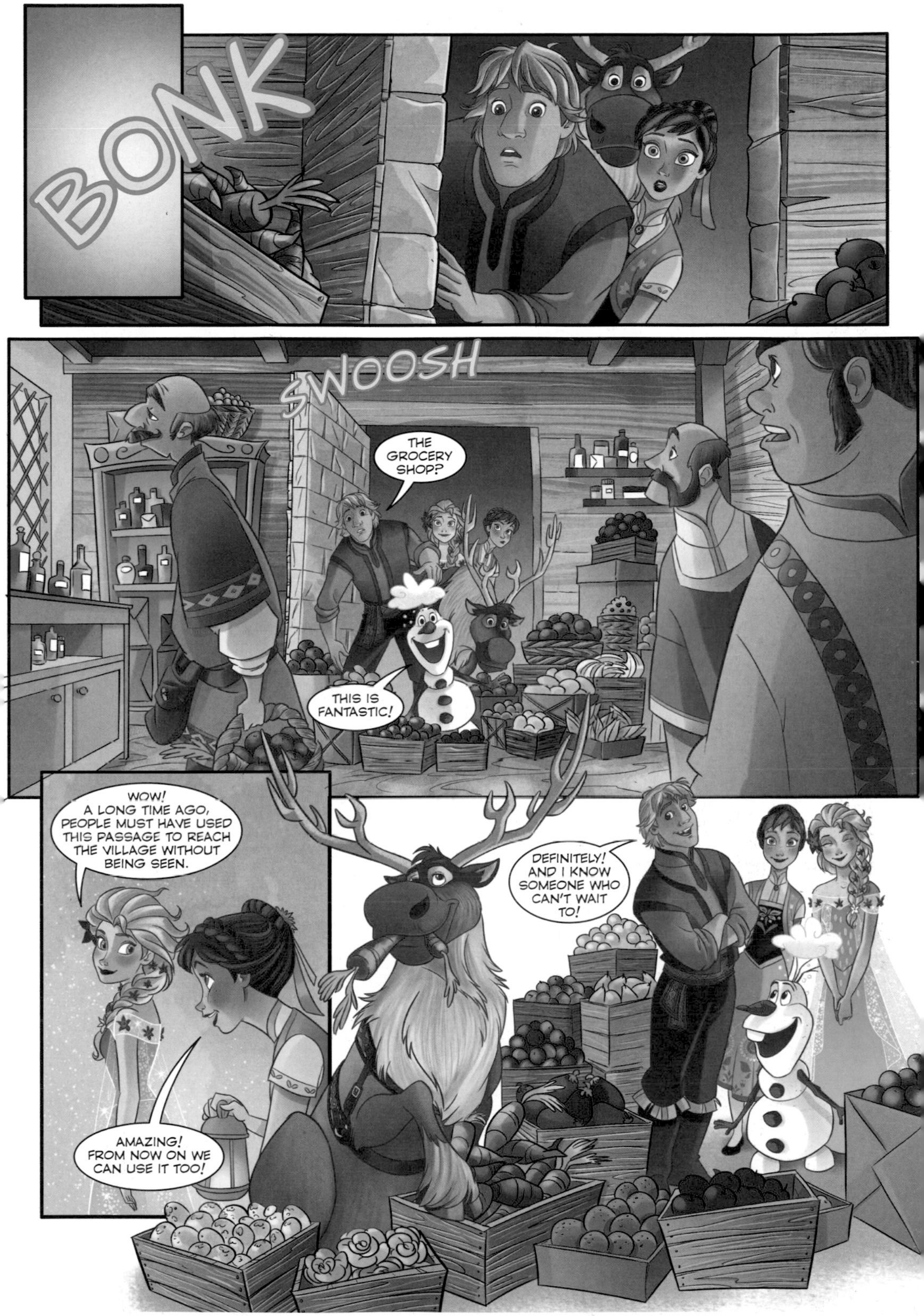
BONK
SWOOSH
THE GROCERY SHOP?
THIS IS FANTASTIC!
WOW! A LONG TIME AGO, PEOPLE MUST HAVE USED THIS PASSAGE TO REACH THE VILLAGE WITHOUT BEING SEEN.
AMAZING! FROM NOW ON WE CAN USE IT TOO!
DEFINITELY! AND I KNOW SOMEONE WHO CAN'T WAIT TO!

# Melting Gift

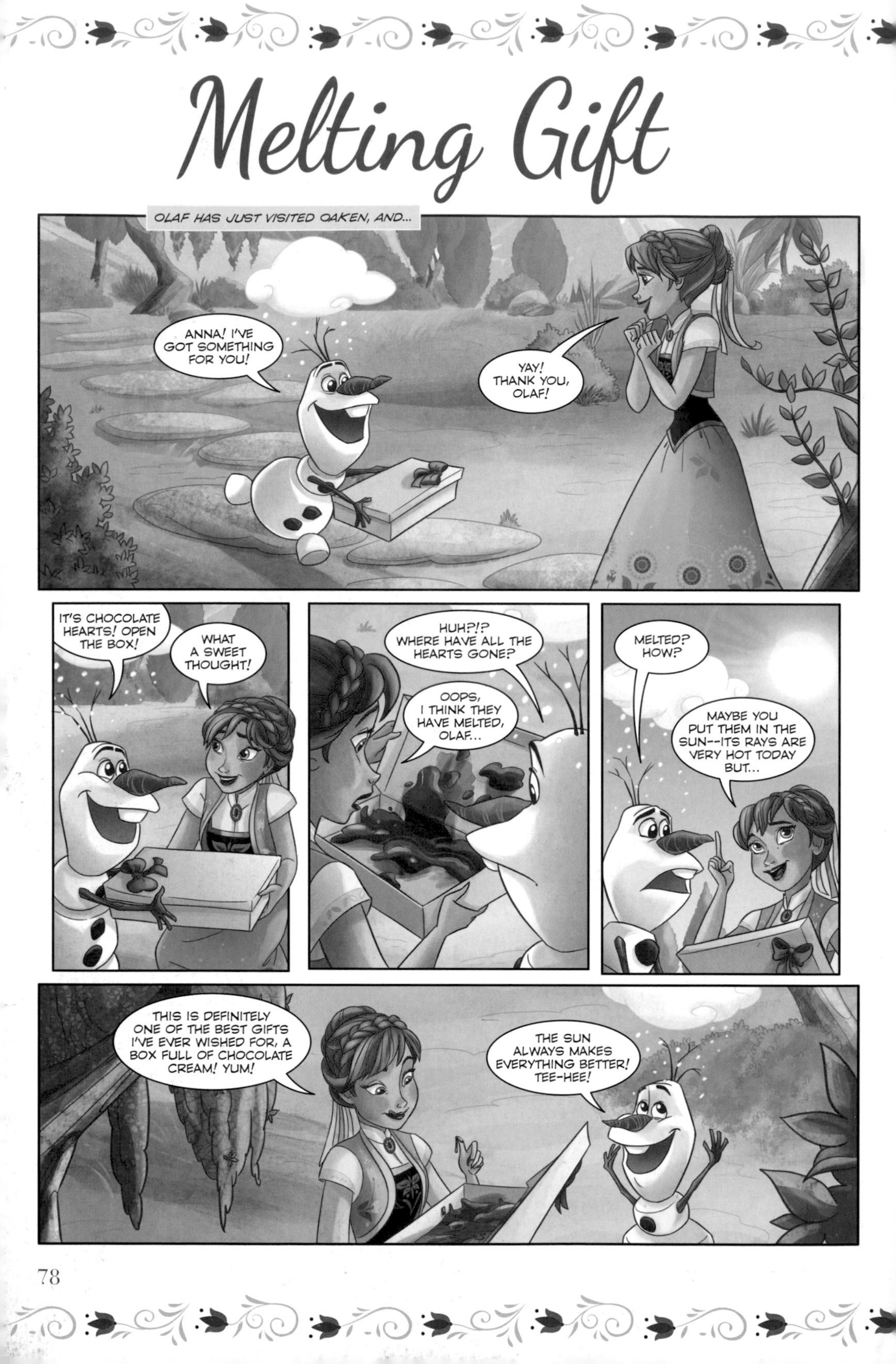
OLAF HAS JUST VISITED OAKEN, AND...
ANNA! I'VE GOT SOMETHING FOR YOU!
YAY! THANK YOU, OLAF!
IT'S CHOCOLATE HEARTS! OPEN THE BOX!
WHAT A SWEET THOUGHT!
HUH?!? WHERE HAVE ALL THE HEARTS GONE?
OOPS, I THINK THEY HAVE MELTED, OLAF...
MELTED? HOW?
MAYBE YOU PUT THEM IN THE SUN--ITS RAYS ARE VERY HOT TODAY BUT...
THIS IS DEFINITELY ONE OF THE BEST GIFTS I'VE EVER WISHED FOR, A BOX FULL OF CHOCOLATE CREAM! YUM!
THE SUN ALWAYS MAKES EVERYTHING BETTER! TEE-HEE!

# A Good Friend

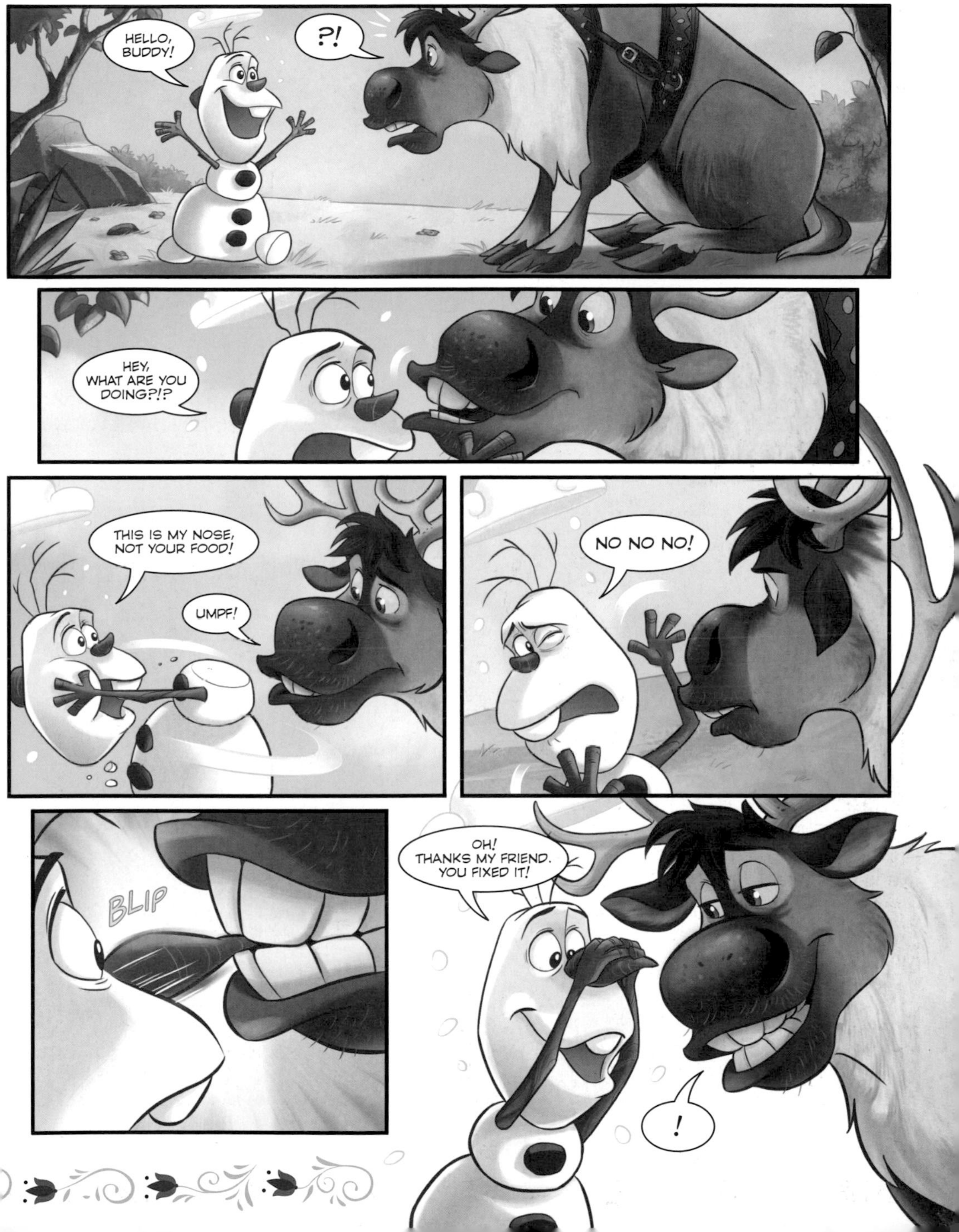
HELLO, BUDDY!
?!
HEY, WHAT ARE YOU DOING?!?
THIS IS MY NOSE, NOT YOUR FOOD!
UMPF!
NO NO NO!
BLIP
OH! THANKS MY FRIEND. YOU FIXED IT!
!

# Buzzing Moments

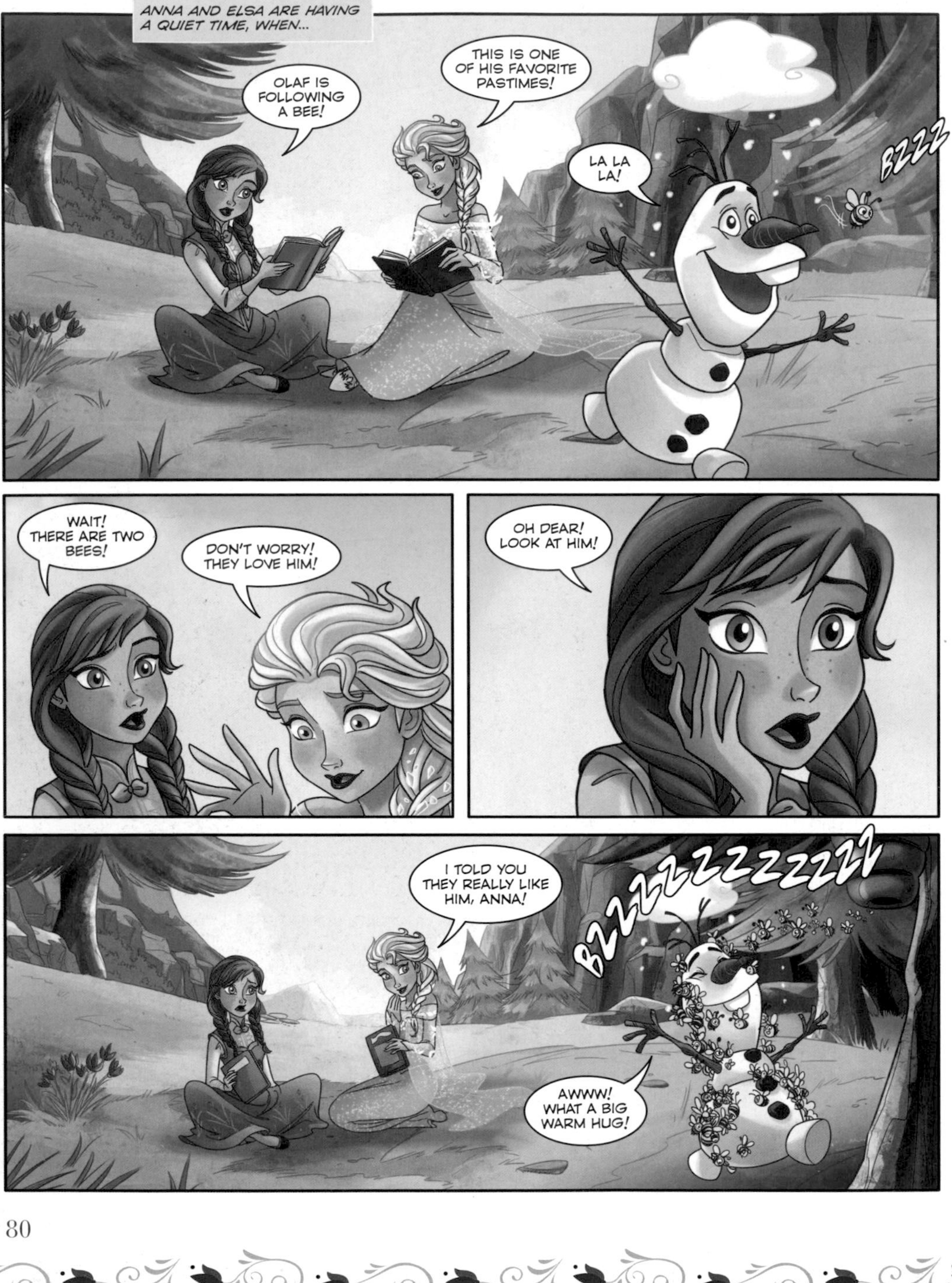
ANNA AND ELSA ARE HAVING A QUIET TIME, WHEN...
OLAF IS FOLLOWING A BEE!
THIS IS ONE OF HIS FAVORITE PASTIMES!
LA LA LA!
BZZZ
WAIT! THERE ARE TWO BEES!
DON'T WORRY! THEY LOVE HIM!
OH DEAR! LOOK AT HIM!
I TOLD YOU THEY REALLY LIKE HIM, ANNA!
BZZZZZZZZZZZZ
AWWW! WHAT A BIG WARM HUG!

# The Icy Playground

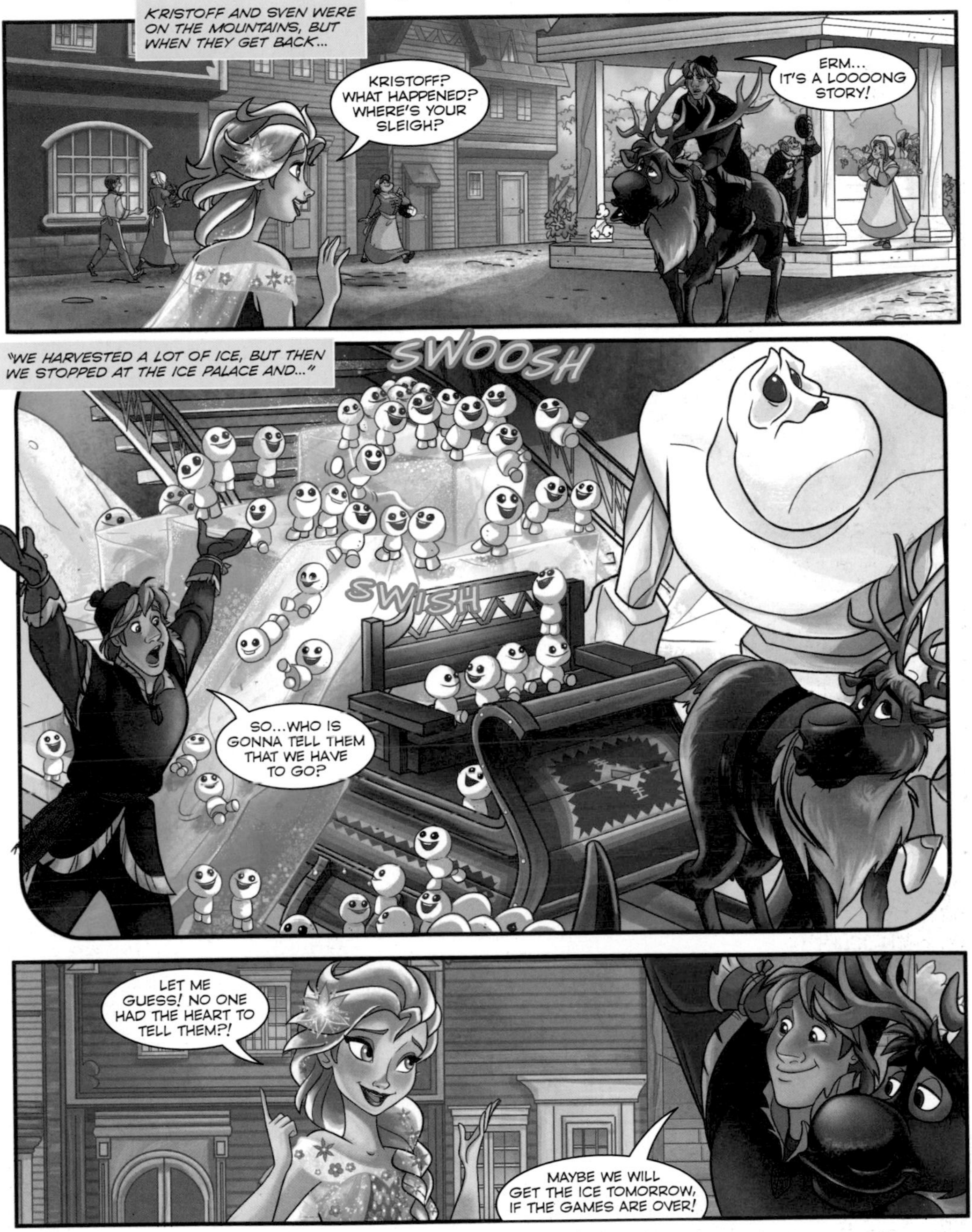
KRISTOFF AND SVEN WERE ON THE MOUNTAINS, BUT WHEN THEY GET BACK...
KRISTOFF? WHAT HAPPENED? WHERE'S YOUR SLEIGH?
ERM... IT'S A LOOOONG STORY!
"WE HARVESTED A LOT OF ICE, BUT THEN WE STOPPED AT THE ICE PALACE AND..."
SWOOSH
SWISH
SO...WHO IS GONNA TELL THEM THAT WE HAVE TO GO?
LET ME GUESS! NO ONE HAD THE HEART TO TELL THEM?!
MAYBE WE WILL GET THE ICE TOMORROW, IF THE GAMES ARE OVER!

# The Most Special Gift

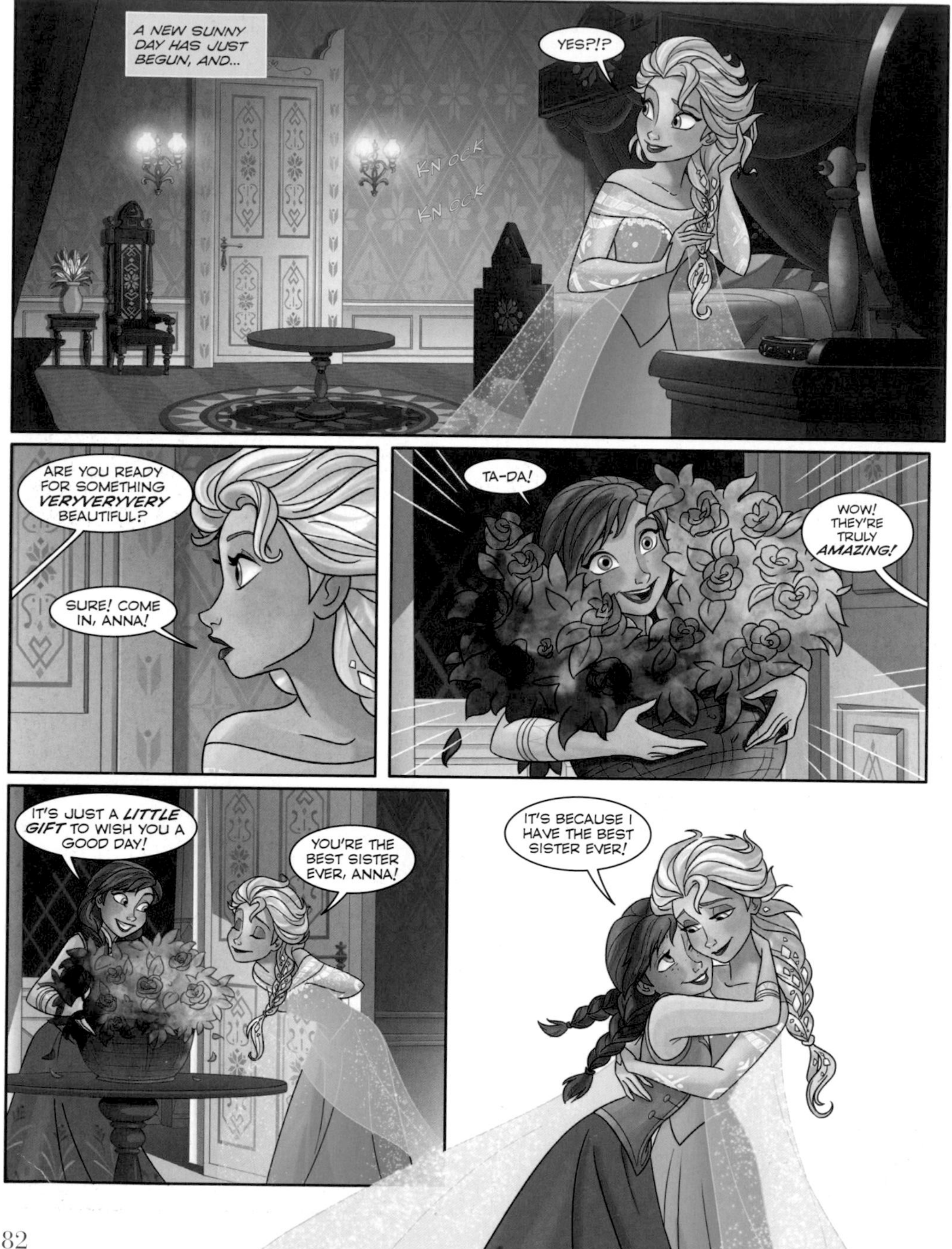

A NEW SUNNY DAY HAS JUST BEGUN, AND...
KNOCK
KNOCK
YES?!?
ARE YOU READY FOR SOMETHING VERYVERYVERY BEAUTIFUL?
SURE! COME IN, ANNA!
TA-DA!
WOW! THEY'RE TRULY AMAZING!
IT'S JUST A LITTLE GIFT TO WISH YOU A GOOD DAY!
YOU'RE THE BEST SISTER EVER, ANNA!
IT'S BECAUSE I HAVE THE BEST SISTER EVER!

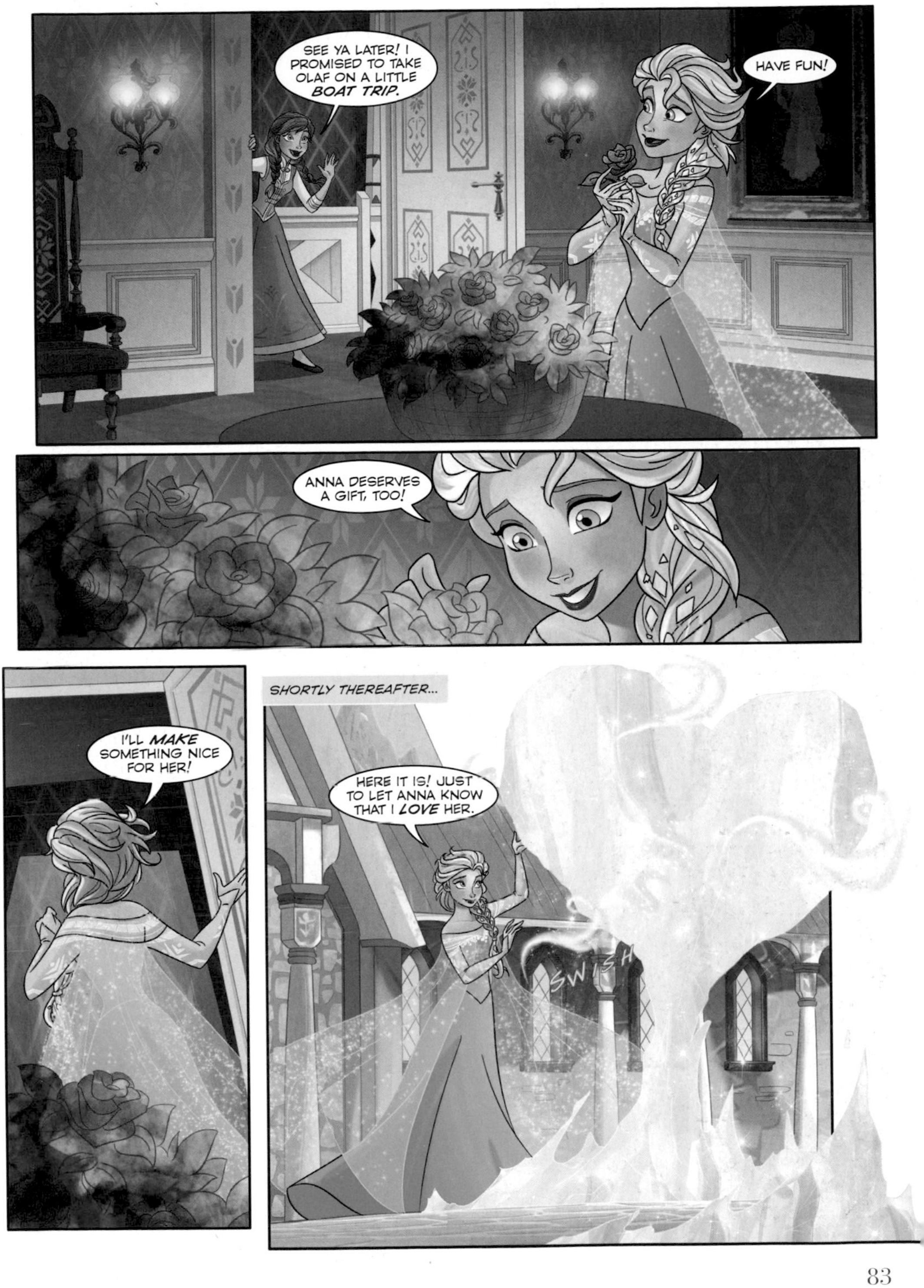
SEE YA LATER! I PROMISED TO TAKE OLAF ON A LITTLE BOAT TRIP.
HAVE FUN!
ANNA DESERVES A GIFT, TOO!
I'LL MAKE SOMETHING NICE FOR HER!
SHORTLY THEREAFTER...
HERE IT IS! JUST TO LET ANNA KNOW THAT I LOVE HER.
SWISH

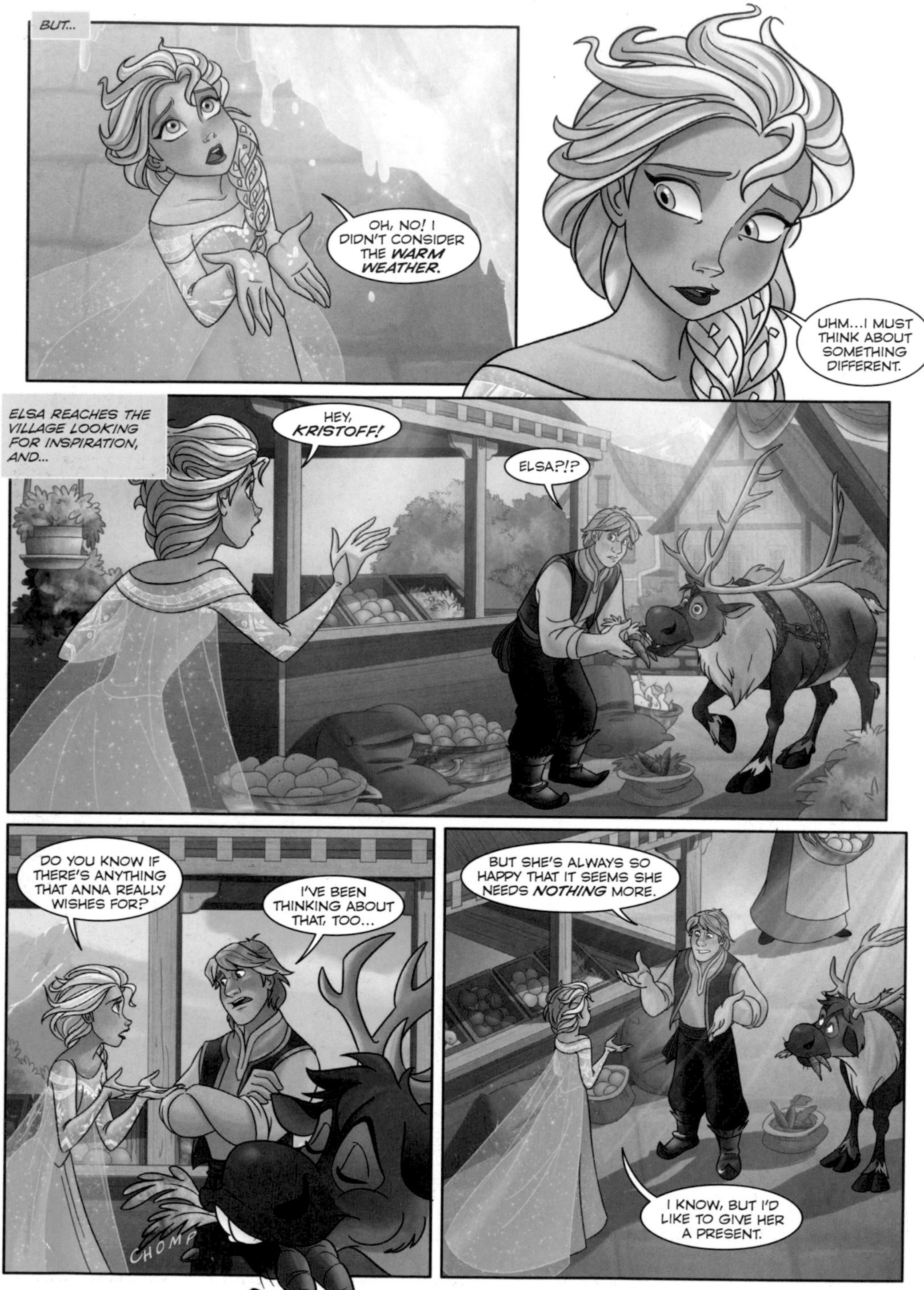
BUT...
OH, NO! I DIDN'T CONSIDER THE WARM WEATHER.
UHM...I MUST THINK ABOUT SOMETHING DIFFERENT.
ELSA REACHES THE VILLAGE LOOKING FOR INSPIRATION, AND...
HEY, KRISTOFF!
ELSA?!?
DO YOU KNOW IF THERE'S ANYTHING THAT ANNA REALLY WISHES FOR?
I'VE BEEN THINKING ABOUT THAT, TOO...
CHOMP
BUT SHE'S ALWAYS SO HAPPY THAT IT SEEMS SHE NEEDS NOTHING MORE.
I KNOW, BUT I'D LIKE TO GIVE HER A PRESENT.

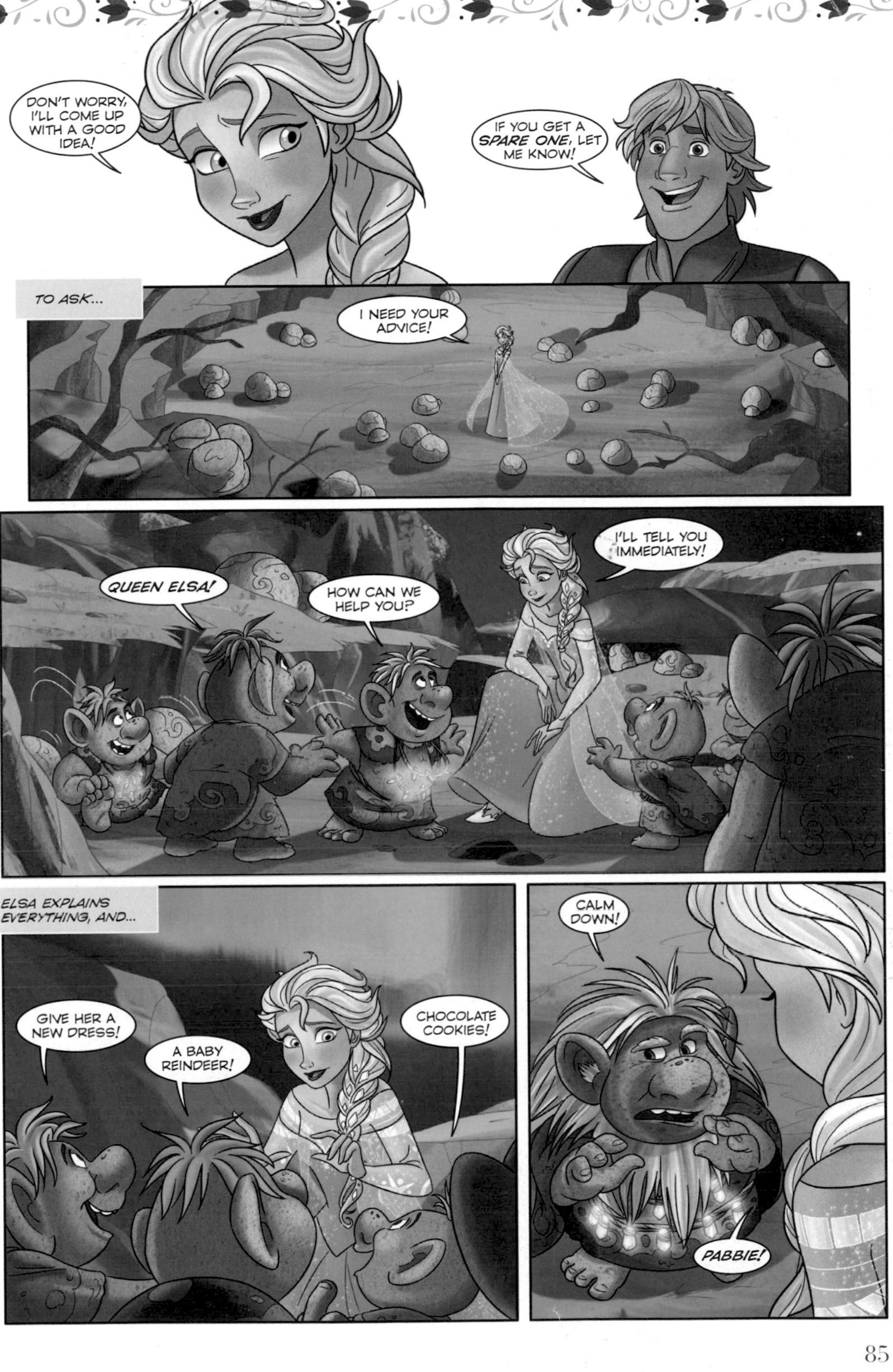
DON'T WORRY, I'LL COME UP WITH A GOOD IDEA!
IF YOU GET A SPARE ONE, LET ME KNOW!
TO ASK...
I NEED YOUR ADVICE!
QUEEN ELSA!
HOW CAN WE HELP YOU?
I'LL TELL YOU IMMEDIATELY!
ELSA EXPLAINS EVERYTHING, AND...
GIVE HER A NEW DRESS!
A BABY REINDEER!
CHOCOLATE COOKIES!
CALM DOWN!
PABBIE!

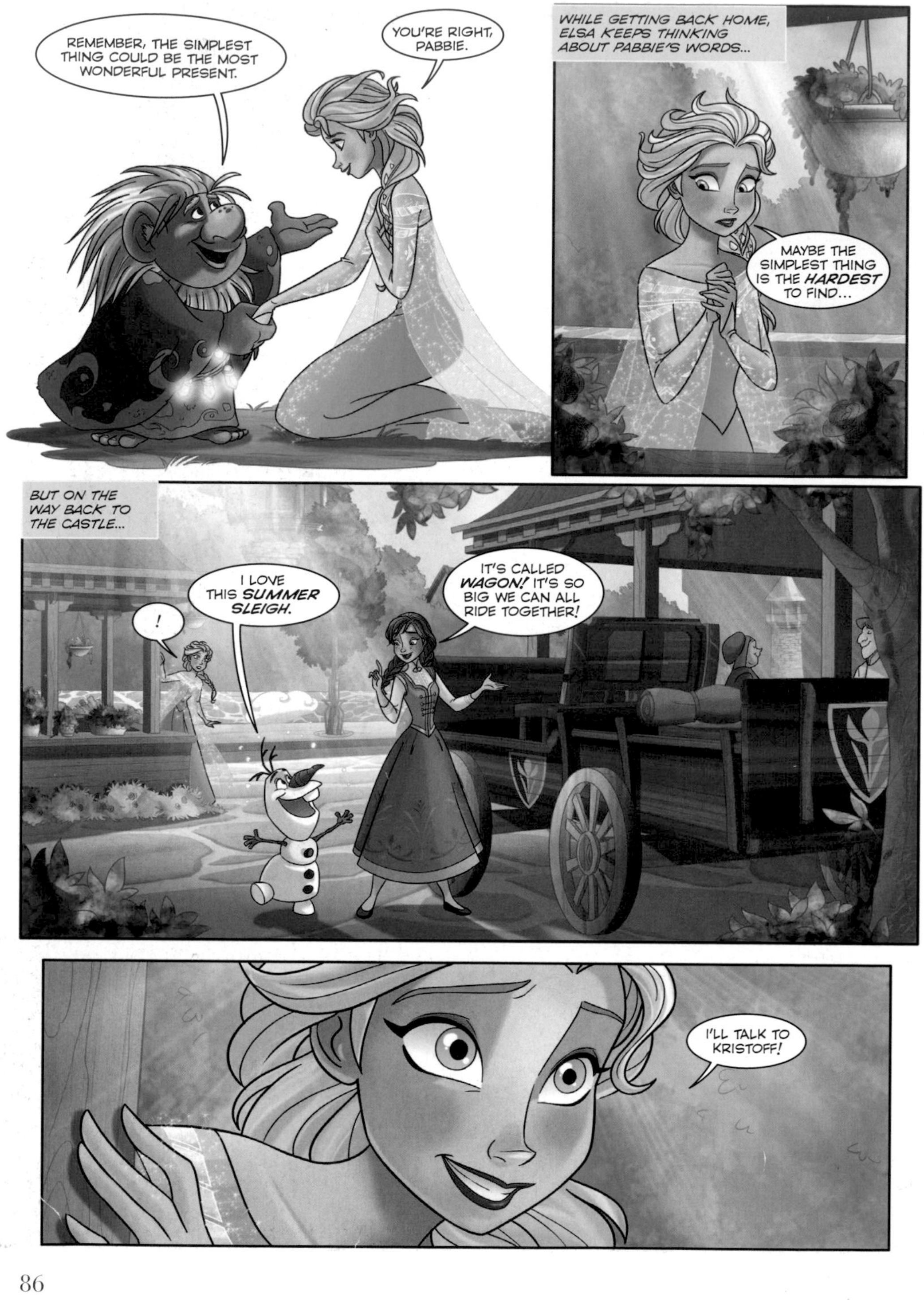
REMEMBER, THE SIMPLEST THING COULD BE THE MOST WONDERFUL PRESENT.
YOU'RE RIGHT, PABBIE.
WHILE GETTING BACK HOME, ELSA KEEPS THINKING ABOUT PABBIE'S WORDS...
MAYBE THE SIMPLEST THING IS THE HARDEST TO FIND...
BUT ON THE WAY BACK TO THE CASTLE...
!
I LOVE THIS SUMMER SLEIGH.
IT'S CALLED WAGON! IT'S SO BIG WE CAN ALL RIDE TOGETHER!
I'LL TALK TO KRISTOFF!

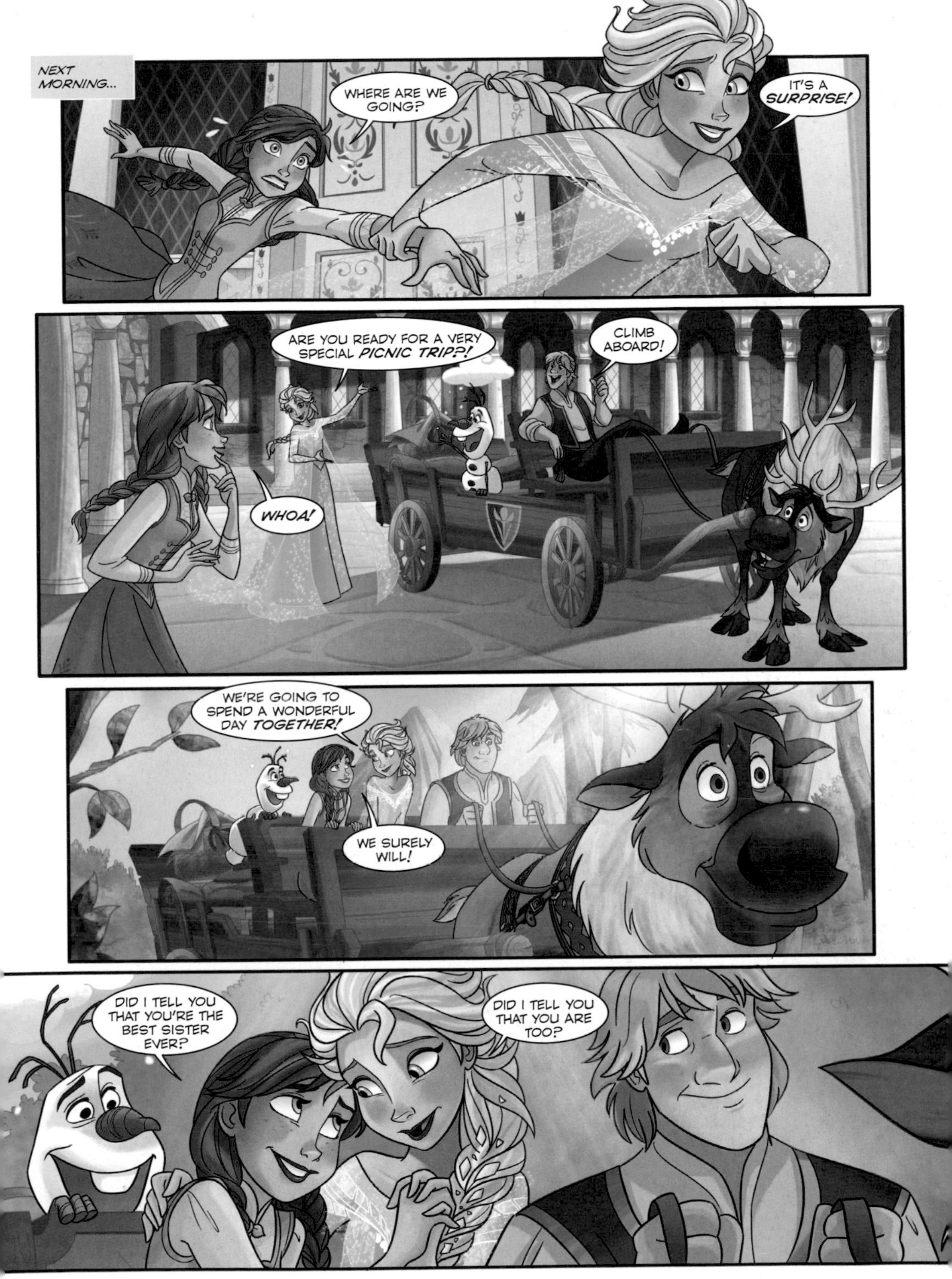
NEXT MORNING...
WHERE ARE WE GOING?
IT'S A SURPRISE!
ARE YOU READY FOR A VERY SPECIAL PICNIC TRIP?!
CLIMB ABOARD!
WHOA!
WE'RE GOING TO SPEND A WONDERFUL DAY TOGETHER!
WE SURELY WILL!
DID I TELL YOU THAT YOU'RE THE BEST SISTER EVER?
DID I TELL YOU THAT YOU ARE TOO?

# Olaf's Pastime

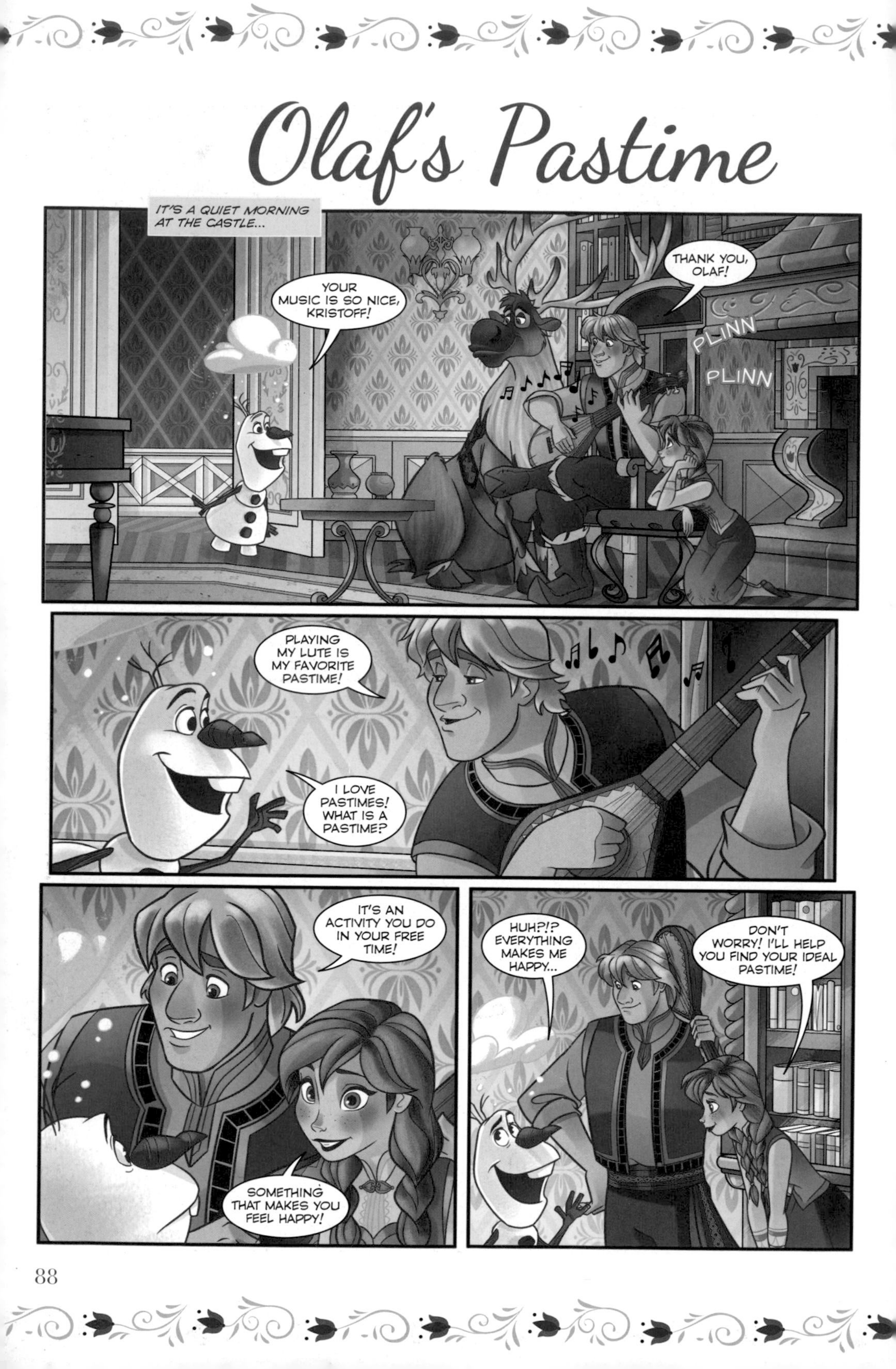
IT'S A QUIET MORNING AT THE CASTLE...
YOUR MUSIC IS SO NICE, KRISTOFF!
THANK YOU, OLAF!
PLINN
PLINN
PLAYING MY LUTE IS MY FAVORITE PASTIME!
I LOVE PASTIMES! WHAT IS A PASTIME?
IT'S AN ACTIVITY YOU DO IN YOUR FREE TIME!
SOMETHING THAT MAKES YOU FEEL HAPPY!
HUH?!? EVERYTHING MAKES ME HAPPY...
DON'T WORRY! I'LL HELP YOU FIND YOUR IDEAL PASTIME!

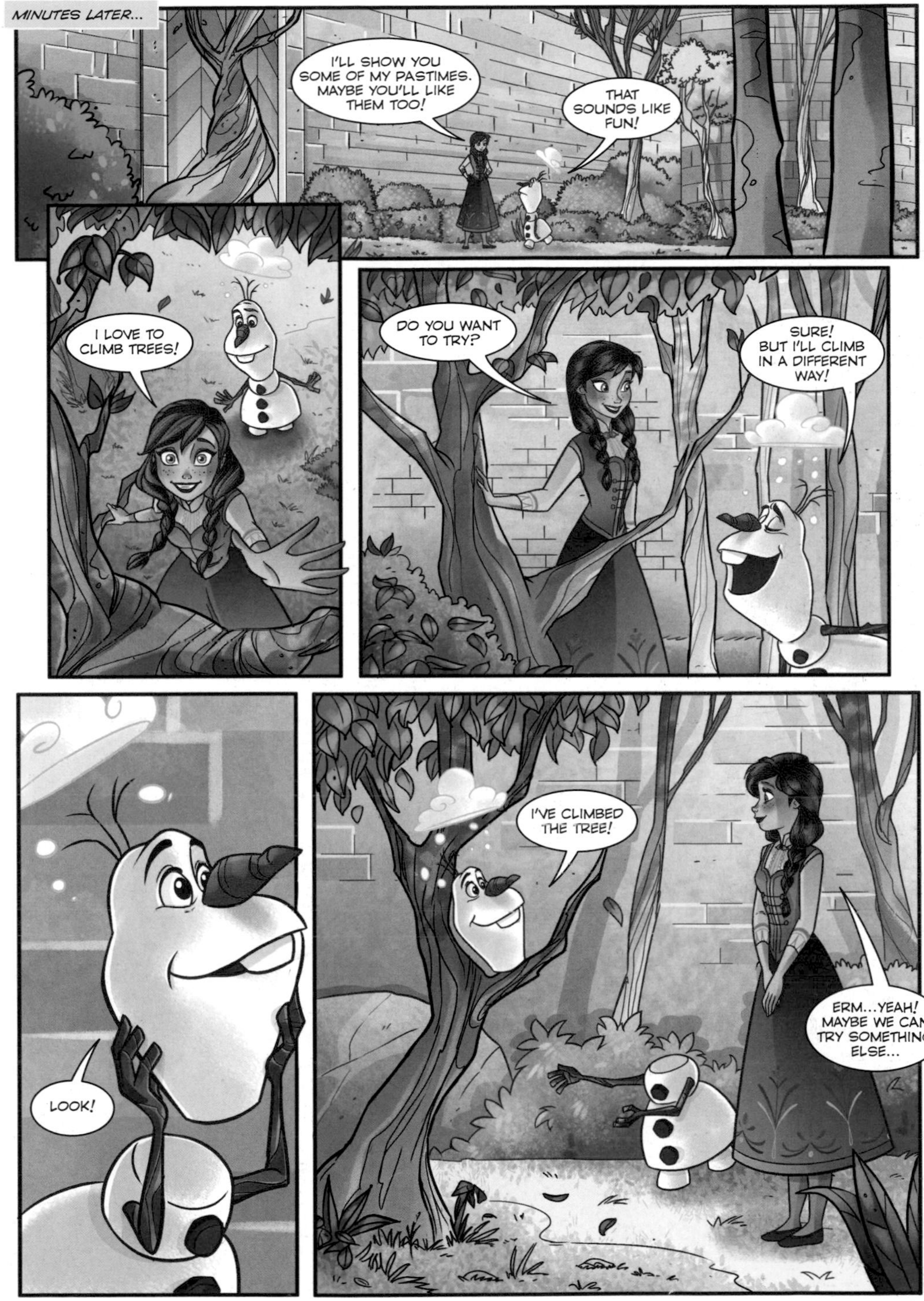
MINUTES LATER...
I'LL SHOW YOU SOME OF MY PASTIMES. MAYBE YOU'LL LIKE THEM TOO!
THAT SOUNDS LIKE FUN!
I LOVE TO CLIMB TREES!
DO YOU WANT TO TRY?
SURE! BUT I'LL CLIMB IN A DIFFERENT WAY!
LOOK!
I'VE CLIMBED THE TREE!
ERM...YEAH! MAYBE WE CAN TRY SOMETHING ELSE...

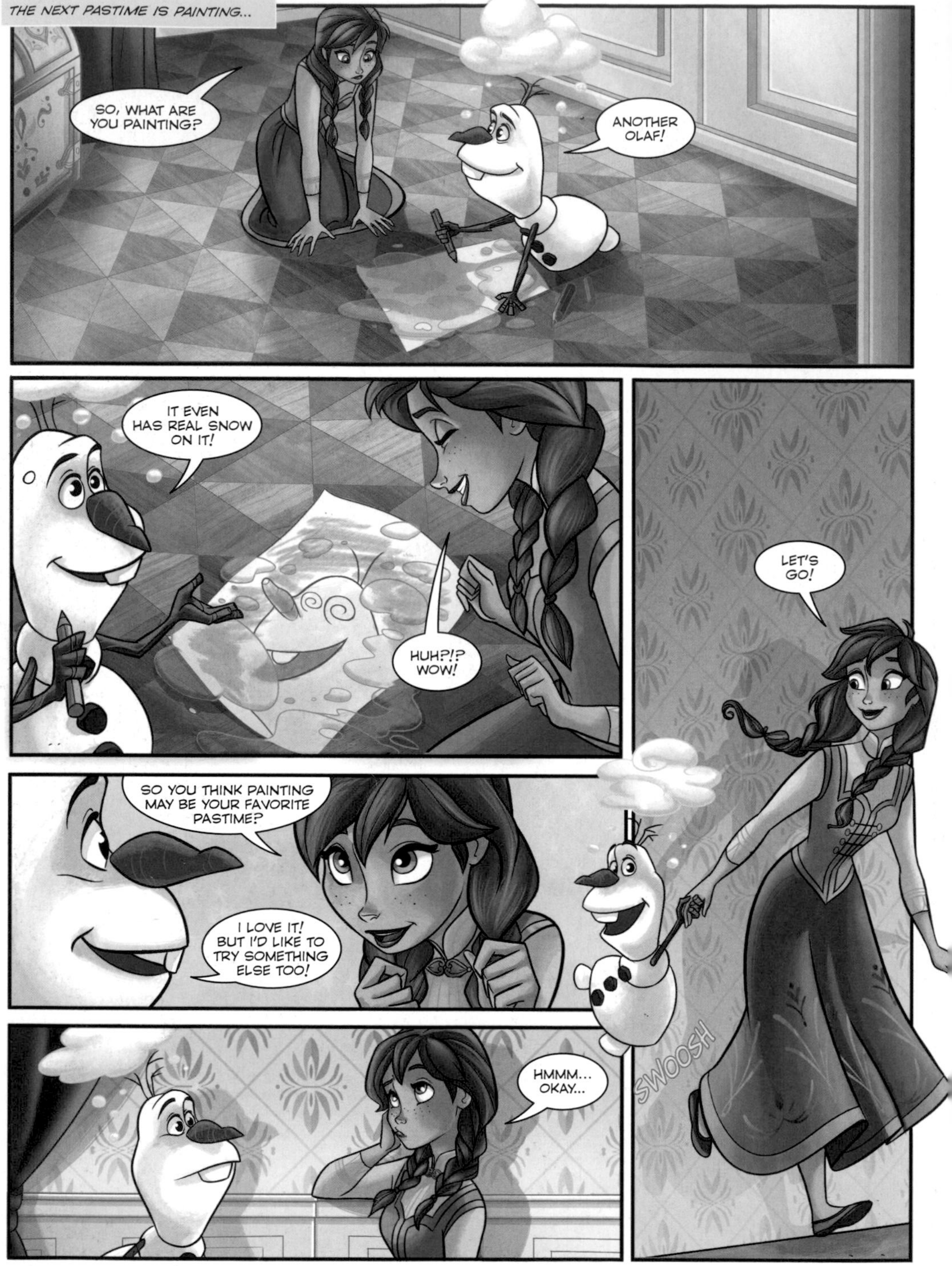
THE NEXT PASTIME IS PAINTING...
SO, WHAT ARE YOU PAINTING?
ANOTHER OLAF!
IT EVEN HAS REAL SNOW ON IT!
HUH?!? WOW!
SO YOU THINK PAINTING MAY BE YOUR FAVORITE PASTIME?
I LOVE IT! BUT I'D LIKE TO TRY SOMETHING ELSE TOO!
HMMM... OKAY...
LET'S GO!
SWOOSH

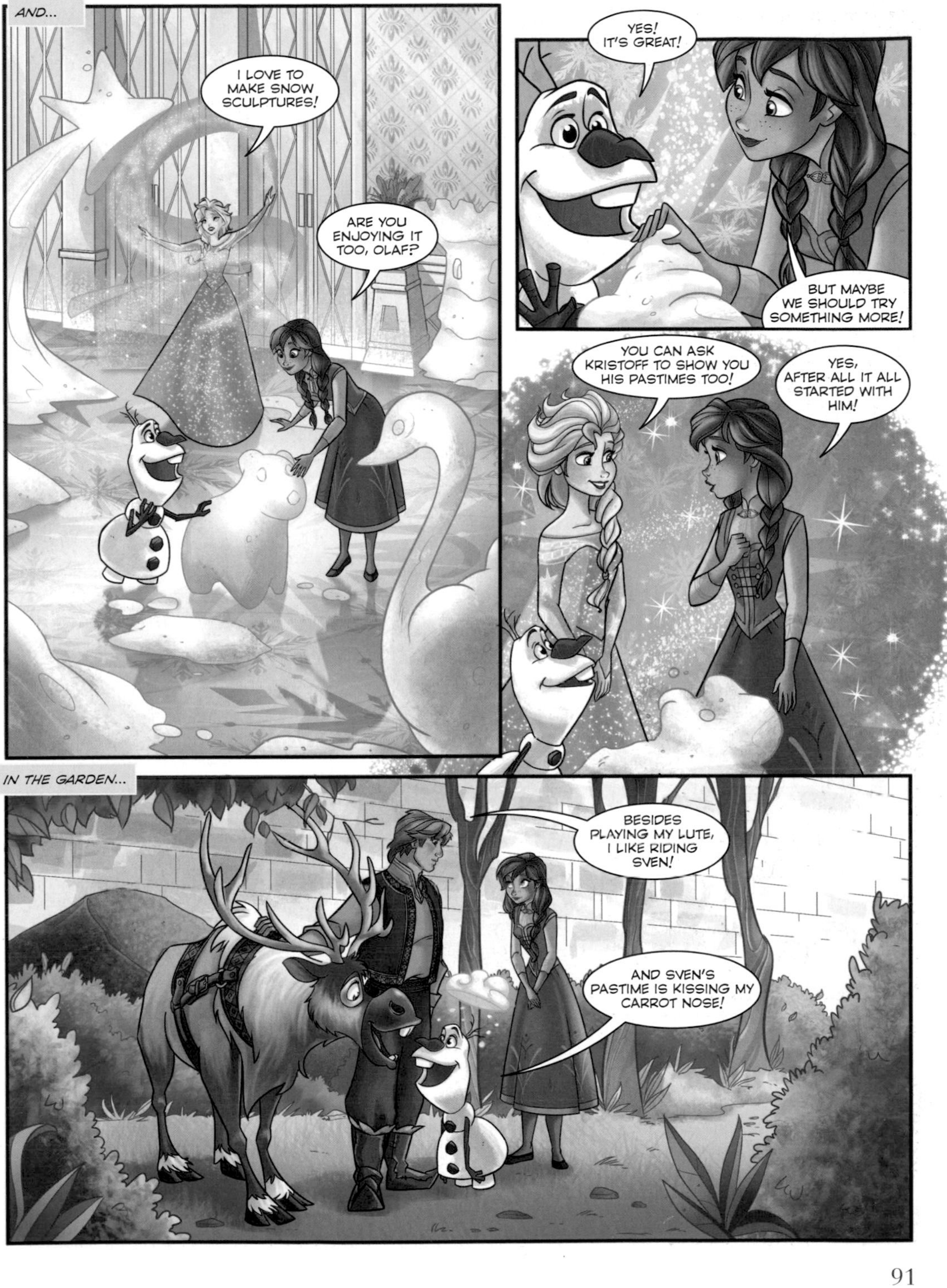
AND...
I LOVE TO MAKE SNOW SCULPTURES!
ARE YOU ENJOYING IT TOO, OLAF?
YES! IT'S GREAT!
BUT MAYBE WE SHOULD TRY SOMETHING MORE!
YOU CAN ASK KRISTOFF TO SHOW YOU HIS PASTIMES TOO!
YES, AFTER ALL IT ALL STARTED WITH HIM!
IN THE GARDEN...
BESIDES PLAYING MY LUTE, I LIKE RIDING SVEN!
AND SVEN'S PASTIME IS KISSING MY CARROT NOSE!

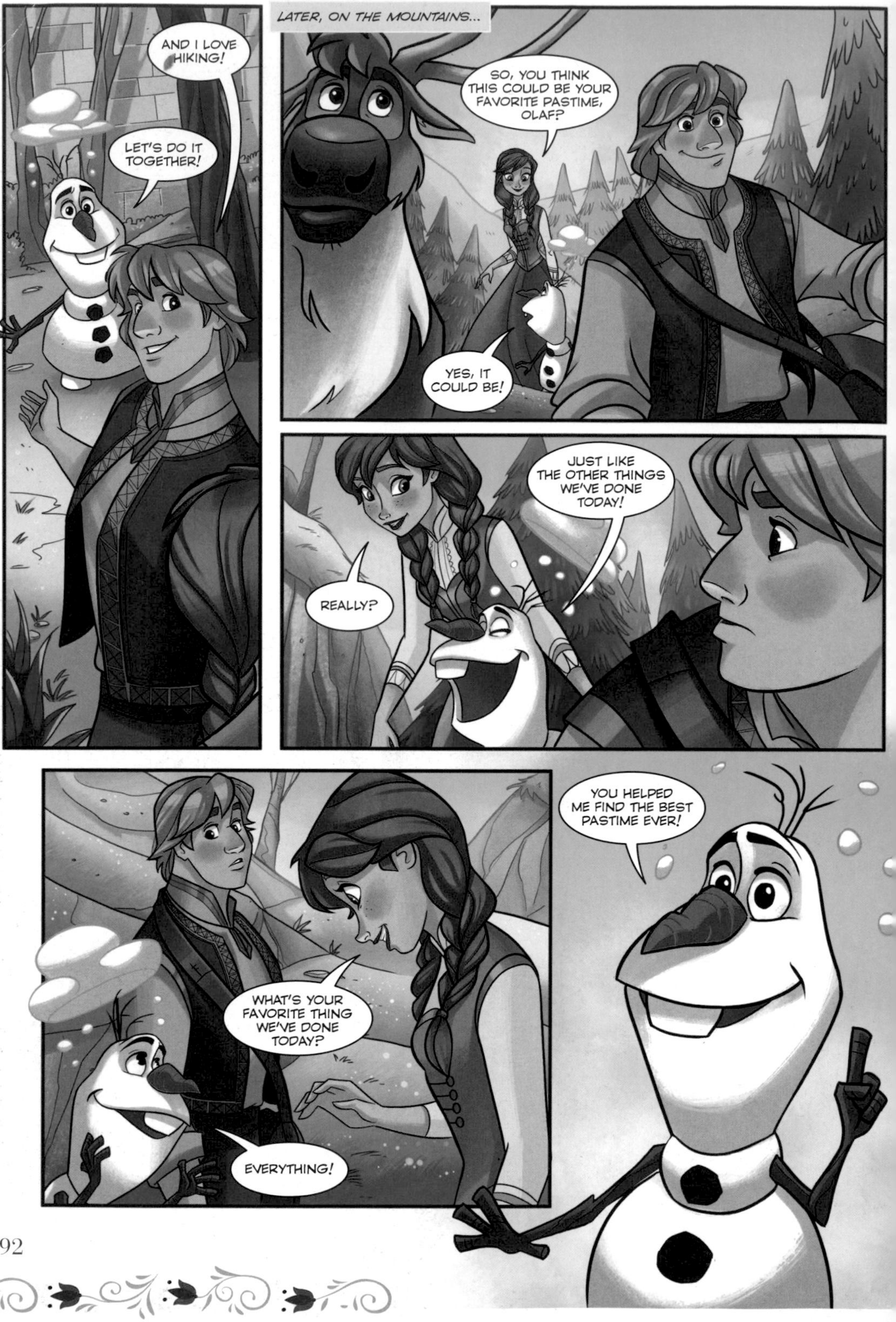
AND I LOVE HIKING!
LET'S DO IT TOGETHER!
LATER, ON THE MOUNTAINS...
SO, YOU THINK THIS COULD BE YOUR FAVORITE PASTIME, OLAF?
YES, IT COULD BE!
JUST LIKE THE OTHER THINGS WE'VE DONE TODAY!
REALLY?
YOU HELPED ME FIND THE BEST PASTIME EVER!
WHAT'S YOUR FAVORITE THING WE'VE DONE TODAY?
EVERYTHING!

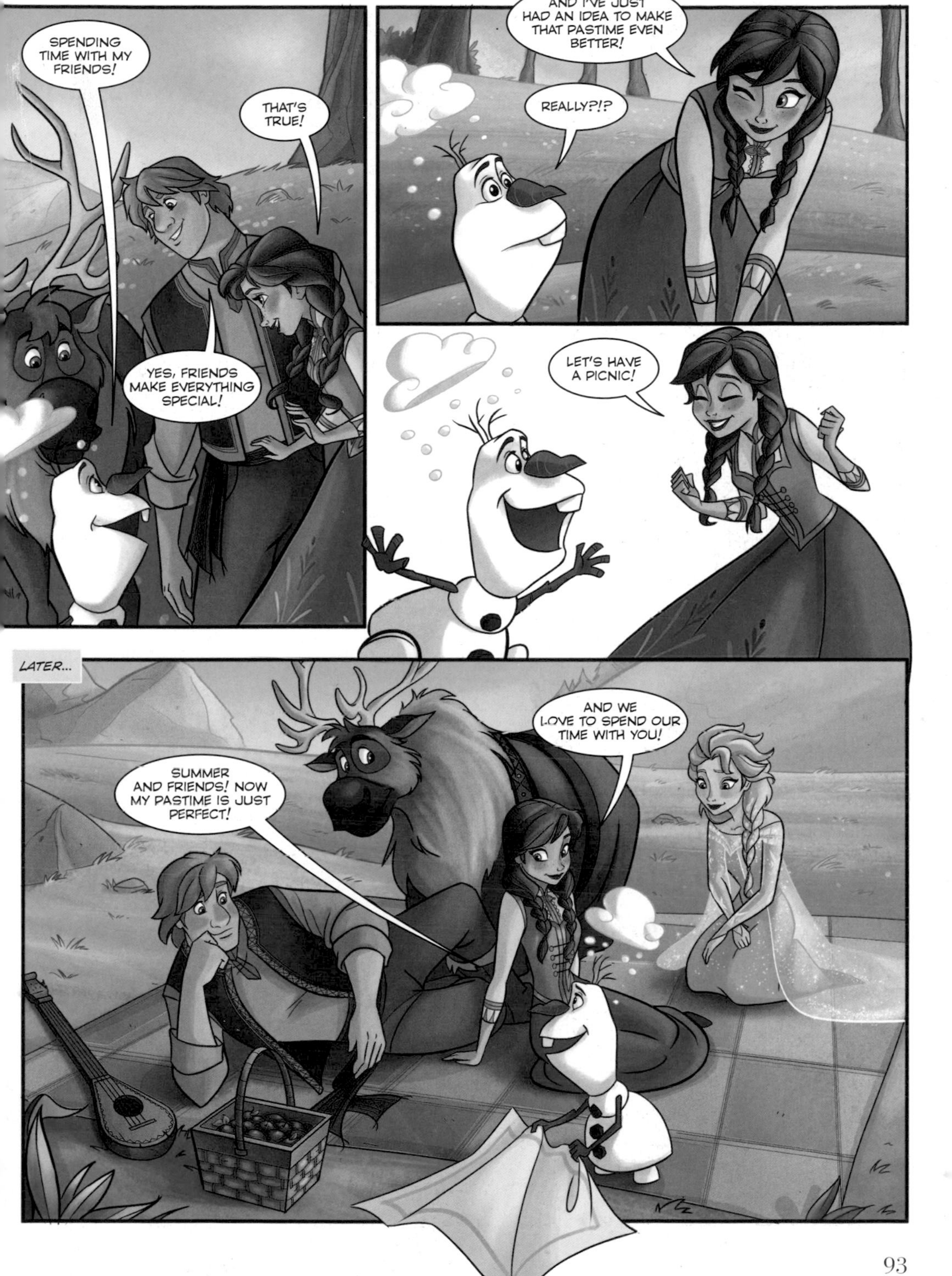
SPENDING TIME WITH MY FRIENDS!
THAT'S TRUE!
YES, FRIENDS MAKE EVERYTHING SPECIAL!
AND I'VE JUST HAD AN IDEA TO MAKE THAT PASTIME EVEN BETTER!
REALLY?!?
LET'S HAVE A PICNIC!
LATER...
SUMMER AND FRIENDS! NOW MY PASTIME IS JUST PERFECT!
AND WE LOVE TO SPEND OUR TIME WITH YOU!

# Only at Night

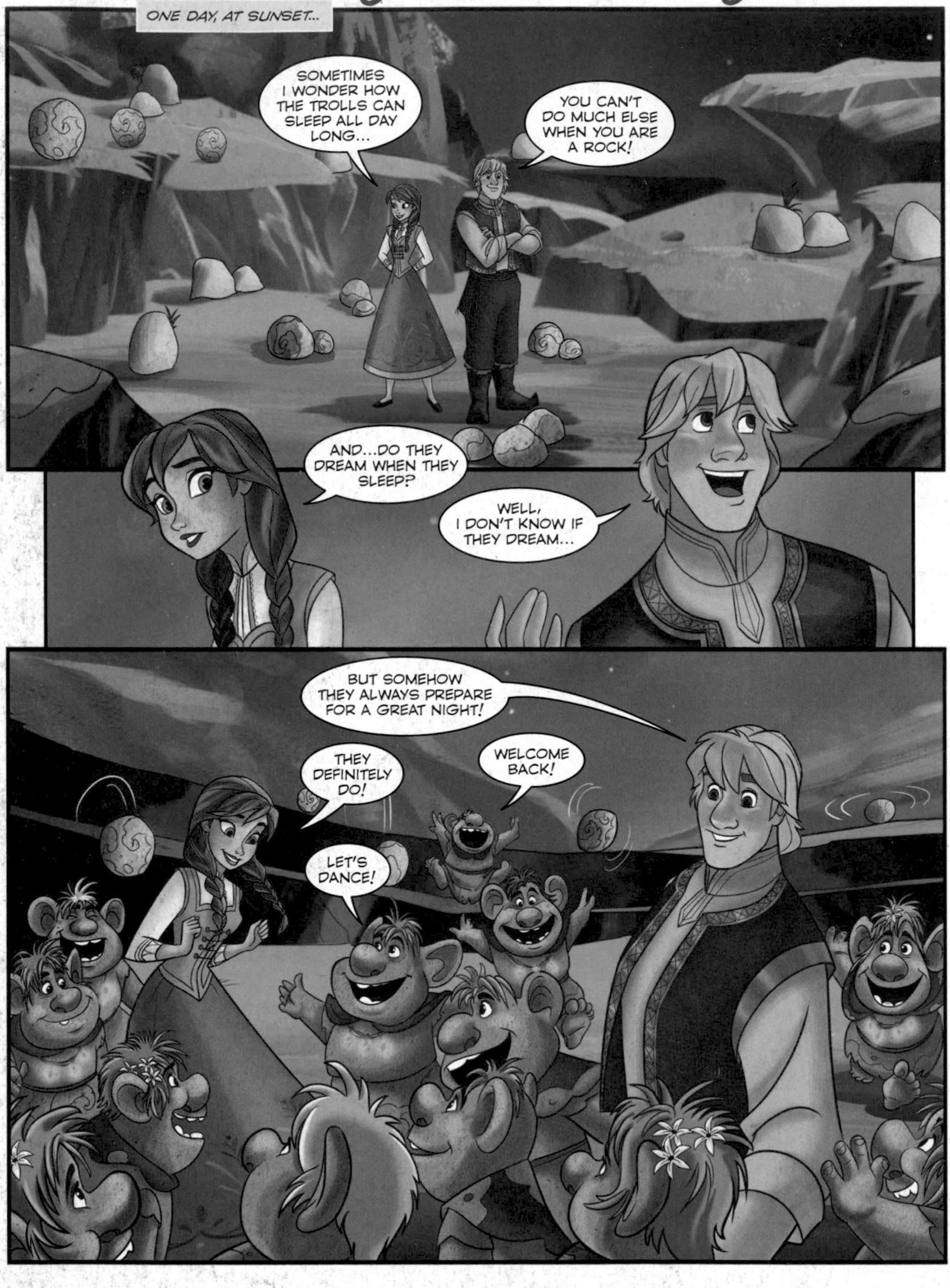
ONE DAY, AT SUNSET...
SOMETIMES I WONDER HOW THE TROLLS CAN SLEEP ALL DAY LONG...
YOU CAN'T DO MUCH ELSE WHEN YOU ARE A ROCK!
AND...DO THEY DREAM WHEN THEY SLEEP?
WELL, I DON'T KNOW IF THEY DREAM...
BUT SOMEHOW THEY ALWAYS PREPARE FOR A GREAT NIGHT!
THEY DEFINITELY DO!
WELCOME BACK!
LET'S DANCE!

# FROZEN COMICS COLLECTION CREDITS

**"Special Break"**
STORY: Tea Orsi
LAYOUTS: Emilio Urbano
CLEANUPS: Nicoletta Baldari
COLORS: Dario Calabria

**"Morning Bike Ride"**
STORY: Tea Orsi
LAYOUTS: Emilio Urbano
CLEANUPS: Veronica Di Lorenzo
COLORS: Dario Calabria

**"A Mysterious Invitation"**
STORY: Tea Orsi
LAYOUTS: Nicoletta Baldari
CLEANUPS: Veronica Di Lorenzo
COLORS: Patrizia Zangrilli and
Antonia Angrisani

**"New Branches"**
STORY: Tea Orsi
LAYOUTS: Emilio Urbano
CLEANUPS: Rosa La Barbera
COLORS: Dario Calabria

**"Almost Ready"**
STORY: Tea Orsi
LAYOUTS: Marino Gentile
CLEANUPS: Nicoletta Baldari
COLORS: Dario Calabria

**"Question of Balance"**
STORY: Tea Orsi
LAYOUTS: Marino Gentile
CLEANUPS: Nicoletta Baldari
COLORS: Dario Calabria

**"Spring Trolls"**
STORY: Tea Orsi
LAYOUTS: Emilio Urbano
CLEANUPS: Chatal Christine
COLORS: Stefania Santi

**"A New Reindeer Friend"**
STORY: Alessandro Ferrari
LAYOUTS: Elisabetta Melaranci
CLEANUPS: Veronica Di Lorenzo COLORS:
Dario Calabria and Silvano Scolari

**"The Right Season"**
STORY: Tea Orsi
LAYOUTS: Emilio Urbano
CLEANUPS: Nicoletta Baldari
COLORS: Dario Calabria

**"A Touch of Spring"**
STORY: Tea Orsi
LAYOUTS: Emilio Urbano
CLEANUPS: Rosa La Barbera
COLORS: Dario Calabria

**"The Carrot Guard"**
STORY: Tea Orsi
LAYOUTS: Emilio Urbano
CLEANUPS: Veronica Di Lorenzo
COLORS: Dario Calabria

**"A Great Spring Game"**
STORY: Tea Orsi
LAYOUTS: Emilio Urbano
CLEANUPS: Miriam Gambino
COLORS: Dario Calabria

**"A Funny Show"**
STORY: Tea Orsi
LAYOUTS and CLEANUPS: Nicoletta Baldari
COLORS: Dario Calabria

**"Heavy Climbing"**
STORY: Tea Orsi
LAYOUTS: Marino Gentile
CLEANUPS: Marino Gentile
INKS: Cristina Stella
COLORS: Patrizia Zangrilli

**"The Spring Reindeer"**
STORY: Tea Orsi
LAYOUTS: Manuela Razzi
CLEANUPS: Nicoletta Baldari
COLORS: Dario Calabria

**"To the Rescue!"**
STORY: Tea Orsi
LAYOUTS: Marino Gentile
CLEANUPS: Marino Gentile
INKS: Cristina Stella
COLORS: Stefania Santi

**"The Lost Map"**
STORY: Tea Orsi
LAYOUTS: Nicoletta Baldari
CLEANUPS: Veronica Di Lorenzo
COLORS: Stefania Santi

**"The Best Drink Ever"**
STORY: Tea Orsi
LAYOUTS: Emilio Urbano
CLEANUPS: Manuela Razzi
COLORS: Dario Calabria

**"A Fuzzy Rest"**
STORY: Tea Orsi
LAYOUTS: Emilio Urbano
CLEANUPS: Manuela Razzi
COLORS: Dario Calabria

**"Sailing Sisters"**
STORY: Tea Orsi
LAYOUTS: Nicoletta Baldari
CLEANUPS: Nicoletta Baldari
COLORS: Dario Calabria

**"Scary Noise"**
STORY: Tea Orsi
LAYOUTS: Nicoletta Baldari
CLEANUPS: Miriam Gambino
COLORS: Stefania Santi

**"A Day on the Beach"**
STORY: Tea Orsi
LAYOUTS: Alberto Zanon
CLEANUPS: Veronica Di Lorenzo
COLORS: Manuela Nerolini

**"Let's Help Oaken!"**
STORY: Tea Orsi
LAYOUTS: Elisabetta Melaranci
CLEANUPS: Manuela Razzi
COLORS: Dario Calabria

**"A Very Hot Day"**
STORY: Tea Orsi
LAYOUTS: Manuela Razzi
CLEANUPS: Veronica Di Lorenzo
COLORS: Dario Calabria

**"A Snowflakes Surprise"**
STORY: Tea Orsi
LAYOUTS: Elisabetta Melaranci
CLEANUPS: Nicoletta Baldari
COLORS: Dario Calabria

**"A Great Song"**
STORY: Tea Orsi
LAYOUTS and CLEANUPS: Elisabetta Melaranci
COLORS: Dario Calabria

**"The Para-Snow"**
STORY: Tea Orsi
LAYOUTS: Emilio Urbano
CLEANUPS: Miriam Gambino
COLORS: Dario Calabria

**"Oaken's Mystery Box"**
STORY: Tea Orsi
LAYOUTS: Alberto Zanon
CLEANUPS: Rosa La Barbera
COLORS: Stefania Santi

**"Through the Wall"**
STORY: Tea Orsi
LAYOUTS: Alberto Zanon
CLEANUPS: Miriam Gambino
COLORS: Patrizia Zangrilli and
Manuela Nerolini

**"Melting Gift"**
STORY: Tea Orsi
LAYOUTS: Emilio Urbano
CLEANUPS: Miriam Gambino
COLORS: Dario Calabria

**"A Good Friend"**
STORY: Tea Orsi
LAYOUTS and CLEANUPS: Elisabetta Melaranci
COLORS: Dario Calabria

**"Buzzing Moments"**
STORY: Tea Orsi
LAYOUTS: Emilio Urbano
CLEANUPS: Veronica Di Lorenzo
COLORS: Dario Calabria

**"The Icy Playground"**
STORY: Tea Orsi
LAYOUTS: Emilio Urbano
CLEANUPS: Nicoletta Baldari
COLORS: Alessandra Bracaglia

**"The Most Special Gift"**
STORY: Tea Orsi
LAYOUTS: Elisabetta Melaranci
CLEANUPS: Veronica Di Lorenzo
COLORS: Dario Calabria

**"Olaf's Pastime"**
STORY: Tea Orsi
LAYOUTS: Alberto Zanon
CLEANUPS: Nicoletta Baldari
COLORS: Manuela Nerolini, Ekaterina
Maximenko, and Ekaterina Myshalova

**"Only at Night"**
STORY: Tea Orsi
LAYOUTS: Alberto Zanon
CLEANUPS: Nicoletta Baldari
COLORS: Stefania Santi